RETURNED BROKEN

RETURNED BROKEN

A NOVEL

Judith Keller

TIFFIN-SENECA PUBLIC LIBRARY
77 JEFFERSON STREET
TIFFIN, OHIO 44883

Alpharetta, GA

This is a work of fiction. Names, characters, businesses, places, and events are either the products of the author's imagination or are used in a fictitious manner. Any resemblance to actual persons, living or dead, or actual events is purely coincidental.

Copyright © 2016 by Judith Keller

All rights reserved. No part of this book may be reproduced or transmitted in any form or by any means, electronic or mechanical, including photocopying, recording, or any information storage and retrieval system, without permission in writing from the publisher. For more information, address BookLogix, c/o Permissions Department, 1264 Old Alpharetta Rd., Alpharetta, GA 30005.

ISBN: 978-1-61005-643-4
Library of Congress Control Number: 2015921361

10 9 8 7 6 5 4 3 2   040716

Printed in the United States of America

∞ This paper meets the requirements of ANSI/NISO Z39.48-1992 (Permanence of Paper)

CHAPTER 1

NEVER WALK THE STREETS OF SYRIA ALONE. THAT WARNING, engrained in Clair's mind from the moment her plane landed, was one she tried to abide by. But today it was just her, stepping out through the hospital's double doors and into the steamy air.

There was little traffic as she crossed the street, and with her mind on David, she slowly walked two blocks before turning right at the corner of Trablos and Al Dabla.

As she neared the mosque, the halfway point between the hospital and hotel, she slowed. The street ahead was lifeless and eerily quiet. Even the wind that earlier had whipped her hair into knots was now still. Tall buildings that lined the way blocked what was left of the sun, and shadows darkened her path.

A car appeared from out of nowhere and coasted on the road beside her. It moved suspiciously slow. Her stomach fluttered, and she picked up her pace.

She had grown accustomed to persistent men shouting from their passing vehicles—the equivalent of American catcalls. But this was different. The three men looked straight ahead, feigning disinterest in her while they struggled to keep their car from passing her by.

The shops had closed for the day but she urgently tugged at their doors in a useless attempt to find help. The nearest occupied building, her hotel, stood two blocks away.

Tires screeched as the car accelerated and whipped into the alley ahead, blocking her path. Fear poured into her like a trembling flood. It pumped through her veins and turned her legs to jelly.

A man leaped from the open rear door with a two-by-four. Frantically, she looked in all directions for somewhere—anywhere—to run, then spun around and headed back toward the hospital, her chest tight and her heart hammering as she ran, dizzy with panic.

"Stop or I'll shoot," he yelled.

Liar. You would have shot from your car if you wanted me dead.

The man was gaining ground on her. She screamed as she ran, "Help! Somebody please . . . help me!"

Nearby, a horn sounded.

If I can make it to the corner—

"Stop," he ordered, closer than before.

One more block.

When she looked over her shoulder, he swung. The whoosh of the wood as it cut the air resonated while pain exploded in her head, and the world around her faded into darkness.

* * *

As consciousness seeped in, her pain-ravaged mind flashed fragments of her abduction. An engine droned close by and the hot, stagnant air, laced with the distinct smell of gasoline, made her light-headed and nauseous. Except for the dim light that squeezed through a crack, the trunk was dark.

The car came to a halt, launching her to the front and into a tire-iron. A sharp, piercing pain ripped through her ribs. With her head lifted, she strained to hear anything that might give her a clue to what was happening.

Outside, men talked, but she didn't know the language well enough to comprehend. And then, the sound of gravel underfoot, fading slowly away until nothing but the wind, blowing sand against the car. Who were these men, and what did they want from her? She tried to stay alert and listen but the heat, along with the pain sapped her strength. Her eyes closed, and her head dropped back, hitting the floor of the trunk with a thud.

* * *

She woke cold and thirsty. Through bleary eyes she spotted a window near the ceiling, giving light to the otherwise dim and gloomy room. Besides the cot she lay on and one wooden chair, the place was empty. The dirt floor and concrete walls smelled of mold and added a chill to the room. Despite her throbbing head and tender ribs, she slowly sat up.

The room swirled around her while she dropped from the cot to her knees and with closed eyes, rested the crown of her head in the dirt. When the reeling eased, she sat and moved her hands over her body, looking for any damage beyond the deep gash across her forehead. A purple lump, the size of an egg, had grown along her ribcage, and her every move brought with it sharp pain.

The cold room, coupled with her fear, had her teeth chattering. Someone had stripped her of the lab coat she'd been wearing, along with her cell phone in its pocket. She took long, deep breaths and tried to pull herself out of the fog she was in and think. Had she seen these men before? Had anything happened today that led to this?

The last thing she remembered was being at the hospital. She had stayed over to consult with Dr. Schmidt and sent the other volunteers on without her. A patient there, a young girl with pneumonia, wasn't responding to her medication. They were running out of options. Medicines were in pitifully short supply throughout the country and diminished further when several of Syria's pharmaceutical manufacturing plants were shelled. David had warned her about the conditions she would work under.

The thought of David made her wonder if he knew yet that she was missing.

Without a doubt, he'd fight with every ounce of strength in his body to get her out of here. She just needed to stay alive until he could.

The door flew open and hit the concrete wall with a bang. Clair's head jerked up and she squirmed to the far end of the cot, as a man entered the room. He stood tall with his hands on his hips and glared down at her. His dark skin so smooth and clear it glowed, his body lean and muscular. She recognized him right away—the one driving the car.

He wore a dirty white T-shirt, tan camouflage pants, and black boots. Dark stubble marked his hard, angular jaw line and his unkempt hair spilled over his face. But what captured her attention most were his high cheekbones and narrow eyes that seemed out of place on this Syrian man's face.

With her muscles tight she sat straight and stiff while he gazed at her with scrutiny. She crossed her arms, pressed her knees together, and pleaded silently there'd be no more violence.

"Tomorrow you will be put to work, mending our wounded soldiers. This room is your home now. Welcome."

He spoke matter-of-factly about something so devastating that, for a moment, she thought he must be joking. She pictured her life here, working for this egotist, away from her husband and home.

"You won't get away with this. I'm an American—people will be looking for me. Besides that, I'm a pediatrician, not the surgeon that you need."

With long strides he moved lightning quick, and before the words were out of her mouth, he crossed the room. With his fingers clamped tight around her arm, he yanked her off of the cot and slammed her into the wall. The cut she'd gotten earlier broke open and warm blood trickled from her forehead, down the side of her face. His body pressed tight against hers, and his hot breath swept across her face as he whispered, "We do not make mistakes."

When he stepped back, her limp body dropped to the ground like a rag doll. The door slammed shut, and the deadbolt slid into place while she lay in a heap and sobbed.

Every cell of her body screamed in pain—but worse, she was being held here by a mad man and had no idea where she was or how long they would keep her. She only knew why— they needed a doctor.

To her this felt like a scene from a nightmare where you keep saying to yourself, *This can't be happening. I'll wake soon and this will be over.* If only it weren't so real.

On hands and knees she crawled to the cot and lay down. All the while trying to convince herself that this couldn't last. Soon the sound of footsteps as again someone lumbered down the steps. Remembering her last visit, she sat up, wrapped her arms around her knees and braced herself for more torment. And then she watched, as the handle turned and the door slowly opened.

CHAPTER 2

DAVID STIRRED, ROLLED UPRIGHT, AND TRIED TO SHAKE THE cobwebs from his head. He hit the alarm clock, but the ringing wouldn't stop.

Who's calling at four in the morning?

"Hello," he answered, his voice hoarse.

"Mr. Stevens?"

"Yeah."

"This is Marcus Cook. I'm the coordinator with Doctors Without Borders. I apologize for calling with such terrible news, but your wife is missing."

David's body sprung forward, stiff with shock.

"Missing? What do you mean? She isn't at the hospital?"

David wasn't sure what time it was there and wasn't awake enough to do the math.

"She worked the day shift as usual. It's eleven now. We've been looking since she was reported missing, around six."

"She's been gone for five hours and I'm just now hearing about it?"

A helpless anger began to simmer inside him.

"We have protocols to follow. In the morning, if she's not found by then, we'll go to the embassy in Damascus and report it. They'll contact the FBI once she's been gone twenty-four hours."

David desperately wanted this to be a prank, some sick joke, or a nightmare he would wake up from.

"We were told she'd be safe. What happened?"

"She was safe, well . . . I'm sure you know of the unrest—"

"I heard things were heating up, but you're there. If you saw it wasn't safe, why didn't you get the volunteers out of there?" He was hot. His wife was missing and someone would pay for this. "Did you talk to her coworkers? She didn't just vanish, somebody knows something."

"We've talked with everyone she works with; they weren't much help. We're doing our best to find her. I'll be in touch when I know more, but right now, that's all I can tell you."

David hung up the phone and thought of Clair, far away and without anyone who cared about her. It was a bold move on her part to go without friends or family and volunteer in a foreign country. It went against her nature. But she had a skill that could make a difference and that outweighed her fears. He went downstairs and paced the kitchen floor.

She would never have gone off on her own.

He took a deep breath, rubbed his eyes with the heel of his hands.

I don't know who has you, but if they hurt you . . .

He snatched his phone from the counter and punched in the number of Clair's friend Darcy.

"I need a favor," he said the second she answered.

"David?"

"I just got a call from Doctors Without Borders. Clair's missing."

"What!"

"For at least six or seven hours now. No one has a clue. I wonder if it's for money. Maybe somebody knows of her parents' wealth and wants a ransom. I don't know."

"This is terrible. My God, poor Clair. What can I do to help?"

"You dated an FBI agent, didn't you?" he asked.

"Yeah. It didn't end well."

"I need you to call him. See if they can get involved now, instead of waiting a day. The longer they wait, the further away she might get."

"Okay. I should still have his number."

"Marcus Cook's heading up the search, for now. Pass that on to him. I'm going to make some calls, get as many people involved as I can."

After he had ended his call, David went to the computer, desperate to find more ways he could help.

Wherever you are, stay alive.

After spending all morning on the phone, David grew discouraged. He was hoping by now he would have something positive to tell Clair's parents and had dragged his feet on calling them.

I might as well get it over with.

As he picked up his phone, it rang.

"Mr. Stevens? I'm Brent Freeman with the FBI."

Thank you, Darcy.

"I'll be your contact person throughout our search. Do you mind if I ask you a few questions?"

David's jaw ached, and his head throbbed, but he shook it off. What he told them could make a difference.

"I want my wife back. I'll tell you anything you need to know."

"Did your wife mention anything unusual that had happened? Anything that she was concerned about or anyone she was suspicious of?"

"No, nothing. Her time there was almost over. She's scheduled to come home soon." David's throat grew tight, and it took a minute before he could speak. "Her parents are loaded. Her mother inherited old money and her dad's vice president at Proctor and Gamble."

"So you think someone's after the money?"

"It's the only thing I can come up with."

"I'll keep that in mind, but so far there's been no ransom note, no calls. Unless . . . shit. Have her parents been contacted?"

David released a loud sigh. "I haven't told them yet."

"You better, and make it quick. I doubt if this is a ransom, but if someone is after her family's money, they need to be prepared for the call. I'll give you a few minutes, and then I'll need to contact them, make sure they know what to do if a call does come in."

"I'll call them now. But please, let me know what's going on, I don't care what time it is."

Hanging up, David inhaled deeply and prepared to make the most difficult call of his life.

CHAPTER 3

CLAIR SAT ON THE COT, TIGHT AGAINST THE WALL WITH HER legs curled beneath her. A man entered the room, short and chubby, his stiff right leg lagged behind. With a small smile on his lips, he offered her water.

Parched, she lunged at the cup, spilling a few precious drops before gulping it down.

"You know they'll come for me. And when they do, they'll take you down, along with the others."

His blank stare made her wonder if he understood English. She tried again.

"If you help me, I'll speak on your behalf and they'll go easy on you."

He stood with the bland, expressionless stare of an overgrown baby. Then took the cup from her, gave her a slight bow and turned to go. At the door he held up a bucket. "For you," he said, as he placed it on the ground.

So, you do speak English.

She walked over and picked it up. The bucket had mud caked along its inside walls and small bugs crawled in and out of its cracks. Her toilet she presumed, and dropped it in the far corner.

Her head still throbbed, and her vision blurred. With a weariness she had never known, Clair curled into a ball, closed her eyes and thought of happier times, when she and David were together . . .

* * *

Her parents had rented the second floor of a high-end restaurant to celebrate their accomplishments. She had just finished her residency while David completed his dissertation and received his PhD. David called to her, his voice barely audible above the band's thundering bass. The room was filled to capacity, and it took a minute before her eyes met his. His hand raised and waved. Diligently, she swam through the sea of partiers, past friends, relatives, and people she hardly knew, toward David. Their eyes locked as if they were the only two in the room.

He pulled her into his arms and kissed her.

"I thought you'd never get here."

He took her hand and led her out of the room, away from the crowd and the noise, to a stairwell. The steps led down, but he pointed to the fire escape, its metal ladder steered upward, to an opened trap door.

"After you," he said with a wide smile.

"What are you up to?" she asked as she reached for the first rung of the ladder.

"Trust me, you'll like it."

He followed close behind, and at the top, they climbed onto the restaurant's roof. A table, covered with a white cloth and two plates heaped with food, was positioned near the roof's edge. It overlooked the river that wound through downtown.

"Oh David."

He was full of surprises but this blew her away.

"You know, there's a party downstairs?" she asked, half laughing.

"I want to have our party, just the two of us."

He picked up a bottle of champagne and popped its cork, pouring two glasses.

"To the woman I can't live without. I love you, Clair."

She swallowed hard. "I love you too."

They drank, then David set his glass down.

"Do you have to go?"

Her shoulders dropped, and she sighed.

"You've known that I would do this. Just yesterday, Doctors Without Borders confirmed my destination and my start date. In three months, I leave for Syria."

"Syria? Is it safe?" he asked.

"They assured me that it is. And I've already committed to this."

He reached into his pocket and pulled out a small box.

"Commit to me first. Clair, will you marry me?" He lifted the lid off the box and revealed a stunning diamond, surrounded by sapphires.

Her mouth fell open as she gawked in disbelief.

"Are you sure? We won't be married long before I leave."

"I'm sure. It will make it easier for me to be without you, knowing that after this, we'll be together forever. When your job in Syria is over, you'll be coming home to your husband."

His open mouth came down on hers. When the kiss ended, he buried his face in her neck. A small, breathless whisper escaped her lips. "I love you."

With his finger, he lifted her chin and gazed into her eyes.
"So . . . will you marry me?"
Her heart swelled in her chest.
"Yes. A thousand times, yes."

* * *

Darkness filled the room while she slept, and she woke more frightened than before. Sounds of movement kicked in from above along with men's muffled voices. Then the slow tromp of someone descending the stairs.

In walked the man with a limp. If she were anywhere else she might have thought him kind, but here he was an accomplice to her kidnapping. He carried a basin of water, a towel, and a flashlight, and wore the same small smile as before.

"Sargon has asked that you wash. I have bandages for your cut." He placed the basin on the chair.

As she stood, the searing pain of razor blades ripped through her rib cage. Grimacing, she bent over and walked gingerly toward the chair.

"Sargon. Is that the name of the man who was here this morning?" she asked through clenched teeth.

He lowered his eyes, nodded his head.

"Who are you people? And why do you have so many wounded that you need your own doctor?"

"We are members of ISIS," he said, the pride in his voice undeniable.

ISIS? From what little she knew, they hoped the civil war would succeed in overthrowing the current president, Bashar al-Assad.

But they also had an agenda of their own and would capture cities to claim for themselves. Here, the hotbed for militants and extremist, many groups formed. Too many to keep track of.

With soap in hand, she began the task of removing the dried blood. All the while, thoughts of ISIS and what they would do with her festered inside her head.

She washed her arms, went under her shirt and wiped her underarms, and the back of her neck. When she wrapped and secured the bandage around her head, she turned to the man.

"What's your name?" she asked.

Beads of sweat rested on his upper lip as he stood with downcast eyes.

"My name is Ashur," he said in a soft voice.

"Can you tell me, Ashur, how long they plan on keeping me?"

"I do not know."

"I have a husband and parents who'll be worried about me. I have a life. Don't you see how wrong this is?" She implored him to understand.

"I am sorry. I should not be talking to you."

He picked up the basin and towel and seemed eager to get away from her.

"Wait." She had an idea. "I'd like to speak to your leader, Sargon. Will you tell him I have something important to talk to him about? Information that he should be very interested in."

He backed away from her, toward the door, and nodded.

Sitting on the chair, she tried to think if she'd heard of a rebel leader named Sargon, but nothing came to mind. She wished she had paid attention to the conversations around the hospital lunch tables. For those who lived and worked in Syria, the events that caused their country to be in such turmoil were all they talked about.

At the time, Clair had been more concerned with doing her part. To go home with a feeling of pride that she had given six months to an impoverished country. Except, she wasn't going home. Not yet anyway. Held here by the Islamic State in Iraq and Syria.

With much of the fighting taking place in border towns, Clair felt somewhat safe working in Homs, a city centrally located. But if they brought her to a place where battles waged, it's possible she could be near Turkey.

Somehow she had to find a way out. She thought of her mother, who would not handle this news well. She had already lost one child. When her sister died, her mom had stayed in her room for months.

They had a maid to do the cleaning, and a cook to fix their meals, but Clair missed her mother and grieved for her sister. After losing Megan, they were no longer a family, but individuals who shared the same house.

Clair tried to keep things together, as well as an eleven-year-old could. She would suggest outings for the three of them, but it took years for her parents to regain their interest in her. By then she was a teenager and not into hanging out with mom and dad. Now, this news would devastate her parents.

I'll talk to their ring leader, offer him the one thing that speaks every language—money. Hopefully it can all be arranged quickly, and have me back home soon.

Later, Ashur brought her a plate of rice. The tasteless mush would have repulsed her back home. But she had never been this hungry and made quick work of it. When Ashur returned for the plate, he gave her a blanket and some water.

The blanket was worn thin and embedded with strong body odor. She ignored the stench, covered herself, and gazed into the darkness. The pounding pain in her head kept her awake. That, and the paralyzing fear of what lay ahead for her, as a prisoner of ISIS.

CHAPTER 4

SARGON ELBEZ WAS NO FOOL.

A leader in the fastest growing, most powerful militant group in the world does not allow criticism from anyone, let alone an American woman. Hard to believe that a year ago, he was nothing. Moving from one dead-end job to another, with no hope of a better life. But ISIS rewarded him for his dedication to their cause, and he rose quickly up the ranks. Before ISIS, he was just another loser, begging for any job he could get. But those same people who thought him unworthy to employ now respected and feared him.

He sat at the kitchen table, eating breakfast. Ashur stood at the counter preparing food for the doctor. He did not like hurting her, but it was necessary. She needed to understand he could not be manipulated and would not tolerate back talk. They needed a doctor, and she was it, although not the one they had wanted.

As they waited outside the hospital for the man they were expecting, two men in a parked car across the street watched them. When time passed, and still no doctor, he grew anxious and decided they would take the next doctor who came out the hospital doors. Had she taken off her badge, they may have mistaken her for a nurse.

Some would call it chance, but he didn't believe that. It was Allah's will that brought her to them. In time she would learn to accept her new life.

He got up and headed to meet with her.

"What is this important news you have for me?"

He stood with his arms crossed looking down on her.

Tentatively she rose from the cot and faced him. The bandage that ran across her forehead couldn't hide her red and swollen flesh. Her clothes were dirty, and her dark hair tangled, but her troubled green eyes, deep and brilliant, overshadowed all that was flawed.

"I would like to arrange for my release," she began. "My father is very wealthy, and he'll pay whatever you ask for me. If you like, I'll give you his name, and you can confirm that. Once you have, I'll give you the number where you can reach him to begin the negotiations."

Her trembling hands exposed her false bravado. He stared stone-faced for several minutes until he could no longer hide his amusement, and a snort burst past his wide grin.

"You Americans think you can buy everything." He sobered and moved close, inches from her crimson face. "Why would I sell what I need most?"

He watched as her face drained of color—so shaken that he almost felt sorry for her. But he would need to be strong to break her will and subdue the fight in her. It was the only way. She stepped back from him, crossed her arms beneath her breasts, and looked down at the dirt. He left her silent and quaking.

Upstairs, he met with his comrades, as he did every morning.

"I will be gone two days. Supplies are low and with another mouth to feed, we will soon be out of food. The doctor is here to care for the wounded and is not to be harmed in any way." Sargon glared at the men, he meant business and wanted them to know it.

Most of the day was spent behind the wheel of his truck. As he drove, he thought of all that must happen before they became one Islamic State. Having control of Azaz was important, but it wasn't the only border town they would need to secure if they hoped to win this war.

There have been many wars in his country, but this one was different. This time they fought with a sophistication never seen here before. They used computers to recruit and spread their ideals, their training was intense and their leaders intelligent. He had never felt so optimistic about the future for the people of Syria.

The miles sped by, and his mind drifted back to the American doctor who would learn who was in charge here. And would, in time, realize that this is where she lives. Like it or not, she was now one of them.

CHAPTER 5

WHEN CLAIR OPENED HER EYES THE NEXT MORNING, ASHUR stood over her holding a plate. It took a moment before she remembered where she was, before the fear poured back into her. Hungry, she drank the weak tea and ate the dry bread, leaving the mold that grew along one edge.

"You must eat fast. There are many soldiers for you to see," he said, as he paced the floor.

When footsteps sounded above them, Ashur opened the door. "Come."

Her insides quivered as she climbed the rickety steps. At the top, she entered a kitchen. The sound of her shoes as they stuck to the dirty linoleum floor was amplified by the silence around her. Two soldiers who cradled machine guns sat at the table, their glare made her face burn.

Ashur gently pushed her, kept her moving forward into the next room. There, across the floor, seven men lay on mats while others sat leaning against the wall. A child's scribble in purple crayon decorated the wall. Evidence that a family had once lived here.

Clair stood and took it all in. She chewed her lower lip with such vigor that she tasted blood. The men that lay before her, those who were awake, looked at her with cold, hard stares. Those who sat whispered amongst each other while sizing her up with defiant eyes.

How can they expect me to take care of all these men? I'm only one person, and a pediatrician for heaven's sake.

Ashur held a basket with an array of medical supplies, thrust it into her hands and pointed to a man on the floor.

Clair knelt next to him. His face was striped with cuts, and black soot smeared his nose and forehead. He held his thin arms close to his body while he pressed a bloody rag over the wound in his abdomen.

With care she lifted his shirt. All the while his eyes shot daggers at her. The long cut, most likely from a knife, looked severe. She put on gloves and raised his flesh to get a better look. Immediately, he grabbed her wrist and twisted. His face contorted with hatred and disgust.

"Stop it," she cried. Wincing in pain, she nearly lay on top of the man as she fought to free herself from his grasp.

Ashur spoke and begrudgingly, he released her.

"He will not hurt you again," Ashur said.

She took a deep breath, batted away her tears, and lifted her chin. She would not let them see her cry.

"Can you put on gloves, take gauze, and soak up his blood so I can get a better look?" Even with Ashur's help, she could only hope that she found all the damage and adequately repaired him.

So began the first day of her new job. Although she was being held against her will, she felt obligated as a physician to do her best to save them, but she had never had to do so much with so little. All her years of medical school hadn't prepared her for this.

Despite their injuries, when time for salat, or prayer, those who could kneeled and prayed. It surprised her to see the soldiers at midday stop what they were doing, lay down their guns, and pray. For all she knew they asked for forgiveness, but their devotion to God, regardless of their lifestyle, intrigued her.

Hours later, after she had treated her last patient, she was returned to her room in the basement. Ashur brought her water and a plate of rice and vegetables.

When she finished eating, Clair lay on her cot. Her back and shoulders burned from the hours working on the floor, hunched over the soldiers.

Someone will come for me. I just need to be patient and know this won't last.

It wasn't easy to calm herself after the day she had. With so many men with weapons, one wrong move could set them off. In addition to that, the vegetables she ate had seen better days. Her stomach rolled as she lay cold and nauseous. Darkness filled the room and the sounds of night, those unknown noises that in the light of day prove harmless, haunted her, keeping her awake and terrified as she waited for dawn.

CHAPTER 6

IT WAS NOT EASY TO CARE FOR THESE MEN. THEY WERE ANGRY. Life had been unkind to begin with, and now they were brought here with life-threatening injuries. Some never left. Their bodies, carried to the field behind the house, were thrown into a deep hole—communal burial at its worse.

While she worked with Ashur, she noticed the lewd glances coming from one of the soldiers who lived there.

"Ashur, who's the man sitting in the kitchen?" She crossed her arms across her chest in a tight hug. "He keeps looking at me, smiling."

"Mohammad. He has recently joined us."

"Yesterday he brushed against me, and ran his hand down my back."

Ashur turned his head toward the kitchen. His brows bunched together as he watched Mohammad smile at her.

"I will mention this to Sargon when he returns. He would not want anything bad to happen to you."

"I'm sure he doesn't." *Kidnapped doctors are hard to replace.*

They worked side by side, changing bandages, serving food and water. When Clair walked to the supply table, she noticed they were out of gloves.

"Ashur, can you get us more gloves please?"

"That box was half full. You can't be so wasteful." His eyes were wide with disbelief. "Only one pair of gloves each day. You wash them between patients."

Clair felt as if she had been put in a time machine and sent back one hundred years.

"Okay. From now on I'll do that, but can you get me another box for now?"

"I will look in the supply shed out back."

He was gone only a minute when Mohammad approached her. He stood close enough that she could smell his foul breath. With a crooked smile, his eyes swept over her landing on her breast.

"It is time you and I get to know each other." He ran his fingers over her cheek.

"Leave me alone." She slapped his hand away. He grabbed her wrist, ripped her blouse open, and squeezed her breast— stopping her heart. Her free arm crossed over her chest and pulled her blouse closed.

His wide open laugh revealed his broken and yellowed teeth. Stepping back, she squirmed out of his grip and spun around, hoping to find Ashur. Instead, she collided with a soldier, the one who had sat with Mohammad in the kitchen. He wore the same menacing grin as Mohammad when he aimed his gun at her.

"If you make any noise, I will kill you."

* * *

When Sargon arrived at the house, it was midmorning. He looked forward to eating, relaying the orders to his men, and getting a few hours of sleep.

As he entered, he passed through their makeshift hospital and thought it odd that neither the doctor nor Ashur were there. In the kitchen, he dropped the supplies on the table, then paused. A muffled cry rose up from the cellar. He jerked open the door and flew down the steps, two at a time.

The doctor and two of his men were on the floor. One held her arms while the other lay on top of her, his pants bunched around his ankles as he tugged urgently on hers.

With one swing of his leg Sargon kicked, landing a punishing blow to Mohammad's ribs. He rolled off of her moaning in pain.

"What are you doing? I told you to leave her alone."

Looking down at him, Sargon raised his booted foot and stomped his face. Blood exploded from his nose.

Ashur rushed into the room.

"What is . . . ?" He stopped short, looked at the doctor on the floor, Mohammad beside her, and the blood that poured from his face.

"I'm gone two days and you allow this to happen?" Sargon shouted at Ashur. He then turned to Mohammad's cohort. "Get him out of here."

Ashur followed them up the stairs.

Barely clothed, the doctor lay like a mannequin, her dead eyes stared into space. He crossed the room, retrieved her shirt, and helped her stand. He waited while she put it on, then guided her to the cot.

"What did you do to make them want you?"

He could see the hate in her eyes as she regained her focus and glared at him.

"This will not happen again."

He paced the floor, trying to defuse his fury. No matter what their needs, he had given them an order. Their disobedience would not be excused.

Ready to take her upstairs, he noticed the rip in her shirt, which made visible a good portion of her stomach. He dashed up the stairs, and on up further to his bedroom, rifled through his clothes, and came back with a shirt.

The doctor still sat where he had left her, crying.

"Put this on."

She stood, turned her back to him, and took off the tattered shirt. He couldn't help watching, and noticed the curves of her waist and hips, her dark hair lying against her cloud-white skin.

His voice turned raspy and deep. "Come. There is much to be done."

CHAPTER 7

SITTING ON A BENCH BENEATH A SHADE TREE, DAVID, LIKE everyone else on campus, had taken his lunch outside. Summer semester would end soon. Clair had been missing for four weeks, and the helplessness he felt was eating him alive. He had to do something more to find her.

If things had gone according to plan, Clair would be here, starting her career at Mercy Hospital and maybe their family as well. He couldn't wait to be a father.

David had been offered positions elsewhere, but they both wanted to stay in Ohio. Heidelberg University seemed the best fit for him and Tiffin seemed the perfect place to raise a family.

Clair loved children. While in college, she would sometimes babysit for her professors' kids and David would join her. He remembered one night when she watched three boys, all under the age of ten. By the time David arrived, Clair had set up an elaborate soccer field in the living room. They split up into teams and for two hours the competition waged.

Clair, however, was a cheat. Whenever David had a clear path to the goal, she would tackle him to the ground. He'd scream foul, but the boys loved it, laughing and piling on top of him.

She's such a loving and selfless person. Not everyone would give away six months of their lives. He had been wrestling with the idea of heading up his own search. Now, with his resolve strengthened, he stood and walked straight to the dean's office.

Looking down at the plump receptionist, he waited while she swallowed the last bite of her sandwich.

"Is Dean White available, Mary?"

"Good afternoon, Professor Stevens. He's in his office. I'll see if he's free." The pity splashed across Mary's face irritated him. But it wasn't just her, he saw it everywhere. People assumed Clair already dead and looked at him—the poor bastard—as if he waited in vain. Mary stood and walked across the room to the adjoining office. A few minutes later, she returned.

"You can go in now."

David marched in the office and felt, for the first time since his wife's disappearance, empowered. For weeks he'd been at the mercy of other people, practically begging the different agencies to help him. Well, he'd given them their chance, and got nowhere.

"Thank you for seeing me. I'm sorry to barge in without notice."

Dean White stood to shake David's hand. "Not at all. What can I do for you?"

David sat down in the soft leather chair and looked at his boss across the large mahogany desk. He would not be intimidated.

"You know the situation with my wife. Well, I'd like to take a couple weeks off and go to Syria. With summer semester almost finished and the break before fall begins, I would only miss a few days. I know this is short notice, but honestly, I can't sit here doing nothing much longer."

He paused to take a breath, he knew he'd been rambling but wanted to lay it all on the table.

"So with your permission, I'll ask Mary to arrange for my substitute and make plans to leave as soon as possible."

Leaning back in his chair, Dean White studied David's face. He ran his hand through his thinning gray hair, his brows furrowed.

"I'm sure you're aware of what's happening over there. In the past, war-torn countries would honor all humanitarian efforts. Health care providers, missionaries, groups who brought food and clothing were all off limits, considered safe from intentional harm."

He stopped to pour himself a glass of water, took a few sips before he continued. "Syrian rebels are now making their own rules. Within the last few weeks, hospitals have been bombed, people killed at an alarming rate. Most volunteers have left the country."

David rose from his chair, took a deep breath, and then let it out in a huff. "I know all that. But what kind of man continues to live life as usual when his wife's missing in another country?"

"I'm not telling you this to discourage you from thinking she will come home one day. I am, however, trying to dissuade you from going there. It's much too dangerous."

David sat, his jaw tight. "I have to do something," he said, "or die trying. Can I have the time off or do I need to look for a job elsewhere?"

He would resign his position without a single regret if it came to that. Career suicide? Maybe. But without Clair, what difference would his career make?

Dean White pointed to the empty chair across from him. "Sit down please."

He waited for David to sit before he went on. "I understand your frustration. And I don't mind if you take some time off. In fact, I insist on it. But the chance of you going to Syria, finding your wife, rescuing her from whoever took her, and bringing her home is miniscule."

A knock on the door silenced him. Mary stuck her head in and looked at her boss.

"Excuse the interruption, but the contractors for the new library are here, and they ran into a snag. They would like a word with you."

Dean White sighed. "This shouldn't take long."

David laid his head back on the chair and gazed out the window at the students who walked by. It was true, the likelihood of him finding his wife was slim. But slim felt better than none. He had to do something to get her back; life was meaningless without her.

* * *

Standing in the doorway to their bedroom, David watched her. Busy packing, Clair hadn't noticed him. A tear spilled from her eye before she quickly swiped it away. She started to close her suitcase but suddenly stopped, walked to the nightstand and picked up a framed photo of the two of them, taken while on their honeymoon. She paused to gaze at it while her fingers traced over their image, then wrapped it in a sweater and placed it in her luggage. When she turned to leave the room, she almost ran into him. "I miss you already," he said, his voice thick with emotion. While he carried her to bed, her eyes, glazed with need, never left his. Her hair rippled across the pillow as she lay waiting for his touch. His body covered hers and he hungrily took possession of her mouth. They made love like never before, knowing it would be their last until she came home. Neither knew then that their time apart would last this long.

* * *

Dean White returned carrying two cups of coffee. Handing one to David, he sat before he launched his proposal.

"I have a son-in-law, Joe Donaldson, who's a senator from Indiana. Why not let me talk to him, see if he can pull a few strings, and get some information for you? Then at least you'll know what's being done to find her. I think you can do more from here than you could if you were in Syria."

Pulling out a clean sheet of paper he picked up his pen. "Tell me everything you know about what happened the day she went missing, and everything you've learned since. I'll pass the information on to him, see if he thinks he can help you."

David paused, this turn of events unexpected.

"I guess it's worth a try."

"Great. Who's your contact person?"

"Brent Freeman is the legal attaché agent assigned to the region. He serves as a diplomatic liaison to Clair's case. I call him about every other day, but all he tells me is that they're looking at everything, and it takes time."

David rubbed his face with his hands. Racked his brain to think what information would help.

"There's a doctor, from Germany, Dietrich Schmidt," David said. "The last one known to have seen Clair. He spoke with her after her shift ended, around five o'clock, the afternoon of June 6. He mentioned she had been in good spirits but also concerned about a sick girl. They talked for close to forty-five minutes, she asked him to look in on the girl, and then she left."

David drank coffee from the Styrofoam cup he'd been given, trying to remember any details that might matter. "All the volunteers stayed at the Alriad Hotel, roughly five blocks from the hospital. Most everyone walked the short distance. Dr. Schmidt also told me that things were heating up between several rebel groups, and expressed concern about one in particular, ISIS. At the time I talked to him, there were battles over territory in the north. He felt safe enough in Homs but worried that in time, ISIS would move south toward Damascus. I don't know the outcome or even if that bears any relevance to Clair's disappearance, but he seemed worried about it—the fact that the war was gaining momentum."

David watched as his words repeated across the paper.

"When I talked with representatives from Doctors Without Borders, their biggest concern was to save face. It doesn't bode well for future volunteers to hear about missing doctors."

Dean White added a few more notes before looking up. "I'll be sure to tell this to Joe. And will call you when I have any news. Meanwhile, keep in touch with Mr. Freeman. I'll ask Joe to contact him as well. And David, I want you to take a few days off. Get some rest. Come back on Monday ready to work." The dean stood, making clear this meeting had come to an end. "The rest will do you good."

David nodded, thanked him, and left. As he stepped out into the sun, his mind filled with plans for his trip to Syria. And what he would do once there.

CHAPTER 8

After work, David drove home while his mind played random scenes of Clair and their life together. The details faded with each passing day, but the feeling they brought remained strong as if they were happening now. He parked the car in the garage and walked toward the back door.

The bordering shrubs needed trimming and the flower bed Clair had worked so hard planting had been taken over by weeds.

When did all this happen?

Near the back door, a soft whimper came from behind the shrubs. Hidden by the overgrown bush, a small dog curled in a ball, lay shaking. David whistled, trying to coax the dog out, but it wouldn't budge so he scooped him up and set him on the concrete. Its coat was filthy, and it held a hind leg close to its body as it limped back toward the bush.

"You came to the right house. I'm a sucker for animals in need. I'll get you food and a vet but once you're fixed up, it's back to your rightful owner."

He carried the dog into the house and to the laundry room, then made a bed for him out of an old blanket.

"I could use the company," he said while looking for some food for him.

With the dog settled, David checked his cell, made sure the ring volume was turned up. He didn't want to miss any calls.

He pulled a beer out of the refrigerator and leaned against the counter as he drank. When he finished, he grabbed another and headed upstairs to their walk-in closet. A box of photos sat on the floor under Clair's clothes rack. Their wedding pictures were in a large envelope, waiting for her to come home and put into albums or frames.

He flipped through them until he found what he was looking for. The photo, not shot by the photographer, but by Darcy, was David's favorite. Taken long into the reception and after much champagne, they were on the dance floor embraced in each other's arms. The love in her eyes as she looked up at him caused his throat to tighten every time he saw it.

He slipped the pictures back into their envelopes, held on to the one Darcy took, and got up. He reached out, ran his hand over her clothes, neatly hung and grouped by color. A faint scent of Giorgio Armani's "Beauty" floated in the air—his gift to her last Christmas. He closed his eyes and inhaled deeply. *Come back to me Clair.*

Downstairs he settled on the sofa and called Darcy.

"Hey. Any news?" she answered.

"My boss offered to help. He has a son-in-law who's some big shot senator. Thinks he might be able to get information on Clair. Maybe push to get more done to find her."

"That's great news. We needed a break like this." Darcy said.

He looked at the picture—his eyes fixed on Clair's beautiful face.

"I'm going there."

"What? You can't be serious."

"My boss gave me a few days off. Add the weekend, a couple of sick days if necessary, I'll be back in a week."

"What do you hope to accomplish? Where do you start looking? This is a bad idea," she argued, worried that something bad could happen to him.

"You sound like my boss."

"I thought you were going to let him help you."

"I am. Let him think I'm taking a few days off to get myself together. He can get his son-in-law on this. I'll work from the inside and let him work with what's available to him. I have to do this. I have to try."

She sighed. "If I can't talk you out of this, please be careful. And call me as soon as you get back."

He hung up, took his cell and Clair's picture to his desk. After booking his flight, he called the hotel where she stayed and booked a room there. Then he called a vet and made arrangements for the stray. Hopefully, they could fix his leg while they had him.

The last time he spoke to Clair they talked about what they would do together her first night home. Mostly lots of lovemaking and plenty of food and wine. He wondered if, like him, she dreamed of that day, holding it in front of herself like a carrot before a horse, urging her on through each day that they were apart.

* * *

With the sound of David's voice still fresh in her head, Darcy longed to be near him. For years she had ignored her feelings, but with Clair gone, and his frequent calls, it became more difficult each day.

She had met David when paired with him for a history class project. She liked him from the start. At first, they did most of their work at the campus library. But after a few meetings, they took their project to an area coffeehouse and soon became friends.

He would always walk her home, making sure she got there safely, even though it was out of his way. And boy, could he make her laugh, and she him. She thought they would be perfect together until she introduced him to Clair.

Darcy often wondered if, knowing how she felt about him, Clair would have backed off. But it no longer mattered. She hadn't mentioned it, and the rest is history.

The attraction David and Clair had for each other was obvious from the start. Before long they were dating on a regular basis, and she became the funny pal who, on occasion, tagged along.

Making matters worse, she and Clair were practically sisters, living in the same Cincinnati neighborhood since early childhood. This secret they would never share.

Darcy had dated other men, but they all fell short. After David, the bar was set high, and none of them came close. Without a serious relationship, she was lonely. But not Clair, she had it all. Darcy didn't like having these thoughts of David, especially while Clair was missing or possibly dead. And although she prayed Clair would come home, she couldn't stop dreaming of a life with David—if the worst actually happened, and she never returned.

CHAPTER 9

STILL SHAKEN FROM THE ATTACK, CLAIR TRIED NOT TO THINK of what could have been, had Sargon not come in when he did. Her arms were bruised and her breasts sore—she could live with that. It was the nightmares and the chance of another rape attempt that kept her awake nights. But for two days, the only man she saw was Ashur. And only when he brought in her meals.

As a child, she thought she knew lonely. But this? This constant, slow-moving solitude that weighed heavily on her arms and chest was unbearable. Could David possibly be this miserable? If he knew of their attempt to rape her, he'd pay them back in spades. If only he were here.

* * *

It was finals week, their junior year of college. Clair had a terrible head cold and put off seeing David all week. She needed to study and with being sick, she didn't have the time or the energy.

While she prepared for her anatomy exam, David called her.

"Whatcha doing?"

"Trying to stay awake. By tomorrow I need to know the names of every bone in the human hand," she said, her voice scratchy. "All twenty-seven."

"Do you think you have the strength to unlock your door?"

"Please, don't tell me you're here."

She looked down at her sweatpants and oversized T-shirt, ran her fingers through her bed-head hair.

"Your neighbors are getting suspicious. Please let me in before they call the police."

She threw aside her blanket, rolled off the couch and waded through the used tissues that littered her floor.

He entered, wearing rubber gloves and a surgeon's mask, carrying a takeout container of chicken soup. Laughing, Clair couldn't believe it.

"No wonder the neighbors are leery. You look crazy."

"Go to bed. After I rid this place of its germ infestation, I'll bring you dinner," he said.

"I can't let you do that. I can take care of myself. Besides, I need to study."

He crossed his arms and glared at her. Although his mask covered it, she could see the smile in his eyes.

"Don't make me use physical force."

Just then, Clair broke into a coughing fit. David pulled a wooden spoon out of a crock on the counter, and poked her with it, moving her into the bedroom without touching her.

An hour later, her small apartment clean, he brought in her soup.

*　*　*

She loved him so much. That love would keep her sane until they were reunited.

While she lay daydreaming, her eyes settled on a spider, spinning its web in the corner of the window frame. The bright sun lit up the sparkling threads and intricate patterns, too beautiful to be the death trap that it was.

She stood, walked over for a closer look. That is when as if seeing it for the first time, she noticed the window.

At two feet wide and two feet high, it was just large enough for her to squeeze through. It stood eight feet from the ground with a deep ledge that preceded the glass. The longer she looked at it, the more certain she became—this window would be her way out.

So began her scheme to escape. Her confidence soared as each step of the blueprint came together in her mind. Her next meal would be dinner so unless she were needed upstairs she should have several hours uninterrupted.

Excited by her idea, she moved quick, before she lost the courage, and dragged the heavy cot across the room and under the window. Then, she turned the chair on its side and with her foot on a spindle, kicked until it broke in half and fell out. She slid the piece of wood in her back pocket, placed the chair on the cot, and stepped her way up to the window ledge. With her arms inside the ledge, she pulled herself up. If she were any larger, this wouldn't be possible. Even now, it was difficult to move in such a small space. With shaky hands, she used the splintered wood to meticulously shatter the window, one small piece at a time. Her arms ached from holding them up so long.

As she worked, steps sounded from the kitchen. The screech of a chair being pulled from the table made her stop. She held her breath and waited.

Please, don't come down here.

Her heart raced as she listened for more sounds. The hollow thud of boots on the wood of the stairs began. She needed out now but the opening in the glass wasn't large enough yet.

With her head through the small hole, the broken glass sprayed the ground as she barreled out, and the door opened behind her. Outside, she dashed to the underbelly of the nearest truck. Sweat trickled down her face, her breath came fast, and her heart sprinted out of control.

To the left, open space, weeds and rocks framed the narrow road leading west. The house blocked her view to the right. Across the road, she spotted a dilapidated shed. It stood behind a ransacked home, the door wide open and most of its windows broken. She could see furniture turned over and holes in the wall. The shed looked safer.

Trembling, she crawled out from under the truck and sprinted across the street, diving head first behind a juniper bush. There, she listened. But the only sound was her heart as it beat like a drum in her ears.

What's going on in there? And why hasn't someone come after me?

Strange how quiet it was for a mid-morning weekday, and except for the house that had imprisoned her, the area appeared devoid of life. On hands and knees she made her way through the brush and at last, to the shed.

Inside, she sat on a rusty bucket and peered through a crack. The old looking house, dusty trucks, and large oak tree, sat as innocent as a Norman Rockwell painting. One would never guess by looking, the evil that lived inside.

Blood trickled down her neck. She swiped it away with a shaky hand, then closed her eyes and took several deep breaths to calm herself.

But her peace was short-lived as the sound of revved up engines shattered her calm. She dropped to her knees and watched through the crack as Sargon stood in the stones with his hands on his hips. His gaze slowly combed the area.

She held her breath and her heart fluttered like a caged bird as she waited for his next move.

Sargon shouted obscenities and kicked at the stones before he jumped in the truck and sped off. A second truck followed close behind. Tires spun and dust filled the air, as she watched them disappear down the road.

Flooded with relief, she shuddered, then eased herself to the floor, and took a deep breath. Her insides trembled, but there was no turning back. Soon, she would start out, moving away from the horror across the street.

It was Ashur who had gone down to her room. His step-and-slide gait gave him away. Had he deliberately delayed telling Sargon she was missing, giving her a head start? Maybe one person in this godforsaken place wanted to help her.

After sunset, she stepped out of the shed, leaving the security it provided behind. Concealed in darkness she crept through the city's neighborhoods like a thief in the night, inching forward toward freedom, and David.

The further north she moved, the greater the rubble. Buildings that had once housed hundreds, now lay in ruin, thanks to the war. And their impenetrable mass of brick and concrete made Clair's journey all the more difficult, taking her out of her way to move beyond them. Every so often she would spot a scarf, some shoes, or a child's toy. Evidence that this once was a community and its people either left in a hurry or were buried beneath it all.

While she weaved through the mess, a blur of motion in one of the buildings caught her eye. She dropped to her knees behind the ruins, listened, and waited.

When she peaked out, she saw a girl, standing on a third story balcony of a shelled apartment building. As Clair stepped out from hiding, their eyes locked. Neither flinched, both caught in an all-knowing trance of the suffering they shared. Behind Clair, gunfire startled her. When she turned back around, the girl was gone.

She continued across the sandy gravel of Syria's landscape and became less sure of herself with each step. Not only did she have Sargon after her, out here a war was being fought—you'd have to be crazy to be out at night. Or incredibly desperate.

Moving past most of the destruction, she entered into an area of homes. Some looked abandoned, while others displayed dim lights, their brave owners defiant in their decision to stay. As she walked, a noise from behind, startled her.

She stopped and listened, looked around. Street lamps that no longer lit the way lined the deserted brick road. A newspaper, propelled by the wind, floated past.

She moved away from the street to the pathless ground and picked up her pace. When again the crunch of gravel sounded behind her, even closer than before, she ran.

She moved through backyards, under clotheslines and around parked cars, past chained dogs barking—she ran. Uncertain if she was being followed, but too afraid to stop, her arms pumped and her lungs burned as she sprinted through the dark.

When she couldn't go on, she stopped. Bent over with her hands on her knees, she sucked in air as she scanned the area for a hideout. Steps that led to an underground entrance looked promising. She took them two at a time before she slipped, tumbled to the bottom, and splashed into cold water. From her knees she turned the rusted knob and pushed. The door wouldn't budge, leaving her no choice but to squat in ankle-high water that smelled of sewer.

Huddled in the corner, the rapid rise and fall of her chest her only movement. The sound of footsteps in the distance, each step louder than the last, moved close then stopped. Her heart pounded so loudly that she feared it would give her away.

Lightheaded and dizzy, she felt as if this was a dream. But the cold water that filled her shoes made it all too real as the possibility of terror loomed at the top of the stairs.

Suddenly, a voice cut through her obscurity and stopped her heart.

"I know you are here."

CHAPTER 10

THE GIRL?

"I need your help. Are you an American?" the voice asked.

Clair remained motionless. She could be working for ISIS or any number of criminals that roamed the streets at night.

"I want out; can you help me?"

She would know the lay of the land, maybe we could leave this country together.

Clair stood and creeped up the steps. The girl was alone.

"I'm here."

Their eyes met, a forced smile pasted on the girl's dirty face. The scarf that covered her head framed the teenager's worrisome dark eyes.

"I live back there, amongst the fighting. My mother is dead and my father, a Freedom Fighter, cares only of the war. Most days I help my father make bombs. I want to get away from here, go to school."

Clair laid her hand on the girls arm.

"I'm running myself. I'm not sure I can help you."

"There is a man from Turkey," the girl pressed on, "who comes here selling medicines black market. He knows a family there who will take me in. I would go to school and work in their shop after. But freedom is never free. The man wants money. You are an American; you must have money."

Clair dropped her head.

"None here. A couple of months ago, I was kidnapped by ISIS and am trying to get out myself."

"Maybe you have friends here who have money?" she said hopefully.

If I had friends here, who would give me money, we wouldn't be standing in the middle of a war, having this conversation.

"When will this man be here?" The wheels started to turn in Clair's head. "I'm a doctor and have money back home. If he'd take the both of us, I'll send money once I'm free."

The girl shook her head.

"He won't be here until Thursday next week. But he doesn't give loans, and he doesn't mess with ISIS."

The forlorn look on the girl's face was enough to make Clair cry.

"We could go together, the two of us. You know the way, with each other's help we can do this."

The girl sighed heavily and shook her head.

"ISIS will not easily give up their search for you. Young girls like myself are taken and sold all the time. I cannot risk being with you."

She looked at Clair with sympathetic eyes as if ignorance of the ways of this world was something to be pitied.

"I will show you a home, where a man lives. He is very kind and might help you."

"What will you do?" Clair asked.

"I'll go back home, help my father, and continue to look for a way out."

She started off, motioning for Clair to follow. They walked ten minutes before she pointed to a house, nestled between two exact replicas.

"I wish you luck," she said.

They embraced. Clair waved goodbye as the girl walked away with dejected strides.

"Wait," Clair shouted, as she ran to her. "Will this get you out?" She held between her thumb and forefinger the symbol of David's love.

With eyes like saucers, the girl looked from the ring to Clair and back again. The large diamond reflected the moonlight and seemed to mesmerize her.

"That ring is worth a fortune. I cannot take it."

Clair held the girls hand, laid the ring in her palm, and folded her fingers around it.

"I want you to have a better life, and maybe help others. It's your only ticket out of here. Take it."

How much is a life worth? David will understand.

With teary eyes, the girl pocketed the ring.

"You don't know what this means to me."

While they hugged, Clair whispered, "Yes, I do."

* * *

Behind the house, concealed by a clump of olive trees, Clair sat and waited for dawn. Gunfire blast in the distance. A gray lizard popped its head out of the ground, spotted her, and then withdrew back into its hole.

The temperature had dropped drastically, the unbearable heat of a few hours ago, gone. Clair pulled her arms inside her T-shirt and sat shivering, her clothes still damp from the plunge. Loud gurgling erupted from her empty stomach, pleading for food. With her head against the house, she closed her eyes.

If the man of this house helped her, she would be home soon. Back into the house that she loved, in bed with the man that she loved. She'd never leave the states again.

The first thing she'd eat would be a big greasy cheeseburger. With a thin slice of Vidalia onion, smothered in mayonnaise. Add a side of fries and a thick chocolate shake, so thick she'd have to use a spoon. After that, a visit to the spa would be nice. A pedicure followed by a full body massage, complete with aromatherapy.

Maybe they would get pregnant soon—and often, if David had his way.

He looked so gorgeous, the day she left. Every day really. As they waited at the airport, she saw the way the teenage girl looked at him, as she rang up his coffee. The snug-fitting shirt showed off his chiseled chest and arms. And with his dark eyes and thick wavy hair, who could blame her?

"Soon David. I'll be home soon."

After sitting for hours, the sun finally began to show itself, and the fog that covered the mountains began to burn off. She could hear people moving about inside, and the smell of fried eggs floated out the window. Her mouth watered, as she closed her eyes and imagined omelets, filled with ham and cheddar cheese. Soon, she could have eggs and anything else she wanted, whenever she wanted it.

The front door slammed, Clair moved close to the porch and listened. Although they were talking in Arabic she could differentiate their voices. Two, maybe three children and a man, probably their father. He spoke to them in a soft voice and whatever he said made them laugh. Soon the children walked off the porch and down the street. She approached the front entrance, and with a shaky hand, tapped on the door.

CHAPTER 11

CLAIR STOOD OUTSIDE THE DOOR AND CHEWED THE LAST OF HER nails. He was in there, she knew it, and knocked again. When the door finally opened, his eyes skimmed over her from the cuts on her face to her torn and dirty clothes, he wore suspicion like a mask.

"Hello. Do you speak English?" she asked.

"I want no trouble," he said.

"I need help. Can I please come in?"

He looked past her to the street, then hesitantly stepped aside and allowed her to enter.

Clair followed him through the house to the kitchen, where he pulled a chair away from a round wooden table. The small room was spotless and the cracked linoleum, polished to a shine. Instead of cupboards, a row of shelves were mounted above the stainless steel sink and held food. A brown Formica countertop sat on more wooden shelves that housed the dishes. A plate with leftover eggs sat by the sink.

"Why are you here?" he asked, handing her a glass of water. Clair told him why she was in his country and how she'd been taken and held by ISIS.

"If we're close to the border, any border, could you take me there? I don't need help once there, but I can't go by foot. I don't know the way, and . . . they're probably still looking for me."

When he remained silent, she pushed on.

"Can you tell me where we are?"

"We are in Azaz. It is a neighbor to Turkey." He shook his head. "I have no car."

Clair had come too far to give up now. "Do you know of someone who does, who would be willing to help me?" Then added, "I'll pay."

Lifting his arm, he ran his fingers through his thick dark hair and paced the kitchen floor. A large circle of sweat had already formed in the underarm of his burgundy T-shirt.

"I have a brother who owns a truck. Wait here, I will ask him to take you."

Clair drew in a deep breath as her hand flew to her chest. "Thank you. If you give me your name and address, I'll send money for your trouble."

He shook his head. "No. Sit. I will be back in one hour."

Clair felt so grateful she could have kissed him. The girl had been right. He walked out of the house and left her sitting, intoxicated with thoughts of going home to David.

She glanced at the counter—the cold eggs beckoned. With her fingers, she scooped every remaining crumb into her mouth. Then found soap and washed the dishes before she browsed unsuccessfully for a phone.

David will know soon enough. Authorities in Turkey will allow me to make my calls. I'll have to find the embassy, or maybe start with the police. What is the protocol for kidnapped victims in a foreign country?

The house was small, along with the kitchen the first floor had a living room and, most thrilling, a bathroom.

As she entered she caught a glimpse of herself in the mirror. Standing, staring at her reflection, she didn't recognize the woman looking back at her. Her tangled hair, greasy and flat, matted to her head in strands like wire. Her face, red with scratches and cuts, topped off with a large scab across her forehead. She looked like something out of a horror film, and as anxious as she was to see her husband, she wasn't happy to take her freak show on the road.

After using the toilet, a luxury she'd soon enjoy again, she washed her hands and face. The warm water felt so invigorating she considered jumping in the tub. Even though she'd gotten used to her smell, she knew her body put out an offensive odor. But after going six weeks without a shower, she could wait another day, and instead washed at the sink.

Back in the kitchen she paced the floor, biting her nails. It seemed to be taking longer than an hour but then, maybe his brother wasn't home or the car needed gas. The waiting became unbearable. Where were they? While she paced, doubt filled her mind. She wished she had thought of a better plan before she took off. One that didn't rely on the help of others. But alone, she thought, the parasites who lived off of the suffering of others would eat her alive. This was her best option. She just needed to be patient.

The squeak of the front door as it opened doused her misgivings. Two sets of footsteps headed toward the kitchen. She had worried needlessly. With a wide smile, she bounced like a child made to wait for the toilet. Finally she would meet this hero brother. But she needed no introduction. The smile fell from her face as they entered the room. Sargon stood with the look of a champion.

"There are hundreds of ISIS soldiers living in this town; I lead them all. You can never escape us."

"No," she moaned, grasping the chair to steady herself.

I can't go back there.

She spun and headed toward the back door. He moved just as quick and lunged at her legs, both hit the floor with a thud. Her teeth clamped down on his arm. The metallic taste of his blood filled her mouth before he loosened his grip—enough to allow her to squirm from beneath him and crawl toward the door. As she reached for the knob, he dove on top of her and flipped her onto her back. Her hand felt for the shelf above her and found the cast iron skillet she had washed an hour ago. Head up, his eyes moved to her hand—too late. The flat back of the pan hit his face with such force and velocity it bounced off and flew out of her hand. And for one brief moment he looked lost and uncertain. She moved toward the door and pulled it open, just as his hands clasped her ankles.

With a quick jerk, Sargon dropped her to the floor, then straddled her stomach. His hands circled her throat and squeezed.

"Stop fighting and you won't get hurt—understand?"

Inches away, his spit sprayed her face.

Slowly he shut off her air, her eyes bulged, and she floated toward unconsciousness. When she nodded in submission, he loosened his hold. Like a dog, she rolled on all fours, coughed and gasped for air—stars flashed before her. He stood, grabbed her arm, and pulled her up.

"Next time I won't be so understanding."

She felt a hot uprush of hatred and loathing toward him, stronger than before. Sargon took hold of her arm, and as she staggered past her would-be savior, Clair met him eye to eye to shame him. Wringing his hands, he took a step back.

"I am sorry," he whispered.

Sargon held the truck's door while she lethargically dropped onto the passenger seat, filled with despair and humiliation.

As they drove back to her prison she looked at the people along the street who stood watching. They knew what was happening, yet did nothing to stop it. Just like the man who had reported her to Sargon, they had families whose lives would be jeopardized if they challenged ISIS. She couldn't blame them.

Sargon didn't speak as he steered the truck through the streets of Azaz taking her back to the nightmare she thought she had awakened from. Tears dropped from her face onto her lap. It wasn't long before the truck skidded to a stop in front of the house.

All eyes were on her as they entered, and like a student escorted to the principal's office, she felt shame. Walking through the kitchen, her eyes met Ashur's, long enough to see his compassion.

Sargon walked her down the stairs, pushed her into the room, and locked the door. It was dark. Not dark, black. She couldn't see her hands in front of her. The window, her escape route, had vanished as if it had never existed.

Crawling, she ran her hand back and forth across the dirt like the blind with a walking stick, seeking the cot. Once her hand hit the metal frame, she felt her way to the mattress and lay down.

The smell of dirt, stronger than before, filled her nose. The darkness weighed heavy on her chest, and her breath became labored. Today she saw firsthand the enormous amount of power these men had. Any thoughts of another escape would be ludicrous. Her only way out now in the hands of other people. Never had she felt so powerless.

CHAPTER 12

DAVID'S PLANE LANDED IN DAMASCUS, FOLLOWED BY A BUS ride to Homs. The long winding road, full of rocks and gullies, nearly jarred him out of his seat. The six other passengers seemed immune to it—some even slept. A rancid smell filled the air, but it was the bullet holes in the windows that sickened him.

Is anyone safe here?

He hailed a cab at the bus stop that took him to the Alriad Hotel. As he carried his bag toward its entrance, he imagined his wife walking these very steps, determined to make a difference here.

After checking in, he went to the hospital in hopes of talking to people she worked with. At the entrance, the receptionist directed him to the pediatric unit on the second floor. There, he spotted a nurse busy writing as she leaned against the wall.

"You speak English?" he asked.

"I do. Can I help you?"

"My wife, Dr. Stevens, was a volunteer here. She disappeared a couple months ago. Did you know her?"

"Yes. Dr. Stevens was a very caring physician."

Still is.

"Did you work with her on her last day here?"

"No, but Dr. Nassar did. Would you like to speak to him?"

"Yes, thank you."

While he waited, David paced the dingy floors and looked around. Babies cried in the distance and young patients on gurneys were parked in the halls. The warm air that blew in through the windows gave little relief from the heat—or the smell.

"Mr. Stevens," the nurse said. "Dr. Nassar will speak with you, but he can't today. He could meet with you tomorrow, during lunch hour."

"I'll come back tomorrow. Thanks."

Instead of the elevator, David took the stairs and passed by the gurneys on his way. He stopped to swat away flies that had gathered on a girl's blood-soaked bandage. They returned within seconds. At the entrance, he again interrupted the receptionist from her work.

"Excuse me. Which exit would the staff use?"

"Most use the rear door, closest to the parking lot," she said.

"The volunteers who stay at the hotel, do they go out the back as well?"

"No. They go out the doors here." She pointed to where he came in.

"Thank you."

He went back to the hotel, stopped at the front desk.

A man who looked to be in his late forties stood sweating profusely in his heavy green suit. David showed him Clair's picture.

"Do you know this woman?"

He glanced at the photo. Nodded his head.

"She stayed here, very nice."

"I'm married to her. She's missing, and I'm trying to find someone who may know where she is. Were you working on June 6?" David asked.

"I told authorities already. She never came back to her room. I know because I was here, and she would always stop and talk to me before going to her room. Always."

If she went out the front of the hospital and never made it back, she was taken somewhere in between. David thanked the man, then turned to leave.

"Do you want her things?"

His words stopped David cold.

"What things?"

"Her luggage. Everything is here, in the back."

He pointed to a room behind him. In his mind-muddled attempt to make sense of all this, David had forgotten about her luggage.

There may be a note or her cell phone in there, a clue to where she might be.

"I'll be back in an hour. I'll pick them up then."

It was a short distance between the hospital and hotel. David wondered how something like this could have happened in such a brief amount of time. As he walked, he looked for anything out of the ordinary that might lead him to her. Movement from a second-story window across the street caught his eye. He glanced up at the blur of a man, then the curtain as it swayed against the empty pane.

Marching straight ahead, David climbed the stairs to the apartment and pounded on the door. The man who finally answered was small in stature and appeared to be in his early sixties. He looked frightened and frail. David told him why he was there, but got a blank stare in return.

"Do you speak English?" he asked.

The man wiped sweat from his brow. Dirt underlined his long nails and his eyes darted like pinballs in their sockets.

David raised his palms toward the man. "Stay here. I'll be right back."

Back at the hotel, David found a baggage boy who spoke English well and offered him twenty bucks to come with him to translate. The kid jumped at the easy money.

David again pounded on the door. They waited, sweating in the sauna of the airless stairway, listening to footsteps from inside. Finally the door opened a crack and fear filled eyes peered out at them.

"Tell him it's okay. I won't hurt him," David said to the boy.

Tentatively, he stepped aside and opened the door. Through the boy, David explained why they were there, and began his questioning.

"Was he home on June 6?"

"He went out in the morning, but was home most of the day," the boy translated.

David showed him Clair's picture. A look of recognition covered the old man's face.

"Something happened to my wife that day. On her way home from the hospital. Did you see anything unusual, anyone suspicious looking?"

The man picked at a rash on his arm as he sat ignoring them. The boy looked at David and shrugged. Finally the man looked toward the window and spoke.

"He watched her, many times walking to the hotel with a group. When he saw her that day, it was just her lying on the sidewalk. A man picked her up, put her in the trunk of a car. Two other men were with him."

David clenched his teeth and walked to the window. Looking across the street, he pictured Clair lying hurt while some monster threw her in his trunk. He cracked his knuckles as he stood dazed, burning inside.

He walked back to the boy. "Ask him if he told this to anyone? Police, US military?"

"He says no one asked him."

Unbelievable. What type of investigation is taking place here?

"Did he know the men in the car?"

The man rattled off a slew of words a mile long. His red face scrunched tight as he paced the room shouting. When finished, he crossed his arms, a line of spit ran down his chin.

The boy nodded, his lips tight.

"He says he does not know the men but has seen one of them before. When ISIS came to Aleppo. They killed his wife when she refused to quit her job at the pharmacy."

God no. ISIS has Clair.

David pulled out two twenties, handed one to each of them, and then dragged himself back to the hotel. Stopping at the front desk, he picked up Clair's suitcase and took it up to his room.

He dumped everything out on the bed. Went through every pouch, emptied every pocket of her pants. Her purse held lipstick, tissues, a comb, and ten dollars in Syrian pounds. No cell phone. Tonight he'd call Freeman, maybe they could ping her phone if they hadn't already. Beneath her clothes, the photo he had watched her pack.

How many times had you sat staring at the two of us together?

Her eyes, so bright and happy, held him spellbound. A rock settled in his stomach.

"I promise you, Clair, I'll do whatever it takes to bring you home."

* * *

The next day he went back to the hospital and met with Dr. Nassar. After introductions, David got to the point.

"I understand that you worked with my wife on her last day here. Did she give any indication that she was worried or afraid?"

"Your wife is a very strong woman. In fact, we've argued. When it came to her patients, she could be very stubborn. Wanted things done her way." He paused, pushed his glasses up with his finger. "But no. Her mood was upbeat that day. All days really."

"Someone I spoke with thought ISIS may be involved."

"I wouldn't be surprised. Their group is growing, and they take what they want. If they needed a doctor, they would take one. Just because she is American does not make her immune to the terror that runs through this country."

David's jaw tightened. He could feel his blood pressure rise as he sat across from this apathetic man.

"Will you think? There must be something you remember."

Dr. Nassar stood. "What do you want from me? I said I don't know."

David stood as well, towering over the smaller man by two inches.

"People drop in our country to feel good about themselves. They stay a few months then get the hell out as fast as they can. You want me to help you, but I can't. To be honest, I think you should go home and accept you will never see her again. People are lost and never found here. Whole families, like mine, are killed in an instant, and no one knows why."

Clearly shaken, Dr. Nassar steadied himself before sitting down.

David looked up at the ceiling and swallowed hard.

"I'm sorry you lost your family," he said in a low voice. "I'm staying at the Alriad Hotel if you think of anything that might help me."

David slowly walked back to his room, more afraid than he had ever been in his life.

He spent the next two days walking the streets, talking to people, but got nowhere. He decided then, to go home early, talk to Brent Freeman. Once intelligence knew for certain that ISIS was involved, they could narrow their search and find her—before his worst nightmare became reality.

CHAPTER 13

STANDING AT THE ROOM'S ENTRANCE, SARGON WATCHED AS she gently cared for the men. Her moves were tentative and her worried eyes always on the lookout for danger. Fear, like a ghostly figure, followed her everywhere. He took a deep breath and closed his eyes. He wished he did not think of her so often, but her beauty had captured his mind. With her long ebony hair and bright green eyes, a touch of gold around their edges, she certainly would have garnered attention back home. And she could be a problem for him here.

If I could go back in time and take a different doctor, I would.

He turned and walked outside to the back of the house. Leaning against the building he pulled out a pack of cigarettes and lit one.

Since her failed escape, she seemed different. More sullen than before. Although they were starting to fade, the bruises around her neck still made him cringe. He had almost strangled her that day. Why did she have to provoke him?

Maybe he needed to get away for a while. He had not been to their camp in Tartus for several days. Being with strong men who never wavered in their beliefs would help him to refocus on what mattered most—the war.

Walking toward his truck, he passed Ashur and called to him, waiting as he waddled over.

"I want you to see that the doctor is given additional food. She is too thin. If she becomes weak, she will be no good to us. Understand?"

"Yes, of course. I will see to it at her next meal."

"And throw her in the shower. She reeks." He laughed as he walked to his truck and drove away.

As always, when he entered Tartus he was greeted by the fresh scent of the sea. The crisp air took him back to his son when he felt the warm sand for the first time. And to his wife's calming touch as they walked, arms linked along the beach. These moments held what little goodness his past possessed. But Sargon didn't—couldn't—have that anymore, not with what he had chosen to become. Everything came with a price.

Sargon drove around deserted jeeps and tanks, past crumbled buildings, to the center of town, and entered their camp. There, he received orders to move weapons ISIS had stored in an old warehouse. It was rumored that the government had discovered their location, and if left there, would take them for their own use.

He hooked a trailer to his truck and, accompanied by two men, began their mission. It took most of the night to load the weapons and they grew tired. They didn't hear the soldiers who had crept their way through the tall grass, surrounding them.

Gunfire blast, Sargon dove beneath the trailer, and within seconds, his two comrades lay dead. Soon the cowards slithered out from the grass like snakes. The four of them moved slow, looking for signs of life from their enemy.

Sargon watched as one set of boots paced the length of the trailer. Moving quickly, he rolled into a stand, grasped a fistful of hair, pulled back the soldier's head, and slit his throat. His movement, so smooth and fast, was second nature.

He crept around the truck, searching for the others. But the moon, wrapped in a shroud of dark clouds, provided little light.

All at once, the sky opened, letting go of its long-held rain. The large drops broke the silence with deafening claps as they battered the truck.

He didn't hear the gunfire but felt the bullet as it entered his arm, the searing pain dropping him to his knees.

He fired shots toward the warehouse as he lunged, falling into the grass, and crawled until he felt safe enough to stand and run. When he could run no longer he stopped to rest. Blood flowed down his arm and dripped from his fingers. Combined with the rain it created small red rivers that wound through the rock-hard ground, bloody streams that sapped his strength and had him woozy. With cloth ripped from his shirt, he made a bandage and tied it tight around his wound with one hand and his teeth.

It was dawn when he dragged himself back to the house. He spoke to Ashur, and then moved up to his room and collapsed on his bed.

CHAPTER 14

CLAIR LAY WAITING FOR ASHUR TO COME DOWN WITH HER breakfast. Last night, for some reason, they had upped the portions and added fruit. For the first time since being here she went to sleep without the pangs of hunger that typically kept her awake.

Living in darkness, she had no clue of the hour, but the onset of noise from above told her another day had begun. She looked forward to going upstairs so she could see again.

On most days, the windows were open and she breathed in the fresh air. It was a welcome reprieve from the musty smell of dirt. That is, unless a strong wind blew in from the north. Then the air passed through the back field, picking up the sickening stench of decaying bodies before blowing it through the windows.

Every so often kerosene was splashed on the dead, a match thrown on top. This was usually done at night while she was in her room, grateful for the cover the musty dirt provided.

At last, Ashur came in with her meal. Strangely, they had become friends, she and Ashur, under the most unlikely circumstances. He was part of the terrorist who controlled her, but he was kind to her and she couldn't help but like him.

"Good morning, Ashur," she greeted him.

"Good morning, Doc," he replied. "I have a surprise for you. Before seeing patients, Sargon has asked that you shower."

Clair stared at him, unable to hide her smile. What she had once taken for granted, now overwhelmed her with delight.

"Quick, finish your breakfast. We don't have much time." He smiled as if pleased with himself for delivering such happy news.

Despite everything, as she walked toward the shower she couldn't help feeling buoyant. Lukewarm water trickled from a rusty shower head, and black mildew grew in the corners. But none of that mattered. The shower was pure bliss.

Picking up the small bar of soap from the shower floor, she washed over her body, then used it on her hair. She washed a second time for good measure, and could feel the hair on her legs and underarms, long and coarse.

By the time she finished, the water had long grown cold, but removing the dirt, sweat, and dried blood from her body rejuvenated her. She stepped into the infirmary ready to work.

While she loaded her basket with supplies, Ashur came to her.

"You are needed in the kitchen."

Do they want me to cook their meals now?

She followed him in. There Sargon sat at the table, his arm bludgeoned between his shoulder and elbow. He looked at her with weary eyes, his face, gaunt and pale. The unbeatable tyrant had the look of a beaten man.

"I need your help."

He held a towel over his wound. Once removed she could see this would not be a quick fix.

"I'll get the basket," she said, her voice as shaky as her legs.

When she came back he had taken off his shirt and waited for her, bare-chested. Fighting her urge to stare, Clair wondered when he found time to work out. His sculptured body likened that of a serious athlete.

With jittery hands, she removed the suture needle from its package, then poured the limited antibiotic solution over his mangled flesh. His hand rested on her leg as she worked, he watched her every move. Although she tried to focus on the job at hand, being this close to him flustered her. There was a feeling of intimacy here, which seemed ridiculous; she'd treated grown men before—lots of men. *Why is this man different?*

"The bullet is still in there. I'll need to remove it."

He nodded in agreement. With nothing to dull the pain, she began the slow process of locating and removing the bullet. Several times he would stiffen in pain, sweat running down his face and neck. Despite that, he remained silent.

Once the bullet was out, the worst was over, and she began to suture the deep gash closed.

"I notice you smell better," he said.

Caught off guard, his comment at first confused her.

"Oh. Thank you for the shower," she said dryly.

"You are happy with the extra food?"

"Yes."

Head down, steadfast she stitched, wanting this to be over.

"Have the men bothered you since—"

"No."

They more than bothered me . . . I was nearly raped.

She stopped often to wipe her face, sweat burning her eyes. Near the end, as she reached for the gauze Sargon took hold of her chin and turned her face to meet his, his course fingers scratchy against her face and neck.

"You will never leave here; it will be better for you to accept it."

And just forget my old life? Pretend I don't have a husband who I love and ache for everyday? Never.

She jerked her chin from his grasp, took out the roll of gauze, and wrapped his arm tight.

"If there's a chance you could get a tetanus shot, I strongly recommend it."

"Unlikely," he scoffed, as he put on his shirt. "Thank you for helping me."

As if I had a choice.

CHAPTER 15

Unable to fall asleep, Clair lay awake and stared into a darkness that seemingly had no end. Danger appeared like phantoms, gathered by her tireless imagination. Every noise became a threat, a menacing presence that taunted her.

But this night the sounds coming from the far corner of the room were all too real. Living in darkness had sharpened her hearing, and she could tell by the sounds of the frantic digging that many were in the room now.

Without light, she could only guess that rats had burrowed their way in. Although she had seen them in the streets and alleyways, she had never been so close to one.

When she clapped her hands, the digging stopped, but they soon caught on to her ploy and ignored her attempts at frightening them. More afraid of them than they of her, she took the blanket and despite its bad smell, covered her head and tucked it around her body.

Throughout the night she let out little screams or whistles that would quiet them momentarily. As time passed they gained courage and moved closer to where she lay.

Determined not to sleep with rodents on the prowl, Clair played mind games to keep herself awake. Naming the presidents in order of office, reciting poetry. It worked for a while but eventually she gave in to her drowsiness and slept.

But her slumber was short-lived. Clair was pulled from her dreams by a piercing pain in her arm and could feel the rats move around her. She opened her mouth to scream but nothing came out—every muscle, tight and stiff. The rat with its teeth in her arm loosened its bite and fled. Its claws scratched her as it ran. Its movements spooked the others and they scurried over her legs and dropped off the cot to the floor.

Uncertain if any were still near, she stood and violently shook her blanket, then tilted the cot, and pounded it against the ground.

Wrapping the blanket around herself she stepped up on the bed, pressed her body tight against the wall, and listened as they ran.

Then, she erupted into full blown hysteria. She screamed, long and loud. Her body shook with the force of it. The rats had ignited a fury that raged inside her. She sucked air into her lungs and screamed again. The anguish she suffered, being held here and deprived of David's love, had finally showed itself.

Trembling, her body slid down the wall to the cot. She wrapped her arms around her knees, pulled herself into a ball, and sobbed. Her body convulsed with each gasping breath, and her anger grew. Not only toward Sargon, but at everyone who should have found her by now, but hadn't. She cried until she grew sick from it, then lay awake, waiting for dawn.

When Ashur came in with her breakfast, her fiery anger had smoldered into red-hot coals that burned inside her.

"I won't be eating this morning. I'm not feeling well," she said from the cot.

His mouth hung open as he stared, unmoving.

She turned onto her side and ignored him.

"I am sorry you are ill . . . but many men were brought here this morning. Even as we speak, men are being carried in. Sargon will expect you to care for them."

"Of course he will," she said, as she threw her blanket and rose from the cot. "We wouldn't want to disappoint Sargon."

"Please, you do not know him. He is a kind man."

She shook her head. "You're right. I don't know him. Not like that."

"When a boy, in Aleppo, his mother died. His father died three years later, shot and killed by government soldiers while Sargon watched. We became friends in a Turkish refugee camp and have been together since then."

Clair walked over to face Ashur. "I'm sorry things are so bad here. He's had a bad life like so many others who live in this country. But that doesn't make it right what he's doing to me."

She grabbed the door knob, flung the door so hard it hit the wall with a bang, and stomped up the steps to endure another day—in hell.

CHAPTER 16

CLAIR WAITED IN THE KITCHEN FOR ASHUR TO COME UP THE stairs then followed him into the infirmary. They stood there, too shocked to move, and drank in the horror that lay before them.

"What happened?" she asked.

"ISIS seized Tabqa Air Base from President al-Assad's army. It is a very important win for us."

Not spoken like a winner, he said this with tears in his eyes as they both stood dumbfounded, staring at the fallout from their so called victory. The room looked like a slaughter house. Wounded men lay everywhere, almost on top of each other. Those who could, stood in the corner of the room, huddled tight together like a clump of grapes.

Where do I begin?

For hours, she waded through bodies, doing what she could. But for many, it was too late. As she worked she avoided their faces, unable to look them in the eye without confirming their ominous fate. Finally, she knelt beside the last of the wounded.

He leaned against the wall with his face in his hands. When Clair touched his arm he lifted his head and his large, dark eyes met hers. She saw his fear.

"I can help you," she said, easing him down so she could take a look.

His lips, cracked and swollen, trembled and his soot-smeared face showed lines where tears had earlier traveled. When she remove his coat she was surprised by how thin he was.

"Where are you injured?" she asked him.

When he didn't answer Ashur repeated her question in Arabic. And when he spoke, with the high, soft pitch of the young, there was no doubt that a child, dressed up as a soldier, lay before her.

She knew from talk at the hospital that boys here were taken, Syria's equivalent to being drafted, and made to fight in a war that to them, held no relevance—forced to shoot, to kill, and be killed. But until now, she had never met one.

"Ask his name," she said to Ashur.

"Hakeem," he said in response to Ashur.

"How old is he?"

Ashur grimaced. "He says he is eleven."

Floored, it took a minute before she voiced her outrage. "Is this common? Someone so young carrying a gun and being shot at?"

"I am afraid it is not uncommon for young men—"

"Young men? He's not a man he's a child. Ask him where it hurts."

When Hakeem indicated an area on his back, Clair went to work. He was lucky; his cut would only require stitches—the bullet had only grazed him. No need to inflict upon him the pain of digging for it.

When she finished her repair, she made sure Hakeem was comfortable. She had never been a mother and now, wasn't sure she ever would be. But here, with a young boy who needed a mother she would play the part.

Sargon had entered the room and was watching her. In a sudden burst, he walked over, took hold of her arm, and pulled until she stood.

"What is all this on your arm?" he asked.

"It appears the lovely room where I'm staying has rats. Very hungry rats."

She jerked her arm from his grasp and sat down, feeling a bit shaken. Until now, her fear had kept her from doing anything to anger him, but the rats had given her attitude. He turned and walked out of the room.

After she had served the injured their dinner, Ashur came to her. "It is time to go down."

"Do you have children?" she asked as they walked.

"I am a father of two young boys. My work here keeps me away from them. But someday, when they are men, there will be peace in Syria, and our time apart will be rewarded."

Clair nodded, thinking him naive.

"When did you last see your wife?"

"Four months ago."

"I bet you miss her."

He nodded. "Very much."

"Just like I miss my husband. The difference is, you chose to be apart from your spouse. I didn't."

With a hand on the door he turned to her.

"But like me, you have a choice, to accept or not, what we cannot control."

She had met many people here who shared Ashur's philosophy. After years of failed dreams and heartache, it was easier. But she refused to give up hope.

After Ashur had left the room, she rolled up in her blanket, tucked it as tight as she could, and prayed that the rats had found a new home. With very little sleep the past night, Clair dozed off quickly. During the night, a blast inside the room jarred her awake. Panicked, her body jerked off the cot and landed hard on the ground. Frozen on her hands and knees in the dirt, she struggled to gain awareness while the explosion roared repeatedly. The room had light, and as the eruption still rang in her ears, Sargon set his flashlight on the chair, walked over to the dead rats and tossed them in a bag.

Glancing her way, he paused long enough to meet her gaze before walking out. With her heart pounding, Clair sat back on the cot and tried to calm herself. The rats were dead—he killed them.

It took several minutes before it occurred to her, she could see. Dashing to the chair, she snatched the flashlight and quickly moved back to her cot.

Why did he leave it? Does he want me to have it, or will he take it back once he realizes he forgot it?

The light shone bright and strong. The shadow puppets she made on the ceiling brought a smile and jogged a memory of nights with her sister. She turned it off, covered herself, and held it close. Soon she slept, her troubles forgotten.

CHAPTER 17

A STIFF BREEZE SCATTERED DEAD LEAVES ACROSS THE PAVEMENT, along with a chill that warned of winter. Clair had been missing for five months now, and David was tired of Freeman's stale excuses.

When David told him that he went to Syria, and what he learned there, Brent warned him that if ISIS had her, it would take time to find her. Their organization spanned three countries. But how much time did they have before a bullet found her, or a bomb?

As he entered Marsh Hall he felt the buzz of his cell as a text came in. Trying to avoid the stampede of oncoming students, David stepped aside before reading it. Dean White wanted to meet with him at four o'clock, he hoped with news on Clair. David entered the classroom and began his last lecture of the day.

Cheerful as always, Mary greeted David as he walked in. "Good afternoon, Professor Stevens. You can go right in."

Dean White stood to greet him. "David, good to see you. Have a seat."

David ran his fingers through his hair. It needed a cut badly, something Clair would have been on him about if she were here. Dean White sat down and picked up the paper he'd been reading. "I have some news for you, from Syria."

David moved to the edge of his seat and waited.

"From what Joe has learned, your wife isn't the only American citizen who's missing. There are two others, both physicians, who went missing a couple weeks after your wife. This is good news for you. The more missing, the bigger a public relations headache it becomes for our government. And, the FBI received a tip from someone who believes ISIS is involved. That source claims to have seen your wife being put in the car with ISIS members."

David shifted in his chair, cleared his throat.

"Um . . . I'm their source, well, I talked to their source."

For a moment Dean White looked confused before he grasped David's meaning.

"Tell me you didn't." His face showed his disappointment.

"I had to go. I appreciate your concern for me, but I couldn't sit and wait any longer. When I told Brent Freeman that I found a witness who saw ISIS take Clair, he seemed more pissed off that I went there than glad for the information. I'm not trying to interfere; I just want my wife back."

"I'm sure he wants that too. The information is slow coming, but it's best to let the experts handle this. And with what they know now, we have reason to be hopeful."

David wasn't feeling it. "I appreciate this new information, but why aren't they moving on it? While there, the man who connected the kidnappers with ISIS told me he'd never been questioned." His hand dropped with a thud on the arm of the chair.

"And while there, you noticed the turmoil the country is in. The military can't put men in situations they aren't prepared for. Try to be patient."

Easy to say when it's not your wife held by terrorists. When you go to bed at night and she snuggles next to you, safe and happy.

David left the office trying to find a silver lining. If a senator from Indiana could get that amount of information, there was probably much more he wasn't privy to.

He drove home and pulled into his driveway. Sitting there, he envisioned his wife at the mercy of ISIS—it made his skin crawl. When he entered the house, his scruffy dog, who he named Buster, greeted him. After weeks of trying to find his owner, David gave up and adopted the mutt. He had to admit, the dog was good company.

After changing clothes he opened the refrigerator, scavenged through it for something to eat and settled on a slice of leftover pizza. With his laptop, he moved to the living room. Buster trailed behind and jumped up on the sofa beside him.

Before his visit to Syria, David found little information on ISIS. Now, they were all over the news, gaining a reputation for their ruthless takeovers and cold-blooded killings. Unbelievably, as their terror grew, so did their membership.

Holding his computer, he became engrossed in the multitude of stories about ISIS. A fragment of Al Qaeda, they were taking over Syrian towns that were once considered liberal, establishing very conservative strongholds on its citizens. Women especially were losing freedoms they had once enjoyed such as education and careers.

If that's how they feel, how will they treat a female doctor?

When he read all he could take, he went outside and sat on the porch swing. He had wanted a table and chairs here but Clair insisted on the swing. She was right, it was a perfect spot for it.

God, I miss you.

Tomorrow would start another long weekend. He went in the house and sat, mindlessly watching television until Darcy called. He answered after the first ring.

"Hi."

"I wondered if maybe you and I could meet tomorrow night in Columbus. It's half way for both of us and maybe get something to eat somewhere. That is if you don't already have plans."

"Nothing that can't be changed. The Melting Pot around seven?"

"Perfect. I'll see you then," she said.

In the kitchen, he grabbed a half empty bag of Doritos before climbing the steps toward his bedroom, looking forward to tomorrow when he wouldn't be eating alone.

CHAPTER 18

SARGON ENTERED THE ROOM AND WENT STRAIGHT TO CLAIR.

"The boy, will he be all right?"

She looked up from where she sat beside Hakeem.

"Do you really care?" she asked.

"I asked you a question—answer me," he barked.

She stood straight and stiff, her chin raised slightly.

"The boy's name is Hakeem, and he'll be one of the lucky ones to leave here alive."

"You may stay longer with him and eat your dinner together."

Her eyes, wide with surprise, met his.

"Okay. Yes, thank you. I'd like that."

Standing so close, he fought the urge to touch her, to hold her in his arms and feel the softness of her flesh. He quickly turned and walked out the back door.

* * *

Since the rat incident he had been thinking of ways to make life easier for her. But why? She was an American who had it easy all her life. He shouldn't treat her any different than what she was, a prisoner taken to benefit their cause. But every day that he witnessed the tender care she gave his men, he grew fond of her. She went beyond what was required of her. And then the boy came and he watched her tend to him with such love, it made him remember his own son.

* * *

Karim followed him everywhere. His wife would scold Sargon, "You have to keep a closer eye on him. He is too brave for his own good."

Sargon would laugh, try to ease her worries. But he had to admit, Karim was a handful. The boy had an insatiable curiosity and had no fear.

One day while at the market, Karim got away from him. He was six and in the city with Sargon shopping for his mother's birthday present.

When he noticed Karim missing, Sargon wasn't too alarmed. It happened so often that he learned to let time pass before getting worried. But when ten, then fifteen, minutes had gone by and he still could not find Karim, panic set in.

A woman whose son said he knew Karim from school saw him heading toward the tall tower. He should have guessed, it had always interested him.

Sargon looked up the tower and called out his name.

Then he heard it. A small, high pitch that could have been the wind. Hearing it a second time it became clear, "Abbun. Abbun." Karim called to him from above.

Taking hold of the cold steel he began his ascent up the thirty-foot tower. Sargon yelled at the top of his voice, "Karim. Don't move. I am coming to get you." His heart raced, just thinking about what could happen frightened him more than anything he had faced before.

When he reached the top, he held Karim tight, so thankful he was alive. But then, anger set in.

"Karim, we will talk about this when we are home, but what you did today was very bad. You could have been killed."

Three years later he was.

Sargon pulled out a cigarette and walked to his truck. He put down the tailgate and sat smoking. The boy being here brought on painful memories. And the woman confused him. Made him think things he should not. He rose and went to the kitchen, fixed himself something to eat. Then, unwittingly, was drawn to Hakeem.

"Are you feeling better?"

Hakeem kept his eyes down and nodded. Assuming the boy had been taken from his family by a man such as Sargon, he couldn't blame him for being afraid.

"You have no reason to fear me."

Hakeem pulled his blanket to his chin. Sargon remembered seeing candy in a kitchen drawer and stood to get it. It would take more than a chocolate bar to win Hakeem's trust but it was a good start. Sitting on the floor, Sargon waved it seductively before him. "Eat this—it will make you strong," he said.

Hakeem turned away from him.

"All right, I will eat it myself."

Sargon tore open the candy. Soon Hakeem pulled his skinny arm out from under the blanket and held out his hand.

"Thank you sir," he said, before taking a bite.

"Hakeem, do you know I have a boy who is almost your age? His curious nature always got him into trouble."

"What is your son's name?"

"Karim. He always brought home lizards and other creatures that would scare his mother. One day, he put a long snake in a drawer in the kitchen and forgot about it. The next day while his grandmother visited, she opened the drawer. Seeing the snake, she screamed to high heaven and ran from the house. I had never seen her move so fast."

Hakeem laughed out loud.

The sweet sound of a young boy's laughter reminded Sargon of what he once had. With a wide smile on his face he looked up and caught Clair watching, disbelief etched on her face. He saluted her, then threw his head back and laughed. Loud, like a boy.

CHAPTER 19

CLAIR STOOD IN THE INFIRMARY, STARING AT SARGON WITH her mouth open.

Is Sargon really being nice? And funny? Giving a boy candy won't change my opinion of him.

She hurried through her last two patients to spend time with Hakeem. It was a relief that Sargon had left the room. He made her so nervous, watching her every move.

With their dinners in hand, she settled in beside Hakeem. He picked up a grape, tossed it in the air, and caught it in his mouth. With a sidewise glance and a wide smile, he reminded her that he was just a boy. He tossed her a grape.

So you want to play—good for you.

She tossed the fruit in the air and opened her mouth but it bounced off her nose. Hakeem laughed. Again she tried and again missed her mark. She picked up another grape and threw it at Hakeem. He expertly snatched it out of the air with his mouth. The joy a simple game brought, not only to Hakeem, but to her, was priceless.

All too soon, Ashur was there for her. As she said goodbye to Hakeem, he became very animated. His words came fast.

"What's he saying?" Clair asked.

"He wants you to know Mr. Sargon had a son his age. He told a funny story about him today."

Not wanting to hurt Hakeem's feelings she smiled and said to Ashur, "Please tell him I'm glad he could laugh today."

Sargon having a son he rarely sees doesn't make him a father, but it did make him a little more human.

Back in the basement Clair turned on her light until she settled in for the night. Long after she had turned it off, she lay awake.

She and David had always wanted children. It was something they discussed before buying their home, a four-bedroom, three-bath American Foursquare. She remembered their conversation, one night, after meeting with their realtor.

* * *

"Do you like the house?" he asked.

"I agree it has character, but it needs so much work."

"We can do it. Besides, it has a huge basement. Lots of room for the kids to play in."

"Oh, we're having kids now?"

"Not right now," he said, placing his fingers on his chin, "but we have space enough for oh . . . five or six."

Laughing, she stepped into his embrace. "The other house would be cheaper in the end."

"I'm not in this short-term. We need a home our kids can grow up in. A house where they'll have good memories."

"You're going to make a wonderful dad."

"So, yes to the house?"

She sighed, surrendering to him. "How can I say no to you?" They sealed their agreement with a kiss.

The night they signed the papers, making it official, they went out to celebrate.

"I can't believe it's really ours," she said.

"I can't believe how far in debt we are."

Giggling, she lifted her wine glass. "To our new home."

He tapped her glass with his. "To our future kids. All six of them."

* * *

Now, she wondered if having children was still possible—if she would ever leave here alive.

Pain welled in the back of her throat as she fought to stifle tears. Her chin quivered and her stomach churned before she rolled over, gave up her fight, and cried long into the night.

In the morning, she dragged herself up the stairs, feeling as if she'd never slept. When she went to Hakeem, his breakfast was untouched. He looked up at her with tired eyes. When she brushed his hair off his face, his brow felt warm. The conditions here were far from sterile and infections were common. When she checked his wound, she saw red streaks shooting out like spider legs. From what she had seen here from other men, this was a small wound. But Hakeem wasn't a man and infections didn't care how big the opening. She hoped he could fight this himself—antibiotics were sparse.

As she went about her day, she kept an eye out for Sargon. If anyone could get their hands on antibiotics, it would be him. But the day passed and he remained elsewhere.

Before going to the basement, she checked on Hakeem one last time, kissed his cheek, and was rewarded with a weak smile.

"Do you know of anyone who could get us some antibiotics?" she asked Ashur when they entered her room.

"No. All medicines are held up by President al-Assad. He gives them out at his discretion. Most often, it is his family and staff, families of his army. It's rare that the people of Syria are so fortunate."

What kind of president keeps medicines from his own people?

It was no wonder people rebelled here. Even if she never stepped foot on American soil again, she had lived better than most people here ever would.

* * *

At breakfast, she sipped her tea while Ashur waited.

"Did you talk to Hakeem this morning?" she asked.

"No, he is sleeping. I thought it best not to disturb him."

When they went upstairs, Clair went to him right away. In sleep, his beautiful face looked like any other boy—serene and well. But when she touched his brow she knew he was seriously ill. Without a thermometer, she wouldn't know his exact temperature, but had felt enough foreheads to know it was dangerously high.

In the kitchen, she soaked a towel with cold water then rushed back to Hakeem. Sargon walked in the room and followed her to where Hakeem lay.

"How is he doing this morning?" he asked.

"His wound is infected and he has a fever."

She pulled the blanket aside and applied the cold towel to his chest and neck. Hakeem fought her and pushed the towel away.

Sargon took hold of the boy's arms.

"Let me help you."

His eyes met hers.

"Thank you. We need to get his fever down, but the bigger problem's the infection."

The two of them worked together for over an hour before finally, Hakeem cooled down.

"We can let him rest now."

As she started to stand, Sargon took hold of her arm and helped her up.

"Do you think you can find Tylenol somewhere?" she asked.

He shrugged. "Everything is limited here but I will do what I can."

He brushed back hair from his hard and handsome face. His eyes gleamed as he looked down at her. Then he slowly raised his hand and ran the back of his fingers across her cheek. Nothing could have surprised her more.

CHAPTER 20

LYING ON THE COT, SHE FELT FOR HER FLASHLIGHT AND TURNED it on. Its light flickered, before settling into a dim glow. Not wanting to waste its precious energy she turned it off. Tonight, she could do without.

After months of living in this dark underground room, she knew her way around. Where the rock protruded from the dirt, if you weren't careful, it would trip you up and send you airborne into the cinderblock walls. And the hole near the middle of the room, it could twist your ankle into a purple ball of pain. She had experienced both.

Now, her brisk walk to the corner of the room was a walk in the park. She stopped just before the wall, and with her arms straight out, she inched forward to the bucket. The dark no longer intimidating, she walked back to the cot and stared into its emptiness.

Do you still think of me David? Have you given up hope like I sometimes do?

Her weariness allowed doubt to creep in, and before she could stop it, she had imagined him moving on, finding someone else to love. Wrapped in self-pity, she oddly found comfort in it and continued down this barren line of thinking for some time until finally, she slept.

* * *

She walked upstairs into the infirmary and was surprised to see David, standing in the middle of the room talking to Sargon. When she called to him, he turned and glared, his upper lip raised in a snarl. He turned and marched out the front door, Sargon right behind. She followed them, begging David to stop and come back—instead he ran. She tried to keep up, running through the streets of Azaz, unable to match their speed. Lost, and standing at a dead end, she heard footsteps and waited for David with a smile. Instead, it was Mohammad. He stopped in front of her, lifted his gun, and fired.

* * *

"Clair, wake up."

Her body jerked forward quick and stiff, she almost bumped heads with Sargon.

"What's wrong?"

"I have these." His palm held four precious pills.

"You found Tylenol."

"Yes, but I need your help. I tried to give them to Hakeem, but he is delirious and fights me."

"Let's go."

Together, they dashed up the stairs.

Before she touched him, she felt the heat that rolled off of Hakeem's body. She crushed the medicine in a glass and added water.

"Can you set him up and hold his arms?"

He did as she asked, and although it took a while, Clair managed to get the medicine down him.

She hurried into the kitchen and came back with a wet towel and the two of them once again rubbed Hakeem's body with cool water. They stayed until his fever broke, then Sargon led the way back to her room.

But instead of leaving her, he sat down on the chair. Clair sat on the edge of her cot, biting her nails.

What now? Yesterday, when he touched my face, I saw the longing in his eyes. He was so angry when Mohammad attacked me. Surely he wouldn't.

"Do you think the boy will recover from this?" he asked.

You want to talk?

"I think he needs medicine. Some bodies can fight off infection, but he's already weak. I just don't know. It's wonderful that you found some Tylenol, and that will be fine for tomorrow, but after that . . ." she said, shrugging. "Again, I just don't know. Can you get antibiotics?"

He shook his head. "I tried today. No one has any."

It was still possible he would get better on his own, but she hated that such an easy fix was unavailable.

"Why are you doing this—this involvement with ISIS?" She risked angering him with her question but wanted to know what made a man join such a group.

He took his time answering, leaning forward and bracing his elbows on his knees.

"It was my brother Jaul, already a member of ISIS, who asked me to join."

He sat up in his chair and looked at her.

"Our president is corrupt, as was his father before him. Syria has a long history of incompetent presidents, an ISIS-controlled country will bring Syrians food and medicine, a better life, even if it is run with an iron fist."

He crossed his arms and leaned back.

"But killing innocent people isn't the answer. Can't you see that you're part of the problem?"

He glared at her, his jaw clamped tight.

"You speak as if you hold a monopoly on wisdom and virtue."

Neither spoke for several minutes. She sat chewing her lip, waiting for his anger to erupt. But instead, he stared at the ground. She squirmed, tugged at the knees of her pants.

"I've led a very sheltered life. If I hadn't come here and seen it with my own eyes, I wouldn't have believed the horror. But there has to be a better way. You are killing Syria, not making her better."

He pulled a cigarette from his pocket and lit it.

"What do you know about suffering? Until you have lived the life of a Syrian, you don't know what you might do to bring about change. It is a bad country right now and will never be better with the government we have. The only way to get him out of power is war. The others, the Freedom Fighters, The Northern Storm, they will never accomplish what ISIS can."

They both sat silent for several minutes. Although her childhood was a far cry from his, she did know something about suffering.

"I had a sister, two years younger. I always knew she was different. Frail. It started when she was four, the coughing, upper respiratory infections that were slow to go away. By the time she turned six, the doctors had tried every antibiotic imaginable. My parents took her to a specialist who diagnosed her with pleura pulmonary blastoma. It's a rare form of lung cancer in children. After that, it seemed like the only place we went as a family was to the hospital."

The story of her sister's illness and death was one she rarely talked about. She found it strange that she poured her heart out like this to him of all people. But for some odd reason, she felt compelled to do so.

"She died two weeks after her ninth birthday. I vowed then to become a pediatric oncologist, but changed my mind and became a general pediatrician. I want to be the one to catch the cancers early on while there is still hope."

"What was her name?" he asked.

"Megan."

Minutes passed in silence before Sargon stood, stretched, and yawned. "It is late, I should go now."

Clair watched as he headed for the door.

"Sargon, thank you."

"For what?"

"The flashlight."

He met her glance and held it.

"Good night, Clair."

Good night, Sargon, you strange and unpredictable man.

When Clair checked on Hakeem the next morning, she found his condition had worsened. His fever spiked and without drinking much he became dehydrated. She gave him the last of the Tylenol.

Throughout the day, Clair took advantage of every opportunity to be with Hakeem, to cool him down with wet towels, or sway him to drink. If he died, he wouldn't be the first child she couldn't save. But to her, he represented something good and innocent, in a place that had neither. Saving Hakeem was as much for herself as for him.

CHAPTER 21

CHECKING HIS CELL PHONE BETWEEN CLASSES HAD BECOME AS much a habit for David as breathing. But for the most part, it was an exercise in futility. Since Dean White called him into his office over a month ago, he heard nothing new about his missing wife. Never had he felt so helpless.

As he entered his next class, David felt his phone vibrate. It was Clair's mother, who called every day. At first, he had liked talking to her. Just having someone who loved Clair was comforting. But lately, she had implied he should do more, go back over there. Without meaning to, they made him feel guilty. He turned his phone off, put it back in his pocket.

When his last class ended, he walked to his car wishing he had someone, other than a dog, waiting at home for him. While driving through downtown, he spotted a sign in the window of a bar announcing "Happy Hour." He needed some happy. He parked and went in.

Sitting alone, he ordered a beer and some nachos. The place was crowded and by the time his food came, he was on his third beer and plenty hungry.

As he neared the end of his meal, his cell phone rang. Having forgotten to lower the volume, David hurriedly answer it, and in his haste, didn't bother to check the caller ID. With a mouth full of nachos, he mumbled hello.

"David, is that you?"

Great, Clair's mom again.

"Hello, Barb."

"Have you heard anything new?"

"No, nothing." As he spoke, the band started up, making it almost impossible to hear.

"Did you watch the news tonight?" she asked.

"No, why? Something happen?"

"What? I'm having trouble hearing you through all that noise."

"I'm having dinner now. Can I call you back?"

"Sure. You have a good time. We'll talk later."

Think what you want, Barb, but I'm not having as much fun as you're probably imagining.

He didn't want to sever the ties between himself and his in-laws, but if they thought he enjoyed his time without their daughter, they were mistaken.

While he finished his meal, one of his students came in and ordered a drink at the bar. The last thing David felt like doing was to have a conversation with a student. Regardless, the young man approached his table and asked if he could join him.

"Of course, James, have a seat."

They talked about the history class he was in and other campus news before James changed the topic to Syria.

"I heard about your wife. Wow, it must be tough. Have they found any clues to where she might be?"

"Nothing yet. Hey, did you see the Browns game last night?" David asked.

"No. I don't watch sports."

"Oh. They lost."

"Did you catch the news today?" James asked.

"What news? I've been in class all day."

"Well maybe I shouldn't say. I don't wanna upset you," James said.

"If you know something, tell me. I'll hear about it eventually."

"Okay, well, I was watching CNN, and they reported that this really radical group took over this town and killed over a hundred civilians. Just lined them up and shot 'em. Crazy."

For a moment David couldn't speak, his lungs quit working, and he had to remind himself to breathe. He knew James meant well, but that sort of news made optimism impossible. All he could do was mumble his thanks for the information, a quick goodbye, and toss a wad of cash on the table. As he neared the door, James shouted, "See ya in class, Professor."

David went home feeling lower than he ever had. He dragged himself into the house and dropped in a chair. For over an hour he sat, thinking of the tragedy that occurred today in Syria. Tired, he decided to go to bed early, but couldn't sleep. He wasn't a religious man, but on this night he prayed fervently that his wife was not among those killed today. And for the families of those who were.

CHAPTER 22

SITTING IN HIS TRUCK, SARGON PUT OFF ENTERING THE HOUSE. The news from his camp was troubling. Turkey worked to get other nations to help them dismantle ISIS. His group grew, however, thanks in large part to foreign fighters who had flocked to Syria to join up. With so many of ISIS soldiers lost, they were needed. The large amount of weapons and shells that were taken from them the night Sargon and his men were ambushed only added to their problems.

He should go in the house and tell his comrades of this news. They needed to know. Besides that, Clair probably waited to hound him about medicine for the boy. With heavy legs, he got out of his truck and lumbered inside.

In the kitchen, he told the men what he had learned today. Not only would they be fighting against the Syrian government and other rebel groups vying for control of Syria, but meddlesome nations as well. Even though he mentioned other countries, it was the United States they blamed for the movement to disband them. It was easy to hate those who had so much. Sargon walked out of the kitchen, leaving his men fired up and ready to take on the world.

In the infirmary, he saw Clair kneeling beside Hakeem.

"Is he any better?" Sargon asked.

She looked up at him. The crease between her eyes ran deep. Her skin looked patchy and dry. The time spent here had changed her appearance, and he was to blame.

"Not at all. His fever is high, and he's dehydrated. He's drinking very little and I've used the last of the Tylenol this morning. Any luck finding antibiotics today?"

Sargon looked around the room, and other than the injured, they were alone. "I had business to attend to. Even if I had time to look, it is doubtful there is any to be found."

She walked to the long wooden table where medical supplies lay, waiting for her to sort. As she worked, she slammed each box of gauze, each bottle of alcohol on the table.

He tossed his hands in the air. "I'm not a miracle worker," he bellowed. "I cannot make something exist when it does not."

She nodded, as she folded some rags into bandages. He stomped out and slammed the door behind him. His friends already had chastised him for the attention he gave to her. If they had seen how she treated him just now, their respect for him would be lost.

As he paced, his mind raged. He should not care about a boy who may die tonight. Many boys have died this year. And he should not care for an American woman. Even if she reminded him, in so many ways, of his wife.

He walked around the house and entered through the back, went upstairs and lay on his bed. He hoped for some peace, if only for a short time.

Late that night, a knock on his bedroom door woke him.

"I am sorry to disturb you, but the boy is very bad."

"Get the doctor," Sargon said with a sleepy voice.

He put on a shirt and plodded down the steps. When he entered the room, Hakeem lay shaking, his head bent back and his eyes open wide. He tried to hold the boy but his stiffness made it difficult. Clair was soon at his side pushing him away to get a better look.

"He's having a seizure," she said. "Without antibiotics, he will die—if that matters to you."

Sargon stood and kicked the supply basket, scattering its contents across the floor.

"What do you want from me?" he ranted. "There is only so much I can do."

She stood, and with her hands on her hips and lips pursed together, she glared at him.

"If he were your son, he'd have the medicine he needs. While Hakeem lays here dying, your son is warm in his bed. While he carries a gun and fights for your cause, your son—"

He seized her arms, lifted her off her feet, and silenced her. Between clenched teeth he hissed, "My son is dead."

She stared at him wide-eyed, her face drained of its color. He released her arms and stormed out the door to his truck.

Deranged, he flew down the dirt road at top speed. The cloud of dust he created trailed behind him like a snake, suspended in the hot, dry air.

Why do I allow that woman to speak to me so brashly? She should have been slapped.

He pulled off the road and with shaky hands, lit a cigarette. Throwing his head against the headrest, he closed his eyes and pictured his son on that last day of his life. Ironically, it was one of his happiest.

He pulled his truck back on the road and drove the many miles to Tartus, hoping there he would find the medicine that would keep this boy alive.

CHAPTER 23

STUNNED, CLAIR STARED AT SARGON'S BACK AS HE WALKED OUT. The possibility of losing Hakeem had propelled her into a fearless, angry woman, throwing words like darts. If only she had known.

Why then had Hakeem told her that Sargon had a son? Maybe there had been a mix-up through Ashur's translation?

It was easy to judge what she didn't know but, what makes a man like Sargon who he is? For that matter all of the men here. What had their lives been like before they committed themselves to do such horrible deeds? And what kind of man, if he lived, would Hakeem grow up to be?

Fatigue took over, and she lay down next to him, his seizures quieted for now. She wrapped him in her arms and gently rocked, pressed her cheek against his forehead and softly hummed. For the first time in months, she would spend the night away from the basement, and its locked door. Spend the night feeling free.

"Doc? Doc? How is the boy?" Ashur said, shaking her awake.

"Not good. At least he wasn't last night."

Hakeem moaned, and when she turned her attention to him, he took her hand, held it, and pressed it to his cheek. She smiled down at him, hoping to convey an optimism she did not feel. As the hours passed, his condition worsened. His seizures occurred often and as much as she hated to think it, this day could be his last. Willing him to feel her love, she held him through the seizures and gently wiped his skin with cold water. Just as her time upstairs neared its end, Sargon entered the house.

Without a word, he walked to her, tossed a small brown envelope in her lap, and continued up the stairs to his room. She tore open the envelope and found ten capsules—the antibiotics. She quickly fed one to Hakeem. Her worst fear was that it was too little too late.

When Ashur came for her, she asked him to give Hakeem a capsule after midnight, and then went to the basement feeling better about Hakeem's survival.

The next day, she sat on the edge of her cot, anxiously waiting for Ashur. She couldn't wait to see Hakeem. But when the door opened, instead of her friend, it was Sargon who entered the room.

Wary of his mood after what she said last night, Clair nervously backed away from him. When he didn't speak, she had to ask, "How is Hakeem?"

"I have not seen him today." He handed her the tea and bread he carried with him.

She took her meal to the cot and ate. He sat in the chair, held his light, and watched her.

"Thank you for the medicine. And . . . I'm sorry about your son."

Sargon closed his eyes and nodded. He looked disheveled and pitifully distraught. His hair was tangled, and his clothes dirty. Life had taken its toll on him. They sat silent for a while, both deep in thought.

He had a far-off look when he said, "He was such a bright child." Then he laughed. "He told everyone he would be president of Syria someday." His focus turned to her. "Do you have children?"

"No. My husband and I were waiting until I finished my commitment here before starting a family."

"You would have made a good mother."

Would have?

Clair bit down on her bottom lip. She wanted more than anything to have David's children and was not giving up on that happening. But every day that passed with her still living here made her less sure of it. Taking a deep breath, she turned the subject back to him.

"I realize you can never replace your son, but you and your wife can have other children."

He looked down at the dirt for such a long time, and Clair wondered if there was something there she couldn't see.

"My wife died along with my son."

"How awful."

"They were at the market getting food for a celebration we were planning. Her parents were coming from Iraq to stay with us. It had been years since their last visit, and we were all excited."

He had brought himself a cup of tea, along with her meal, and drank from it.

"We lived in Damascus; it was rumored that a group there had formed to overthrow President al-Assad. I didn't learn until after that the group used a shop in the market as their cover. The president sent his troops that day to capture the rebels but were not prepared for the number of men they encountered. Instead of a quiet arrest, there was gunfire and pipe bombs. When it ended, twenty-two people were killed."

Clair was speechless. What could she say?

"You are very much like her."

"Like . . . your wife?"

He kept his eyes down, nodded his head.

"She was smart. And beautiful."

He can't be serious.

All at once he got up and took her plate and cup. "We had better go up and check on the boy."

CHAPTER 24

THANKSGIVING WAS JUST AROUND THE CORNER. BUT WITH CLAIR gone, David didn't have much to be thankful for. No news from Syria in almost a month now. The unknown was worse than knowing. Nothing could have happened to her that he hadn't already imagined.

He rolled into the drive, his workday over, got out and leaned against the hood. This house had everything they wanted. It sat on a half-acre of land, its trees tall and full. Clair's flower garden grew along one side. A picnic table sat on the other, shaded by an evergreen tree. They had so many plans for this place, but with her gone, his work on it had come to a screeching halt.

I'm so lost without you.

After feeding Buster he sat, staring heedless at the television, the dog in his lap.

Wonder what Darcy is doing.

He picked up his phone and on the fourth ring she answered.
"Is this a bad time?" he asked.
"No. I was just thinking about you."
"Oh?"

"Would you mind if I came up for the weekend?"

"Mind? Are you kidding? When can you get here?"

"As soon as I throw a few things together I'll head out. And David, if you think its best, I'll book a room before I leave."

"No way. We have three spare bedrooms—why should you?"

"Oh, okay. If you're sure. It would be great if you'd forget your troubles for one weekend and have fun. That is if you still remember how."

She laughed at her joke. David couldn't remember when he heard a voice so light and carefree.

"I'll see you soon."

David moved like a whirlwind, tossing dirty dishes in the dishwasher and bagging the trash. Taking the steps two at a time, he headed for the shower.

Darcy arrived around eight o'clock. They stayed in, had a few beers, and watched TV, both looking forward to the next day.

Darcy had it all planned. They got up early and drove to Cleveland. The day was cool, typical for November, but the sun was bright, and the sky clear. Their first stop was at a local winery for taste testing. They then took a jaunt up a cobblestone path that led to a restaurant. Sitting high on a hill they had a spectacular view of the vineyards and the stream that divided it.

Darcy kept the mood high; she knew how to tell a good joke. But to him, the best part of the day was seeing the Rock and Roll Hall of Fame. It made him feel like a teen again.

It was after midnight when they returned home, both too pumped up from their day to sleep.

"Should we pop the cork on one of those bottles we bought?" he asked her.

"Ooh yeah," she purred.

He carried two glasses and the bottle into the living room.

"Darcy thanks for coming. It's been awhile since I've laughed. I feel a little guilty about it. With Clair gone—"

"Don't. You can't be sad and miserable all the time. Having a day of fun doesn't mean you don't miss her."

After that, they both were content to sit and sip their wine in silence. A few moments passed before Darcy spoke. "David, how are you, really?"

He squirmed in his chair, pulled on his pant legs.

"I don't know. Sometimes I think I'm going crazy. If she's alive, then where the hell is she? And what are they doing to her? That's what I think about the most. Is she suffering right now while I'm sitting comfortable in our home?"

He stopped talking and took a gulp of his wine before speaking again.

"I have a student, who told me about this group over there, killing over one hundred civilians and . . . I can't stop wondering if Clair was among them." His last words were more choked than spoken.

Darcy moved beside him and took his hand. "Listen. It hurts me to say this, but you know it's possible she might not come back?"

That wasn't what he wanted to hear. He refused to stop believing that someday, she'd return to him.

"I want her to come home as much as you do, but I hate seeing what this is doing to you. When we talked last week, it sounded as if you'd been drinking."

David put his face in his hands. She moved close and put her arm around him, laying her head on his shoulder.

Neither moved until David lifted his head and met her eyes. Darcy leaned slowly toward his mouth. The kiss, at first, soft and light, until she drew his tongue into her mouth and moved her body closer.

"Whoa," he said before he stood and took a step back. He looked down at her, and a small laugh flew out from his chest in a huff.

"Must be the wine."

Her eyes twitched before she batted her lashes. When she got up off the sofa, she swallowed hard, then smiled.

"Of course. I can't believe that just happened."

David tried to think of something to say to lighten the awkwardness but drew a blank.

"Clair's a lucky woman."

David dropped his eyes, his hand cupped the back of his neck. *I wouldn't call her lucky now.*

"Can we forget this ever happened?" she asked.

"Sure," he mumbled, stuffing his hands in his pant pockets.

Then they both moved up the stairs, turning their separate ways to spend a night alone, together.

CHAPTER 25

LIFE FELL BACK INTO ITS UNBEARABLE ROUTINE ONCE HAKEEM was no longer with them. Gone two months now, the antibiotic had done its job. Once recovered, Sargon drove him to his village and left him with relatives. He did this as a favor to Clair, but she knew he was fond of the boy and might have done this on his own had she not suggested it.

One evening, Sargon came down to her room and sat with her while she ate.

"I miss Hakeem," she said. "It's hard to believe how close we became in such little time, and without speaking the same language."

"He is a very bright boy and will do well if he can attend school."

"*If* he can attend school. There are so many things we Americans take for granted, school being one of them. Sometimes I feel like I've been dropped on another planet."

Sargon nodded his head in agreement.

"That is how I would feel in the US."

Clair had never thought of it, but there would be things he would have trouble getting used to. Such as the constant noise we Americans seem to need, the rush that everyone is in, and the every minute accounted for business of life.

"Tomorrow I will be taking you out. An important friend of mine, Yusuf Tlas, has a daughter who fell and broke her arm."

Clair fumbled her fork and dropped it. If she were taken outside these walls, escape could be possible.

"Will they have casting materials or should I bring what we have here?" she asked, trying to remain calm.

"Bring what we have. They live close by, in Efrin. We should not be gone long. Ashur will come for you early so you can tend to the men upstairs before we go."

She nodded and kept her mouth shut. Sargon was shrewd, and would detect any unusual behavior. Escape would be difficult enough, the last thing she needed was to trigger his suspicion.

After he had left the room, she tried to sleep, but for most of the night she lay awake. Her mind busy concocting ways to flee once on the outside. Traveling to Efrin would bring her closer to Turkey, she could walk from there.

She was almost afraid to dream of it, but maybe soon she would be home. It had been a while since hope dwelled in her, but this night she was full of it. She imagined David's arms around her, his mouth on hers, and his hands—those strong hands—touching her. This chance may be her last, she had to make it happen.

The next morning as promised, Ashur came for her early. By ten o'clock, Sargon entered the infirmary, ready to go. He carried something in his hand and held it out for her.

"Put this on."

She covered her hair with the black scarf before they walked out. As if on her way to a well-deserved vacation, the adrenaline rush had her jubilant and light-headed. Sargon didn't say much, which was okay with her, and she was involved in a conversation with herself.

Stay calm. Relax. Breathe.

When finally, her nerves settled a bit, she gazed out the window and enjoyed the view. The open sky, bright sun, and majestic mountains were beautiful. She would never again take being outside for granted.

They drove out of Azaz along barren roads, surrounded by brush-covered hills. In Efrin, she watched the people as they went about their business, some waved as they drove by. It seemed surreal. She could roll her window down and scream bloody murder, but it wouldn't help her. Fear is a powerful weapon.

Sargon drove them deep into the city, to cypress-lined streets where children played with balls and shot marbles into circles drawn in the dust. Sargon parked the truck in front of a small house where pansies grew in a window box. The war had not yet left its mark here.

The man who answered the door appeared elderly. He and Sargon hugged like old friends and spoke in Arabic, ignoring her. She followed the men to a small bedroom where a young girl lay, her arm rested on a pillow. Clair went to her side and gave her a reassuring smile.

"Does she speak English?" she asked Sargon.

He shook his head.

"I'm going to examine her arm. Ask her to nod when it hurts."

After determining where the break was, Clair went about setting it and applied the cast. Typical of the young patients she had seen here, this brave girl shed no tears.

When she finished, they walked by the kitchen on their way out. The girl's young mother was busy working and was also ignored by the men. As they headed to the truck she scanned the street, looking for the best route out. On the way here she noticed the busy market—just two streets over. If she could make it there, hopefully she could get lost in the crowd.

"I need to stop for cigarettes," he said.

Okay, change of plans. I won't run there, Sargon will drive me instead.

When they reached the market he parked and got out, signaled for her to do the same. As she stepped out she took in her surroundings. The street was full of noisy activity. Cars, bumper-to-bumper, crawled past, and people moved in and out of shops like ants. Further down she could see tables set up under tents, and people clogged the street. She couldn't have asked for a better setting to get lost in.

In the store, Sargon stood in line to pay. Trying to act blasé, she browsed the shelves. All the while her heart beat like a drum and her hands trembled.

With his purchase made they moved outside and were near Sargon's truck. She was about to take off when suddenly, Sargon collapsed behind her. He lay in the grass like a corpse while she stood with her mouth gaped open. Two men stood over him, one held the barrel end of a pistol in the palm of his hand.

Clair spun around quick and bolted. She traveled half a block before being picked up and thrown in the back of a utility van. Sargon was soon thrown in on top of her, his dead weight crushing her.

The door slammed shut, and the van took off fast. If anyone saw what just happened, they most likely looked the other way. A vigilante wouldn't live long in this country.

She wormed her way out from under him and sat up. The men riding up front talked in whispers. She guessed them to be in their mid-twenties, and all three bearded. One looked back at her, then consulted with the others. With rope in hand, he climbed over the seat and started towards her.

Desperately wanting him to come to and help her, she pinched Sargon's arm. That's when she realized that, within a few minutes' time, there had been a shake-up, and the tables had turned. As unlikely as it seemed, she and Sargon were now on the same team.

The van sped past shops and beyond as one of the men crawled toward her. Despite the heat, she trembled as he grasped both her arms, jerked them behind her back, and roped them tightly together. The coarse cord cut into her wrists. A cloth sack was put over her head and tied. The heat, along with the lack of air, was suffocating.

The man moved to Sargon. The sound of rope as it was pulled through knots and tightened told her he was getting some of the same. When finished, the man crawled over her legs toward the front.

The van came to a stop a short time later. Sargon still hadn't budged. The men got out, leaving the two of them alone for what seemed hours.

The heavy sackcloth, wet from her sweat, clung to her face and made her skin itch. The little air she got came through a barrier that reeked of the sickening, sweet smell of manure.

A tingle started in her hands, then spread upward. Soon, her arms were thick with a needle-prickling numbness that burned. An injection of Novocain couldn't have done better.

When the men came back, the doors opened, and one shouted at her in Arabic. When she sat motionless, he leaned in and hooked her arm, dragged her across the van's floor, and dropped her on the sharp stones outside.

The air was cool compared to the oven she just fell out of. Her shirt was saturated with sweat, and her legs were weak and shaky.

Yanked to her feet, they led her across stones, up steps, and into a building. They moved fast. Her legs hit every obstacle along the way. When the pain slowed her, they yelled something, then tightened their grip and dragged her upstairs, her knees bouncing off each step as they went. With quick strides, they moved across carpeted floor and only stopped long enough to toss her into a room.

She tried to stay alert but her half-baked brain, now a soft mush, wouldn't function. Minutes passed before Sargon's still-unconscious body was dragged in and dropped beside her.

As she started to drift off, she wondered what the odds were for someone to be kidnapped twice in the same year.

CHAPTER 26

"Are you awake?" Sargon said, his voice dry and hoarse.

Clair stirred, keeping her eyes closed beneath the heavy, wet sack. "Yes."

"Where are we?"

With the heat and the thick sack, talking took more energy than she had. She took several breaths before answering. "I don't know. We didn't go far. Still in Efrin, I guess."

"Did they hurt you?" he asked.

"No. How's your head?"

"Throbbing, but I will live."

"Who would want you?" she asked.

"Many would want revenge, I suppose."

"So many enemies you can't even guess?"

"When we are both dead, it will not matter who or why."

After that, neither spoke. They lay for hours, falling in and out of fitful sleeps. She would wake in a panic, then remember where she was, and despair. In and out of consciousness, their bodies thrashed. She would arouse and feel his head on her stomach, or her leg draped over his hip. Like animals, they sought comfort in each other's existence with each touch.

She was awakened by a kick to her side. Someone lifted her hands, cut the ropes, and removed the hood. Her arms dropped to her sides and dangled uselessly like the arms of a sweater, hung over her shoulders. She looked at the men through squinted eyes. Neither was with them in the van. She watched as they freed Sargon.

They were given bread and water. Clair wiggled her fingers, then shook her arms to make her numb hands cooperate and pick up the cup. Her arid tongue soaked up each sip like a sponge.

One of the men came close, his prying eyes poured over her. She lowered her head and avoided his glance.

"What are you doing here?" He asked as if she had come of her own accord.

"I . . . I was taken."

What do you think I'm doing here?

"Why are you in our country?"

"I'm a volunteer, I came to help but was kidnapped by him," she looked at Sargon, who gave her a killer glare, "and brought to this city to set a girl's broken arm. After that your men threw me in their van, along with him." Again she looked at Sargon, his eyes told her to shut up, but she was willing to play this game solo. If she could cut a deal for herself, she would.

"So, you are a doctor."

Ugh.

She closed her eyes, and dropped her head. Sargon tossed his head back and slowly shook it. The damage was done. The minute the men left, Sargon tore into her.

"Are you crazy? Why let them know you are a doctor? Forget any chance of leaving here."

"I know. It was stupid of me."

"I am glad you are smart enough to admit it," he said, his anger toned down.

"Did you recognize either man?" she asked.

"No. But the one who spoke took pity on you. I could see it in his eyes. You may—if you keep your mouth shut and only say what I tell you—be able to get information from him."

"Look, I made a mistake but I'm not an idiot. We need to work together. That man has compassion for me, I agree with you. Now let's decide how to use that to our advantage."

Each small meal was brought to them by the same man. They never learned his name, but behind his back they called him Tenderheart.

The room they were in was small, the size of her walk in closet. The floors were bare wood, the walls painted a bright blue. From the center of the ceiling, one lone bulb hung from a wire and was never turned off. The room had no windows and although it was warm, the van had been worse.

Twice a day they were taken individually to the toilet down the hall. At first, her bladder was shy. She had never used the toilet while a stranger stood three feet away, holding a gun. But like everything else, one adapts.

When Tenderheart brought their food, she always gave him a smile, made small talk.

"Are you married?" she asked him, on their second day there.

"No, no. I am too busy for a wife." He smiled, his large teeth yellowed from smoking or coffee.

"I bet you have lots of girlfriends."

He laughed. "I have my share."

She never learned much but laid the groundwork, hoping to earn his trust. But Sargon was getting impatient and let her know that, once they were alone.

"We need to find out why they are keeping us." Sargon paced the floor, ran his fingers through his hair.

"I'm trying to win his trust first."

"We don't have time for that. You need to be bolder."

At dinner, pita bread and water, Tenderheart stood while she ate. He had come to expect some conversation with her, but to him, Sargon was invisible.

She leaned in close, so only he could hear. "Do you know he is a member of ISIS?" She jerked her head in Sargon's direction.

"Yes, why do you think we are keeping him?"

"I should have known, you are much too smart not to know that." She smiled at him, shocked that she had the haughtiness to flirt with anyone, given her looks and bad smell.

"We are working on a plan," he whispered, "to exchange him for one of ours that ISIS has." He lifted his chin slightly, extended his chest.

"ISIS has a member of your family? That's terrible." She opened her mouth a bit and widened her eyes.

He laughed at her, then moved closer. "It is not my family they have, but a member of our group—The Northern Storm."

"Ooh. I've heard of you. Very important in this war."

He nodded his head then looked down her shirt.

Suddenly Sargon stood. "What is going on with you two? I want to know what you are saying."

"Sit down and shut up or I'll tie you up." Tenderheart threatened. Sargon did as he was told.

"I will see you later." He said to Clair, and with a quick wink, he left them.

They listened to him descend the stairs. Sargon then took her by the arms. "What did he say?"

"His group is The Northern Storm. They are working on some sort of prisoner exchange with ISIS."

"ISIS does not keep prisoners."

"Oh." The implication was not lost on her.

"But let him think we do, it will keep us alive. When you are not mending our wounded, you would make a great spy for us." He smiled, clearly pleased, making Clair drunk with the feeling of accomplishment. Her clever behavior had pulled the words right out of Tenderheart and she beamed with pride as Sargon praised her.

"They will come for us, once they are given this trade offer. No one forces ISIS into anything."

Relief flooded her body. For days her muscles squeezed tight with fear. Now that she relaxed a little, she realized just how tightly wound she had been.

"I think you enjoyed toying with Tenderheart," he teased.

He caught her weak swing at him and laughed.

"Just tell me what you want to know. I'll do the rest, and never mind how much I enjoy it." She giggled, her mood so light. Of course ISIS would come for them. And perhaps in the mayhem of getting them out, she would find a way to wander off. Free of them all.

During the night, the sound of Sargon moaning woke her.

"Sargon, what's wrong?"

"Nothing. Go back to sleep," he said through clenched teeth.

"You're hurting, please tell me what's wrong."

"My leg." He gripped his calf, rocked his body in agony.

She moved close, removed his shoe, and pulled up his pant leg. With expertise, she kneaded his muscle while he covered his face with his arm, stiff with pain.

"It's cramps. Your leg is like rock. It's no wonder, with the scant amount of water we're given."

She rubbed his leg and pushed his toes forward, stretching the muscle over and over, until finally, the pain eased. By then he was wringing with sweat.

"Thank you."

"If this happens again wake me, before it gets bad."

Ready to return to sleep she rolled on her side, used the scarf Sargon had given her as a pillow, and faced the wall. It wasn't long before his hand ran down her arm, slid to her hip, and rested there.

She lay, wide-eyed and stiff. The skin on her arm tingled from his touch. And the short quick breaths he caused appalled her. Minutes passed before he pulled back his hand and turned away. Hours passed before either of them slept.

The next day Tenderheart came in with their breakfast. She leaned against the wall as he handed her water. His crooked smile was so wide, he drooled.

"I have a surprise for you," he said.

"Really? I must warn you, not much surprises me."

His mouth touched her ear as he whispered.

"I know a man who is a soldier in the United States Marines. I will see him tomorrow and tell him about you."

Clair froze. This surprised her.

Right away she felt guilty for tricking this man. He was nice—more than nice. He would go out of his way to save her. And just yesterday she was so smug, jumping up and down with Sargon over their impressive coup.

"You'll really do this for me?"

"For you, yes. And maybe you can do—"

The door burst open with a thud. When Tenderheart turned to look, a bullet entered his forehead, shattering his skull. Bits of his brain splattered Clair's face and arms. An ISIS soldier entered the room, cocked his head, and waited for them to follow. But her feet were nailed to the floor. She stood staring at the wet, gray goo that dotted her arm. Sargon grabbed her hand, jerked her into motion, and led her out.

He took off running the second they stepped outside. But like a ball and chain tied to his wrist, she slowed him. A lone gunman gave chase.

She heard gunfire and bullets whistle past before one found her. It tore through her scalp and knocked her off her feet. Sargon's hand vanished from her grip. His feet pounded the pavement as he kept running.

Her face hit the concrete hard. Warm blood began its way down her crown and onto the road. Lying in pain, she braced herself for a second bullet. Oddly, she wasn't afraid. Instead, just tired of it all. Whatever they wanted to do to her—do it. Death was no longer a threat, just let it be quick.

As she lay waiting, she saw herself with David, with the children that they had in the home they grew old in. It's strange when the life you never had flashes before your eyes. When you see so clearly all that is lost.

Strong hands gripped her arms and lifted her. For a moment she was suspended in air. Her head dangled while her blood splashed the concrete like a leaky faucet. She was then swooped into arms that cradled her against a hard and powerful chest. Sargon had come back for her.

He took off in a sprint, carried her dead weight faster than she had ever run on her own. She watched him as her head bobbed against his shoulder. His face clenched tight and his nostrils flared with each quick breath. Her eyes closed and she drifted away, far from here, to a place where pain and suffering could no longer reach her.

CHAPTER 27

She awoke in bed, in an unfamiliar room. Sharp pain pulsed through her head and someone had bound bandages around it. A cup of water sat on a dresser within reach, and after she had drained it, she lay back on a pillow and enjoyed the soft feel of it.

The paper on the wall cracked and peeled, unmasking an occasional gouge in the plaster beneath it. There were water stains on the ceiling and the room smelled of dust. Thunder roared outside and heavy rain pelted the metal roof above her.

She tried to remember what happened—so much was sketchy. She threw the blanket aside and sat up, just as Sargon walked in with a tray of food.

"Careful. You should not get out of bed without help."

He set the tray on a stand and moved to assist her.

"Where am I?" she asked.

"In my room. It is better that you stay here while you recover," he replied.

Her body sank back into the bed and she closed her eyes.

"I thought that maybe I was free. And that this nightmare had finally come to an end."

"You are. We escaped The Northern Storm and are home now."

"This isn't my home," she cried. Her chin quivered and her eyes floated in tears as yet another opportunity was squashed.

Sargon stood anchored to the floor. She could feel his stare as tears fell from her face.

"Your dinner is here."

When she didn't respond he turned and with his head down, walked out of the room.

Chin up, Sargon, you've won. You've finally broken me.

She was so close to getting out of this Armageddon. And so close to death. Either would be preferable to this.

I need to forget about home, stop thinking of David and what used to be. From here on, I will think like a Syrian, and accept what I can't change.

* * *

Sargon closed the door to his room, leaving her to cry alone. Downstairs, he met with his men. In his absence, it had been decided that ISIS would go into Aleppo, a town they greatly coveted. He would need to prepare for more wounded.

He spent the rest of his day doing small jobs—cleaning his weapons, putting gasoline in their trucks, and helping Ashur with the injured. Having their doctor laid up meant the men would have to wait to get the care they badly needed.

The next morning, anxious to see Clair, he went to his room first thing. Her food lay on the stand, untouched. Asleep, her face cloaked in serenity, she was beautiful. He wished the peace she found in sleep could stay with her always. She stirred and opened her eyes.

"Good morning," he said. "Are you feeling better?"

She nodded, her eyes focused on her hands.

He removed the tape and bloodied dressing from her head, gently pulled the strands of her hair from the adhesive. With the clean bandage in place, he wound gauze around her head. With each round his fingers moved across her face, her hair brushed over his arm.

"You were lucky, the bullet skimmed the surface. The cut is long, but not deep."

She looked up at him, her face just inches away, her full beautiful lips even closer, so that he inhaled her breath and she his.

"You came back for me."

He leaned beyond her, picked up the tape that lay on the bed and secured the gauze.

"Of course I did."

When he left her, he got in his truck and drove to the market, to a place where they served tasty meals. Back home, he put the food on two plates and carried them up to her. He set the tray down and opened the window. The rain had stopped and the cool, clean air that blew in, freshened the room.

Sargon handed her a plate, took one for himself, and sat on the edge of the bed.

"What is this?" she asked.

"Kufta kabobs. Lamb roasted in garlic with vegetables. I think you will like it."

She lifted the stick from the wax paper and took a bite. He watched, anticipating her reaction.

"It is good?"

"It's delicious. I can't remember the last time I ate meat," she said, as she licked her fingers. "I didn't know there were restaurants nearby that are still open."

He smiled wide. "A woman with a wok, a cooler, and a fire pit is not a restaurant, but she sells her food to many at the west side market."

"The west side? You went all that way—for me?" She asked with her mouth full. "Thank you."

"Just eat and get well. That is thanks enough."

The eagerness with which she ate made the long drive worth it. When she finished, she ran her tongue over the wax paper, lapping up the fat that had dripped from the meat.

"Is your head hurting you much?"

She shrugged. A strong breeze blew through the room and rattled the window.

"It hurts. How did we get away from the man who shot me? He was right behind us."

"An ISIS soldier took him out."

"Oh." One more death to add to the thousands already. She lowered her eyes and rested her head on the pillow.

"Are you going away soon?" she asked.

"No, not until you get better."

Taking her plate, along with his own, he laid his hand on her cheek, with his thumb he gently rubbed it.

"Get some rest."

Entering the kitchen he put the dishes in the sink, sat at the table and smoked. He would need to find something for Clair to wear besides the blood-stained clothes she had on. There was a box of clothing in a closet upstairs, part of what was left behind when the family fled during their takeover. Hopefully it held something that would fit her.

The next day he walked in his room.

"I have something I think you will like," he said, handing her a dress.

She held it high, as she looked it over. The gray dress had a musty smell. But since she wore the same pants she came here in, and his shirt, he was sure this would be a welcome change for her.

"Is this for me?" she asked.

"I'm not going to wear it," he said, grinning.

And then, a smile crept onto her face. This was wrong and would only cause more problems for him, but here he was, doing cartwheels to make a girl smile.

"If you are up to it you can shower, down the hall."

"Yes, thank you."

That afternoon, with a spring in his step, Sargon hurried up the stairs. There, she sat on his bed, her back straight and tall. Wearing the dress with its long sleeves and floor length skirt, she appeared regal. Her face glowed from the scrubbing she had given it and her braided hair, tied with strips of gauze, added a youthful aura to her already beautiful face. If not for the bandage atop her head, you wouldn't know she'd been hurt. She stood and faced him. His chest tightened, as he fought his desire to touch her.

"I'm ready to go back to work."

CHAPTER 28

AFTER LYING FOR DAYS, IT FELT GOOD TO GET UP AND WALK. Although she hated every waking moment that she lived here, she really wasn't ready to die yet, and was grateful to Sargon for saving her life.

The men had been neglected in her absence, and some lost a great deal of blood because of it. She rolled up her sleeves and went to work on them.

As she stitched and bandaged, she thought of Sargon.

I can't believe he would drive all that way to get food for me.

She had never tasted anything so good. The lamb melted in her mouth and the vegetables, firm and flavorful. Tonight, she would give him back his room. She was well enough to sleep in her own bed.

Late that afternoon, they heard a ruckus outside. It wasn't often that visitors came to this part of town. They rushed to the windows with their curiosity piqued. Marching past were soldiers, cloaked in black. Dark, hate-filled eyes, their only visible features. They carried guns and were led by a soldier waving a huge black flag.

She stood by Ashur, watching. "Are these ISIS soldiers?"

He nodded his head. "They are gathering here, before moving on to Aleppo, where they will fight for control of that city."

Clair couldn't believe the plethora of men that passed. The line seemingly had no end. As she watched, she felt herself shrink, intimidated by their numbers.

This is the small rebel group that was rarely talked about? How did they attract so many so fast?

The soldiers that lived in the house waved and cheered, thrilled that they were taking the fight to Aleppo. Clair could only see more wounded, more deaths.

When finally, the end was in sight, they watched as a soldier who held an American flag put a flame to it. The men erupted in ovation that neared frenzy. They chanted phrases Clair could only guess the meaning of while some shot hateful glares at her. She turned away and went back to work.

It was later than usual when Sargon came to her, ready to take her downstairs.

"I want to show you something," he said.

He led her out the back door and pointed upward. The sky was drenched in shades of orange, red, and yellow as the sun melted beyond the horizon. Beauty she had never before seen.

"I can't remember when I last watched the sun go down," he said, as he stared mesmerized. "But I noticed it just now, and wanted you to see it."

"It's breathtaking."

He reached for her hand and held it as they stood, sharing the radiance that could only come from nature.

"Someday, when the war is over, I will move somewhere rural. Maybe plant cotton and raise livestock like my father."

Surprised, she looked up at him.

"Someday, I hope you can."

He pulled out a cigarette and offered her one.

"Why not," she said, taking one. She had tried smoking in high school—her rebellious years—but thought better of it and quit. Being here, lung cancer was the least of her worries. Sargon struck a match for her, and she inhaled the poisonous toxins.

"I wish things were different for you."

His words, spoken with regret, hung in the air like the clouds above them.

"Those flowers in the field. What are they?"

"Jasmine. Its flower opens at night, when the sun sets, and the temperature drops."

How strange it felt to be looking at so much splendor, knowing that when she turned her back she would see the ugly reality of death and destruction. He let go of her hand and raked her windblown hair from her face.

"We better get you to bed. Today was too much for you."

"I am tired but I enjoyed the view. Thank you."

He laid his hand on her face and looked into her eyes, then cleared his throat.

"We should go now."

* * *

Sargon followed Clair down the stairs to her room. He held his light and waited while she walked to the cot, then left her. There was a different blanket on her cot and a pillow. He must have slept here while she had his bed. She lay down and covered herself. The cottony material of her dress was warm and soft. It had thrilled her to toss the smelly rags she wore in the trash.

Although tired, she couldn't help thinking about her day. The frightening display of ISIS soldiers, marching as one through town, her new dress, and the sunset.

And his touch.

She thought of her husband and felt shame.

Do you still think of me, David? Does anyone still look for me?

In the morning, she awoke to a strong sweet fragrance that somehow overcame the room's musty air. Quickly, she turned on her light and spotted a bouquet of jasmines at the foot of her bed.

Sargon was here last night while I slept.

He brought beauty into this dismal room, for her. Ashur tromped down the stairs, and alerted her of another day dawning. It was time to go upstairs.

The next few days were busy ones. She still experienced headaches, but with each passing day, they lessened. She saw little of Sargon and when she did he seemed distant. So much so, she began to think she had imagined the spark between them.

Then, one night, he came down and startled her awake. He stood over her while holding his light with a crazed look on his face.

"Sargon, what's wrong?" she asked.

"Everything." His voice was full of anguish. "Tonight we were at a house in Aleppo. A group there wanted to meet with us to talk about joining forces. They had not arrived yet, so we waited. Some of our men decided to go to a hotel further into the city where four French reporters were staying. They were reporting lies about us and needed to be taught a lesson."

Sargon picked up the chair and moved it close to the cot and sat down.

"The men we waited for showed up much later," he said. "But they didn't want to join us . . . they wanted to kill us. When the shooting started, we scattered. I motioned for Jaul to follow me and we ran out the back."

He paused, his lips pursed as he looked up at the ceiling.

"We ran to my truck as they fired. I thought we were safe when we drove away but then—so much blood. He was dead before we reached camp."

He took a deep breath, let it out in a huff.

"He was my brother. I should have kept him safe."

Jaul often hung out in the kitchen, and from what she noticed, did very little. Sargon thought differently.

She knelt before him and put her arms around his hunched shoulders. He held his head in his hands to hide his tears.

Accepting her comfort, he pulled her into him and buried his face in her neck. A minute passed with her arms around him, soothing his sorrow. But then, their bodies so close became more than either could bear.

She caressed his back and shoulders as he kissed a path up her neck toward her lips. Instead of forceful, his kiss was warm and tender. Not at all like she imagined it would be.

He stood, carried her in his arms, and laid her on the cot. Tenderly, he kissed the scar on her forehead while his fingers combed her hair. He covered her with the blanket, kissed her cheek, and stood.

It wasn't until the lock slid across the door that she realized he had gone. Breathless, she lay listening to her heart pound wildly against her chest.

What just happened?

CHAPTER 29

WINTER BREAK. THREE WEEKS BETWEEN CLASSES AND DAVID was on his way to the airport. He had to go back. This time he was more informed. ISIS held northern cities, close to Turkey. His plane landed in Mardin.

He couldn't get any closer without risking his life. He felt safe in Turkey, but just a few miles south, battles raged.

His first night there he sat on his hotel balcony and listened as guns fired in the distance. The flames, leftover from bombings, lit up the sky. And in the air, the sulfurous stench of explosives. He imagined his wife amongst it all.

I should have gotten you out of here sooner.

For hours, he gazed across the border and imagined the nightmare she was living.

The next day he hit the streets, flashing Clair's photo to anyone who would look at it. For the most part, no one was interested, they had problems of their own. But one man took the time to stop, he glanced at the photo.

"She is a beautiful woman," he said. "She deserves a beautiful ring." He reached into his pocket and pulled out a handkerchief that held jewelry.

"No thanks," David said.

"But just look at all I have. I sell cheap." He waved his collection of gems in David's face.

Annoyed, David turned to walk away when something caught his eye. In the midst of the costume jewelry lay a ring. The large diamond, surrounded by sapphires looked strikingly familiar. David held it between his fingers and looked close.

"Where did you get this?" he asked.

"I bought it from a businessman who sells quality jewels. I'll give you a good price. One thousand US dollars."

David had paid four times that amount when he bought it the first time.

"I need to know the name of the man you bought it from. This ring belongs to my missing wife. That salesman may know where she is."

The man's eyes grew large. He rubbed his face and took a few steps back.

"I am mistaken. It is not for sale." He quickly closed the handkerchief and stuffed it into his pocket. Spooked, he turned and started to walk when David took hold of his arm.

"Wait. I'll give you the money. No questions asked."

The man was scared. He obviously dealt in stolen goods, but who knew how many hands that ring had passed through before his. Chances are he knew little about its owner.

"Come with me to the bank. I'll get your money."

The peddler looked at David with narrowed eyes.

"Go get your money. If you come back alone, I will sell you the ring."

It took over an hour for David to walk to the nearest bank, get the cash and walk back. But when he returned the salesman had vanished. Men sat on the street curb, talking, but he wasn't among them.

David paced the sidewalk, mad at himself for letting on that he knew the ring was stolen. He was about to give up when he saw the man, coming toward him. Without a word, the peddler held out his hand. David dropped the envelope with ten one hundred dollar bills in his hand.

After counting the money, he gave David the ring.

"It was a pleasure doing business with you," he said before turning to run.

With the transaction over, David went back to his hotel room. There was no doubt that this ring belonged to Clair. He had worked with his jeweler for months finding the perfect one for her. It was rare. The odds of another just like it, being sold in the streets of Turkey, slim. But whether it was stolen or lost, he would give it back to her, once she came home.

For the next three days he got nowhere. Those who took the time to look walked away without recognition.

His fourth day proved more interesting. He had changed hotels, moved farther west to Urfa, following his plan to cover the border. In a local restaurant while eating his lunch, he talked to his waiter, showed him Clair's picture. A man, who had been sitting nearby, approached them, asked if he could join him. With his foot, David slid a chair from the table.

"I have seen the woman you look for," he said as he sat.

David's heart took off. He leaned forward and spoke low. "Where?"

"She is here, in Turkey, living with a friend of mine."

What?

David tapped the photo that lay on the table.

"Are you sure it's her?"

The man held Clair's picture. With furrowed brows and intense face, he studied her likeness.

"I am certain. My friend found her injured in the street."

"Is she all right?"

"She will be."

With a rush of excitement, David moved close.

"Can you tell me where?"

The man stood tall, with a thick beard and large round eyes.

"I'll take you there."

David weighed his options. It would be dangerous to go with this stranger alone, but he had no choice. If he took the time to get the police or military, this man could be gone along with his wife. You don't find and keep an American woman without reporting it to someone. The man could face charges. But David didn't care how this all came about. He just wanted to get her back.

"Let's go."

David followed him outside and down a side road, through the swarm of humanity that filled the streets and wound deep into the bowels of the city. An hour passed before they arrived at a house, bigger than most with an attached garage.

His guide punched a code into the keypad.

"Why are we going in through the garage?" David asked.

"That is where she is kept."

"Really?"

The door opened. David was shoved in from behind while the door closed. His eyes were slow to adjust to the dark, one dim bulb hung from the ceiling, but taking shape, a room filled with enough guns to supply a small army.

He smelled him before he saw him. A huge, burly beast with a scar that ran diagonal across his face.

The first blow was to his gut that dropped him to his knees. From there, he took a boot to his groin. Pain rocketed from his testicles to his brain and took his breath. He fell forward. His face slammed into the concrete. Both men took turns punching and kicking him until, mercifully, he blacked out.

* * *

The tiny legs of a bug crawled across his face, tickling. He slapped his nose and slowly gained consciousness. His flesh burned and his lips were pasted shut. One eye was swollen closed and from what he could see through the slit of the other, he had landed in hell.

Propped against a tree, his head bobbed side to side, before he gained control and held it upright. A patch of tall grass surrounded him, but nothing else. No homes, no roads, no people.

His mouth felt as dry as the sand that surrounded him. Grimacing, he stood, swooned, and fell. The abrasive sand, glued to his face by his blood and sweat, stung his open wounds. He would die here if he didn't get up.

He stood again, waited for the ground to stop moving, and then staggered across the sand looking for a road. And when he thought he couldn't dredge through the deep sand any longer, he stumbled across one.

He plodded in the direction he hoped would lead toward town. Any town; he needed water. The sun scorched his already inflamed skin and the blisters on his lips oozed pus.

His legs gave out and he fell to the ground. This was the end. He'd never see her again, or hold her in his arms, and would die with the knowledge he had failed to save her.

The hum of an engine woke him and grew louder by the second. At first, he thought the truck coming toward him must be a mirage. But when two men got out and tried to communicate, he found power he didn't know he possessed.

"Alriad Hotel," he whispered.

They spoke to each other, then helped him up and into the bed of their truck. His limp body bounced with each bump in the road as they sped away.

When they parked in front of David's hotel and helped him out, he fumbled for his wallet and pulled out some cash. They shook their heads, refusing his offer.

David lay in bed and drank water from a jug that the bellhop kept full on his nightstand. After three days of chills, sweats, and confusing dreams, he stood and dressed. If he were smart, he'd get on the next plane home. But he couldn't. Not when she was still out there living with a terrorist. He had to give this another try. But from now on, he'd do his snooping in public, not down back roads and alleyways. And he wouldn't trust anyone.

He limped out of his room, and every muscle screamed in pain as he walked. His sunburned skin, tattooed with purple bruises, gave him a clown-like look that people stared at.

For the most part, he sat on a bench or a step. Waved her photo in the faces of those who passed by. He spoke in a language where words were not needed, and everyone understood. While they walked, their eyes rolled from him to the picture, before shaking their heads. All without missing a step as they moved on.

For the next two days, he came away empty and time was running out. Tomorrow he'd be on a plane heading home. Getting her ring made the trip worth it, but the thought of going home without something to help find her was disappointing.

Again, he went into a restaurant, showed Clair's picture, and asked his questions. A group of boys, who looked to be in their late teens, sat at a table nearby. David introduced himself and passed Clair's picture around. They spoke English and all denied ever seeing her. One of them was lying, David could see it in his eyes—the kid knew her.

David left the diner, and waited outside for him. When he walked out, David followed.

"We need to talk," David shouted.

The boy shot a glance at David as he continued to walk.

"What do you want from me? I told you I do not know her."

He picked up his pace. David followed until the boy started to jog. The kid was younger and, right now, healthier than David. He could never keep up.

"I'm CIA," David shouted in desperation. "Stop or I'll have you arrested."

It worked. Even though he looked at David suspiciously, he stopped and faced him.

"I heard what you and your friends were planning. Tell me how you know the woman in the photo, and I'll forget all about it."

It was total bullshit, but the boy, young enough and guilty enough to be scared, fell for it. He gave David a snide glance before he looked up and down the street. He wiped the sweat from his forehead with the heel of his hand.

"If I tell you, will you let me be?"

"Tomorrow I leave for the States. You'll never see me again," David vowed.

"It is true, I never saw your wife. But a woman in Azaz, an American doctor, is being held by ISIS."

"How do you know? Do you live there?"

"My brother does. She was at his house, trying to escape them. That is all I know."

The boy turned and ran away.

"Did she make it? Did she escape?" David yelled.

The kid shook his head while he continued to run. David thought of Clair and how brave she was, fighting to be free, only to be recaptured.

He walked back to the diner. The table where they had sat was empty, except for one boy. David approached him.

"Hello again. Can I ask you one more question?"

He looked at David, his eyes narrowed and he crossed his arms.

"I told you, I do not know her."

"Your friend, the one wearing the baseball cap, tell me the name of his brother who lives in Azaz." As David said this, he slid a fifty across the table, his fingers pressed firmly on top.

The man's eyes swept the room, before locking with David's.

"Fakhir Kaya," he said while pulling the bill out from under David's grasp.

CHAPTER 30

SARGON LAY IN BED, TORTURED BY THOUGHTS OF CLAIR. HE wanted her—badly. She had no idea how difficult it was to walk away from her the night Jaul died.

But no matter what he wanted, she was an American. How could he love someone so rich and spoiled, ignorant of the needs of the world? If he gave into his desires his men would hate him for it. Besides, he had worked too hard to get where he was now. Getting involved with her could spoil everything.

Dawn approached. Sargon rubbed his eyes and yawned, stretched his long body beyond the mattress. Sleep had eluded him most of the night and he rose more tired than when he lay down.

It was hard to look at her without remembering how she felt in his arms, but he would be strong. His life had never been his own, dictated by circumstances beyond his control. And that is how it would be with Clair.

As days passed they would see each other, but things were different. It was as if they had reached an unwritten agreement, look but don't touch. If he passed by her and haphazardly brushed against her, he felt the electricity that ran between them. He thought she felt it too. No one here would understand his desire for her.

He needed to get away from her, so he traveled to Tartus. His mind should be focused on ISIS and his role in this war, not on Clair. ISIS was gaining ground fast and were making the news daily. The world now knew they were a force to be dealt with. Their number of recruits nearly doubled this month, and soon they would control all of Syria. He stayed in Tartus for two days and helped strategize their next move. Before he started back, he went to the market to get food and medical supplies.

As he approached the checkout, he noticed a shelf loaded with fragrant soaps and lotions. He picked up a bar, breathed in the fresh scent of lavender, and with closed eyes imagined it on Clair's skin. He then grabbed a bottle of shampoo, paid for it all and left.

He drove fast, eager to get to the house, and to her. Once there, he carried the supplies in and placed them on the table. Ashur would put everything where it belonged. First, he made certain Clair was not in the infirmary, then headed down the stairs.

Clair sat on the cot looking at the calendar he had recently given her.

"What is it you are studying so intently?" he asked, as he walked toward her.

She smiled, and looked genuinely happy to see him.

"I've lived in this room for over seven months now. I missed Thanksgiving and Christmas. I know it sounds silly to you, but in my family, those two holidays are a big deal."

For a minute, neither said anything, both saddened by what she had missed. Then he handed her the package.

"I saw this in the market today and thought of you."

She took the gift and tore away the plain brown paper it was wrapped in.

"Shampoo," she said in a high pitch. "Thank you. It's been so long."

Her smile was all the thanks he needed.

"There is more," he said, showing her the soap. She unwrapped it and held it beneath her nose breathing in the strong sweet scent of it.

"It's wonderful. What did I do to deserve all this?"

"I owe you more than soap and shampoo."

Their eyes met, locked in an understanding that went beyond words. He regretted taking her and keeping her a prisoner but there was no turning back. The most he could do now was to try to make life easier for her.

He leaned down and kissed the top of her head. "Sleep well," he said, leaving the room to be alone with his wonderful, disturbing thoughts.

He tossed all night, thinking of her until his head nearly exploded. He tossed the blanket to the floor and held his head in his hands. He could no longer fight this. And even though he would pay in the end, for now he would allow himself the pleasure that only Clair could give him.

* * *

The next morning, Ashur woke her.

"Good morning. Are you ready to shower?" he asked.

"I am. You wouldn't believe how often I showered back home, sometimes twice a day."

Ashur shook his head and whistled.

"I'll never take personal hygiene for granted again."

After she had pulled off her dress, she held it under the faucet and scrubbed it with her soap. When she wrung out as much water as possible, she hung it on a hook. Then stepped in the shower.

Piled high on her head, she ran her fingers through the rich lather that covered her head and massaged her scalp. Then with her soap, she washed her body. Its scent so strong, she wondered if they could smell it downstairs.

When finished she put on the dress. Although cold and wet, it was clean. Soon enough the hot air would have it dry.

Sargon was there when she entered the room and approached her right away.

He lowered his face to her neck and inhaled deeply. With closed eyes he smiled.

"I am a boy, running in a field of lavender, free of all worries. You make me feel that."

Clair swallowed hard, her scent bedazzled him. Throughout the day while working, she would feel his stare and meet it. His desire fed hers, and when his eyes caressed her, a slow burn would rise up her neck to her face.

The days passed, each one built upon the other—at first desire, then lust. It soon turned into obsession, and in time, they suffered an addiction to something they had only dreamed of having.

CHAPTER 31

IT HAD BEEN TWO MONTHS SINCE DAVID LEFT TURKEY. THE information he had given to Dean White and Brent Freeman had yet to make a difference. When he left there, knowing he'd scored big, he thought she'd be home in a matter of days. He gave them a name and a town, what more did they need? He had never felt so powerless.

Recently, he joined a campus organization that raised money to fight human trafficking. He was surprised to learn that even in the United States, people were stolen and sold. Someone's spouse or child would suddenly disappear, and like David, the families felt inept and at the mercy of others. David understood their pain, and had spent much time empathizing with family members. It helped them just to know that someone cared. Truth be told, he got more than he gave—a shared tragedy, like a private club, created some tight bonds. Sometimes he'd call a victim's family because *he* needed to talk.

A portion of the money raised was used to hire private investigators. Someone who focused solely on them and their missing loved one. When David heard about this, he tried himself to hire a PI. So far, there were no takers. Syria was as appealing as a week in hell.

He still talked to Darcy on the phone but no more sleepovers. He couldn't trust himself around her. Clair's parents called less frequently and they dropped their accusing tones. After he had returned from Turkey, they stopped by to drop off a Christmas gift. Their stunned looks when they saw the cuts and bruises on his face still made him laugh.

Eight months was a long time. Sometimes he would go days without thinking of her and felt shame because of it. He began to believe he'd never see her again.

It was late afternoon. David packed up his papers and decided to finish the test he was working on at home. He was almost to his car when someone called out his name. Dean White's secretary gasped for air as she ran to catch up with him.

"Mary, is everything all right?"

Her face was red and sweat ran down from her forehead.

"Yes Professor, I'm . . . fine. But Dean White has news about your wife. He tried calling you." Her hand rested on her hip as she sucked in air. "I'm sorry but he's left for the night. I was leaving myself when I saw you."

Whenever someone had word from Syria, the first thing that popped into David's head was that they had recovered her body. It was sick, but he couldn't stop it. It didn't matter that news like that would come only from Freeman.

"Thanks, Mary. I'll give him a call."

"I hope it's good news," she said, waving goodbye.

David got in his car and phoned his boss, who asked if he could stop at his house on his way home. David could only guess at the news that awaited him, and couldn't get there fast enough. After his initial greeting, Dean White led him into his study.

"I received a call today from Joe. He told me that the military has spies throughout Syria and are finally getting some information that bears fruit," he said. "They confirmed what you were told, there is a female doctor in Azaz, a town ISIS has taken over. They're making plans to go in."

"It's about time," David said.

"It's the most promising news we've gotten thus far. Remember when we talked last, I told you that there were two other American doctors missing?"

David nodded.

"Well they found one of them. Unfortunately for him it came too late. But the location where his body was found may lead them to the other."

"When will they go to Azaz to get her?" David asked.

"I'm sure that type of information is classified, but from what Joe has told me they are putting together a plan involving the Navy SEALs. If those boys can't get her out, no one can."

"The two other doctors, were they both male?"

"No, David. The other one still missing is also a woman."

David wished that wasn't the case. It decreased their odds of this being Clair. Still he felt more hopeful than he had in a long time. He thanked Dean White for his help and drove home.

While eating a sandwich, he turned on his computer and studied a map of Syria. Azaz was a small city with a history of revolts and takeovers, and seeing its close proximity to nearby countries, it was understandable why the town would be one of value to a group such as ISIS.

That night, he went to bed with his hopes high. They were close to finding his wife and soon they would be together, their life back on track, just as they planned.

CHAPTER 32

CLAIR KNELT ON THE FLOOR, BUSY SUTURING A SOLDIER'S WOUND when she noticed Sargon entering the room. How could she not, with his height? But it wasn't just his size that grabbed her attention. To her, he possessed a strong attraction, one that she fought against every day. Their eyes met and he tipped his head, she smiled.

After she had done all that she could for the soldier, she moved on to the next one. *Will I ever see the color red again without thinking of blood?*

With her morning work finished, she sat resting on the steps that led to the second floor and looked at the conglomeration of bodies that lay before her. Broken and torn, not only their flesh, but their minds. How many more generations would be reared on war? And how do you break such a hellacious cycle?

Seeing her, Sargon swaggered over to where she sat, a smile on his face.

"I was wondering, do you have any plans for tomorrow?"

She raised her chin and shrugged.

"I planned on getting my hair done and meeting some friends for lunch." She ran her fingers through her hair. "Why do you ask?"

"I have some plans of my own. Ashur will come for you a bit earlier tomorrow. I want you to be showered, waiting patiently for me."

"I don't wait patiently for anyone. What makes you think you're special?" she teased.

He leaned in close and whispered.

"Come with me tomorrow. You will be glad that you did." He sauntered off, leaving her to ponder his meaning.

Clair felt her pulse quicken.

Why does he have this effect on me?

She was in great spirits the rest of the afternoon and could hardly sleep in anticipation of a day away from this house. The added mystery of where he was taking her increased her excitement.

When Ashur came to her room the next morning, he didn't have to wake her. She sat on the cot, ready to start her day.

"Good morning," he said. "Would you like to use the shower before breakfast?"

Clair grabbed her soap and shampoo and started toward the stairs. "Definitely."

It was either the scent of the soap or the way Sargon looked at her that had her feeling like a woman again. She basked in the thrill of it. Her femininity no longer nostalgic, but alive and well.

She stepped out of the shower and rubbed a towel over her scalp, then finger-combed her long strands of hair. David used to rake his hand through her hair. Sometimes he twisted it around his finger.

This is all wrong. I should tell Sargon that I can't come with him today. But yet . . . I want to. Haven't I suffered enough? I just want one day to enjoy. I could be dead tomorrow.

Taking a deep breath, she walked toward the stairs, toward Sargon and all that his promise of a day together held.

CHAPTER 33

On shaky legs Clair walked slow, taking each step of the stairs with deliberate motion. All the while, Sargon stood at the landing, praising her with his gaze. Amazingly, her breath caught and without a touch, he moved her.

"Are we ready to go?" she asked.

"If you are." He stared into her eyes with such intensity she felt the heat creep into her face and turned away. Together, they walked past the men who stood guard, Clair couldn't help notice the disdained looks that they gave her. But no one would rain on her parade. This was her day out. An escape from reality.

They weren't a mile down the road before he turned to her.

"You look stunning."

Stunning? Really? She smiled, his words were like salve on an open wound.

"Thank you."

She tucked her hair behind her ear and straightened her dress beneath her.

"Where are we going?" she asked.

"You really are impatient." He shook his head, in mock disgust. "If you must know, we are going to stop and buy food before going to the beach."

"The beach? Is it close by?" she asked.

"Not close but it will be worth the drive. We are going to the Mediterranean Sea."

She smiled, thinking again how her feelings toward him had changed. Just being alone with him had her warm inside. And when he touched her arm, it tingled, making her yearn for those electrifying hands of his.

As he said they would, they stopped at a market and bought some meat, cheese, and bread, along with some relishes, all for just the two of them. His extravagance surprised her.

She had imagined a large, sandy beach, scattered with vacationers sunning themselves while their children played in the waves. Instead, he turned off the main road and traveled down a dusty path that led to a remote cliff.

Gathering their food, she stepped out of the truck and admired the sea. Her hair, clean and light, waved in the breeze behind her.

Sargon took her hand and led her down a steep hill that turned into a small area of beach. She noticed the beauty he had so passionately talked about while driving. The water pounded the rocks, creating a mist that captured the sun. The combination gave birth to a legion of rainbows, and each floated effortlessly over the sparkling sea. Her senses further came alive with the sound of roaring waves and the heat of the sun on her skin. Although a prisoner, she had never felt so free.

While eating, she couldn't get enough of the imagery around her, soaking it up to remember later, when back in her dark, rancid dungeon.

Sargon broke the spell she was under with a question.

"Is it true what they say about Americans—that you eat all your meals in restaurants?"

He was serious but it made her laugh. "Not all the time, but yes, we do eat too many of our meals out."

"And you have to pay people to help you exercise because you get too fat?"

Now she could hardly contain herself, this portrayal of Americans was not a good one.

"Where are you hearing all this?"

"I get around. I hear things," he said smugly.

"What else do you hear that isn't related to eating?"

He looked out on the water, nibbled on some cheese.

"That the women are easy to bed."

Her mouth hung open. He'd crossed the line. She threw her pickle at him, laughing as it hit his nose.

"This is what you do? You ask me what I hear and when I tell you, you throw food at me."

They both laughed easily, their teasing banter, a form of foreplay. When they finished eating, he got to his feet and held out his hand. "Come."

He led her to the water's edge where they walked over rocks and searched for crab. Clair couldn't remember the last time she had felt this good.

She knew where all this was heading, and how wrong it was, but she couldn't have stopped it if she wanted to. The momentum had been building for weeks—their desire. Together, they sped toward the bottom of the dangerous hill they had climbed. Now, with nothing to impede the inevitable, it was only a question of when.

While bending down, looking beneath a rock, a huge wave crashed into her, plummeting her body into Sargon. He wrapped his arms around her and struggled to keep them both from falling.

Laughing and soaking wet, they headed back to the beach to dry. As they sat she thought of his hands around her waist and remembered their kiss.

Why did he leave after kissing me so passionately?

She sat staring at the water, still baffled by his behavior that night. Glancing up, she caught him looking at her with eyes ablaze. She knew her wet dress clung tight to her body, leaving little to the imagination, and his wanton look told her he noticed.

Pulling her close, he took command of her mouth in a deep, sensual kiss. His hand ran over her throbbing breast and fondled it. Even with her dress between them, his touch had her breathless. Moving his hand to the back of her head he deepened his kiss while easing her down on the blanket.

Clair grew dizzy, helpless with desire. Her mind raced with confusion as she fought for control. She should not want this to happen but she no longer had the strength to fight it. Her body pleaded with her, begged for more. Overwhelmed with pleasure, she surrendered.

It was a struggle, getting her dress off—the wet obstacle frustrated him into a rage. But when at last she lay naked, he scrutinized her body so completely she ached, craving his touch.

Franticly he tore at his clothes, throwing them off as if on fire. Starting with her neck he kissed her, making his way down her body. Her back arched forward, urging him on.

And when her nerve endings fired in a burst of pleasure, she was swept away, into another time and place—another life. In desperation they clung to each other. Both knew their insatiable hunger would not be satisfied in one act of love.

He held her so close, she could feel his heart pound, and his fingers lovingly caressed her arm. She was the first to break the silence. "It's been a long time since . . . what I mean is . . . that was incredible." She struggled to catch her breath.

He leaned on one elbow and looked down at her while his finger traced the outline of her face, stopping at her chin.

"You are a bright light in this country of gloom. Tell me, how does it happen, being good? Can someone come from a place, dark and dingy, and be cleansed by the goodness of another?"

She laid her hand on his face and gazed deep into his eyes. There was a line between good and evil, and he held that line. But she knew the good in him could grow, given a chance. It was possible that he could rise above his past and become an honorable man.

He ran his hand over her hips and glided his fingers softly across her back. The cool breeze joined his touch, making the sensation so erotic—she moaned. Then he kissed her. This time he moved slow and gentle, which nearly drove her crazy. They made love once more, saying the adoring words they both needed to hear. All too soon, it was time to pack up their belongings and go back.

In the truck, Clair felt so content she almost fell asleep. Barring the thought of David, she felt wonderful. But once started, it wouldn't go away, nagging at her, trying to destroy the euphoria that filled her. It didn't matter how they had got to this point, there was no turning back now or undoing what they had done.

David, I'm sorry. If I see you again, I hope you will understand and forgive me.

Sargon pulled the truck off the road, interrupting her thoughts of David.

"This was one of the best days of my life. No matter our future, we will always have today," he said, putting his arm around her.

They sat holding each other, neither in a hurry to return to the house.

"Your life would be much better, free of ISIS," she said.

"Yes, but worse too, in a way you would never understand. Maybe a few months ago I could have walked away. But not now."

"Why, what's changed?" she asked.

"You would be shocked if I told you."

His words challenged her. The kind of words that make you want to know more, but at the same time, make you want to cover your ears and scream—anything to keep from hearing the crimes he may have committed.

"You're right. You couldn't walk away because I couldn't live there without you."

Sargon took her hand and kissed it. He pulled back onto the road and continued toward Azaz. Neither spoke for miles, both lost in thought. Clair looked out her window as the landscape floated by. The mountains surrounded them like a fence that kept her confined. The carefree feeling of the day wore off as they drove back to her prison. And in its place, the weight of guilt and uncertainty. Feelings that would be the cause of her insanity if allowed to cultivate from thoughts of David.

Sargon parked the truck in front of the house. Her world sat before them. He lifted her face to his and gently kissed her. She smiled at him. And with her mouth full of bitter irony she said, "We're home."

CHAPTER 34

BEING WITH HER ALONE HAD MADE SARGON CRAZY WITH DE-sire. Now, most nights, he tossed in his bed, unable to sleep, incapable of getting her off of his mind. And when he did sleep, he dreamt of her.

The days passed, and despite their effort to hide it, their feelings were known to everyone. Clair was hated even more and he became the brunt of their jokes. But it didn't matter. Change was coming.

One night, he went to her room to discuss their future.

"We need to talk."

He sat on the cot beside her, lit a cigarette and handed it to her.

"We can't stay here much longer," he said.

"Why? What's happened?"

"The US is funding the Freedom Fighters. With all the new weapons that money will buy, we would be foolish to fight for Azaz. We are focusing now on Iraq."

He lifted a strand of her hair, tucked it behind her ear.

"Orders have been given that all ISIS soldiers are to evacuate Azaz, and join the others in Tartus."

"Will I go there too?"

Sargon looked away and shrugged.

"I don't suppose they'll let me walk away."

He hated to frighten her, but she needed to know the truth.

"You are an intelligent woman who knows too much."

He sighed heavily, not wanting to put the unthinkable into words.

"I have been given orders to execute you."

He watched, as the color drained from her beautiful face.

* * *

She knew this day would come, but wasn't prepared for the harsh reality that now gripped her.

"Do not worry. I have a plan for your escape," he assured her.

"But if you help me to escape and get caught, they'll kill us both." Her voice rose urgently.

With his arms wrapped around her he tried to comfort her but she couldn't be consoled.

"Escape here is impossible. Is there any chance they will allow me to live?"

He shook his head. She was not liking her options—either way death was possible, but she wouldn't bring him down with her.

"Sargon, I can't let you do this. You are risking your life for me and—"

Before she could finish he put his finger to her lips. "I am going to help you."

He traced his fingers from her hairline along her jaw, to her chin.

"How could we leave here without being caught? Every time I turn around someone is watching me."

Clair looked down at her clammy hands as they trembled. She was now being asked to make a decision for herself, something she hadn't done in months that may cost her life and his as well.

"It would be difficult but not impossible," he said. "I have talked to Ashur and he is willing to help us."

Sweet Ashur, of course he would help us.

"We will leave in two days. Most of our men will be taking supplies and moving to Tartus. Only a few will be left at the house and with Ashur's distraction we will leave out the back."

"The last time we ran together, I was shot," she said.

"We have no choice. We will run, hiding along the way. Ashur will have my truck parked outside of town. We will drive to Turkey, and you will be free."

As he explained their plan, her head filled with doubts, but he remained adamant.

"We can do this. I will be with you all the way. Please, say yes."

Hesitantly and without conviction, she said, "Yes."

Freedom. What will that bring me? A husband who has been waiting for my return, expecting me to be the person he knew before? A lover who would ... what? What would he want from me? Surely he would know I would choose my husband once free.

"Where will you go after I'm in Turkey?"

"Let us try to get out of here first. We can decide our future later," he said.

She sat in a tidal wave of differing feelings, some of hope, some of despair, not at all certain they would leave Syria alive. And if they somehow did, there would be heartbreak in the end. The thought of explaining this—her life here, Sargon, all she had done to David—was dizzying.

She took Sargon's hand and kissed his palm. Callused and rough, it likened the life he had lived.

Bending on one knee he took her hand, trying to ease her anxiety.

"As long as you are here, I promise to be your slave, doing everything you ask of me."

"I'll make you a list," she said. A fake smile on her face.

She appreciated his effort to appease her but her insides were churning and she felt sick.

"I should probably go upstairs now and get some sleep."

Suddenly, a rapid blast of gunfire erupted upstairs, rattling the ceiling above them. Sargon ran toward the door as it burst open and bullets ripped his body. Soldiers entered the room, firing as they walked.

Clair stood wide-eyed, screaming as his body jerked with each assault. The gunfire was deafening. The dirt floor and unyielding walls confined the roar, well after it was over and he lay dead.

Clair fought as Sargon's killer picked her up and toted her out of the room, past his bloodied body that lay motionless, face down in the dirt. She took the image with her as they climbed the stairs.

At the top was Ashur, lying on the kitchen floor with his eyes open wide. The man carrying her stepped over his dead body on their way out the door.

Outside, gunfire resounded through the cool night air. As she was ferried away from the house, the man held her tight and shouted over the noise. "You're going to be all right. Don't be afraid."

An American.

After months of captivity, they finally came for her, freeing them all from the prison that held them.

CHAPTER 35

THE SOUND OF HIS PHONE CHIMING REPEATEDLY PULLED DAVID out of a deep sleep. His hand dropped on the nightstand, fumbled for his phone and tipped over his water glass, drenching his laptop and adding to his annoyance.

"Hello," he snapped, once he found it.

"May I speak to David Stevens please?" a man asked.

"This is David," he said, as he sopped up the water with tissues.

"Mr. Stevens, this is Sergeant Michael Grant of the US Navy SEALs. I was asked by the FBI to call and tell you we have your wife. She's doing well and is with us in Turkey."

David's breath seized in his chest.

"This had better not be some prank," he said.

"No sir. Would you like to speak to her?"

She's really there.

"Sir, shall I put her on?" the sergeant asked.

"Yes. Please."

And then, her soft voice, spoken in a whimper.

"David?"

"Clair. It's you."

She burst into a sob, followed by a sharp intake of breath.

"Everything's all right now. I promise I'll never let anything happen to you again."

"Oh David, it's been so long. I hoped for this day but . . ."

He could hear someone talking in the background.

"Where are you?"

"I'm at the hospital now, they—"

"At the hospital? Are you hurt?"

"No. They want to make sure they don't give me back broken." Her sad, weeping laugh alarmed him.

"You're coming home, Clair. Where it's safe and where nothing can harm you."

"They're here for me. I have to go, but I'll be home in two days."

"Oh, then, I'll see you in two days."

There was more commotion in the background.

"I love you, Clair."

"I love you too."

The sergeant took the phone from her and explained to David the rescue and all that had happened since. When the call ended, David sat on the edge of the bed.

For a moment, he was so full of emotion he couldn't think straight. He sobbed with relief. His chest was tight and pain seized the back of his throat. When he pulled himself together, he picked up the phone and dialed. A sleepy voice answered.

"This had better be important."

"She's alive. Darcy, they found Clair and she's alive."

"What! Oh my God, this is great. Where is she? Who kidnapped her? When will she be home?" she fired.

"Slow down," he said laughing. "She's in Turkey right now. After talking to her, a sergeant with the SEALs filled me in on the rescue. It was, as we thought, ISIS who took her. They forced her to stitch up their soldiers wounded in their war. The SEALs killed the bastard responsible. That's all I know, except that she'll be home in two days. Can you believe it? She's alive and coming home soon."

"I'm happy for you. For you both," she said.

"I'll call you when I get more details but I better call her parents now."

His chest swelled while telling her dad the wonderful news, and listened as both parents cried with relief and joy. Afterward, he sat on the bed, his mind in a whirl. There was much to do. He'd have to spruce the place up, make it look good for her.

David went downstairs and made coffee, still in a daze of unbelieving. After he had showered and eaten breakfast, he turned on the news. As he expected, she was the top story. They showed pictures of the house where she had lived, a large building with stucco exterior and few windows. He imagined her living there, day after day, in fear.

The news anchor talked at length of the many crimes ISIS had committed. In the midst of it all they showed Clair's face. The photo taken by Doctors Without Borders for their directory. He almost forgot how beautiful she was. With her radiant smile and her eyes, a mix of green and gold so unusual they caught and held your attention. It was what he noticed first about her, the day Darcy introduced them. He knew then that he wanted to look into those eyes forever.

As the story of her rescue came to an end, the photo of her abductor aired. Looking at that man, David wasn't a bit sorry he was dead.

Piece of scum. He got what he deserved.

Hearing the thumping of his dog as he scratched himself, David picked him up.

"You're going to love Clair. I just hope she feels the same about you."

Buster licked David's face as if he shared in this wonderful news.

On campus, David parked and headed to Dean White's office. It was still early, and Mary wasn't at her desk yet. He stuck his head in the partially opened door.

"Good morning. Do you have a minute?" he asked.

"David, come in. I heard your good news on television this morning. I couldn't be happier for you."

"I owe a lot to you. Thanks for all that you've done. And thank Joe for me, will you?" David asked.

"I will. I trust she is well?"

"Well as can be expected. When I talked to her she sounded tired but with the ordeal she's been through how could she not be?" David said. "I won't keep you, I just wanted to give you the good news and thank you for all your support."

The two shook hands and David promised to bring Clair by, once she settled in. Walking out into the cold March day, David could hardly contain his excitement, greeting students as they passed, smiling all the way to his classroom.

CHAPTER 36

WITH HER MEDICAL EXAM OVER, CLAIR WAS TAKEN BACK TO the embassy, escorted by a female corporal to a room on the third floor. She was given a pair of running shoes, blue jogging pants, and a matching jacket. Each piece carried the Nike swish, making her feel as if she were headed to the Olympics instead of home.

The room had plush burgundy carpet, leather chairs and sofa, and a wet bar that ran the length of the room.

Am I at the embassy or a country club?

"Help yourself to the bar. There are sodas in the refrigerator, some snacks in the cupboards. A military intelligence officer has some questions for you. He'll be here soon. Is there anything else I can do for you?" the corporal asked.

After the last nine months, Clair felt like royalty, sitting in the soft chair, offered soda and snacks.

"Where can I change into my clothes?"

The corporal walked across the room and opened a door.

"This bathroom is well stocked. Shower, change, and put your old clothes in this bag. We'll dispose of them later."

Once alone, Clair stripped off her clothes and stepped into the shower. She ran the water as hot as she could tolerate. Face soap, body wash, shampoo, and conditioner lined the shower caddie, and she made use of them all.

When she stepped out of the shower, she wrapped herself in a soft, thick bath towel and then spotted a toothbrush, still in its package, on the counter. Of all that she missed out on during her nine months of captivity, a toothbrush ranked high on her list.

Her robust strokes, up and down, then side to side, had her gums bleeding, and turned the white paste red. Its minty fresh taste stung her gums. But never had brushing her teeth felt so good. As ordered, she put her gray dress in the large Ziploc bag and sealed it.

When she walked out of the bathroom, dressed in her new attire, an infantryman sat waiting. He stood when she approached him, decked out in a starched tan uniform with black shoes, spit-shined so bright they could serve as mirrors. His collar was decorated with an array of colored pins, as was his lapel.

"Mrs. Stevens. I'm Lieutenant Colonel Gerard Wolfe, United States Army Intelligence Officer, Human Intelligence Division."

Quite a title.

"Hello."

"I would like to ask you a few questions if you don't mind."

Clair sat on the sofa. A glass of ice and a can of Coke had been placed on the stand beside her.

"How long have you known Sargon Elbez?" he asked.

"Well, as long as I was there, what, nine months?"

"In the nine months that you were there, did he ever talk to you about ISIS?"

She refused to taint Sargon's name any more than it already was. What difference would it make—he was dead.

"No, never," she said. "I mean, I knew that's who they were, but that's all."

"Did he ever talk to you about his personal life?"

"No, not really."

She picked up the Coke and with a shaky hand, poured the soft drink into the glass, spilling some on the fine oak table.

"Did you ever go anywhere with him, maybe to a friend's or to a place where other ISIS members lived?"

"No."

He captured her lies on the small tape recorder he held in his hand. Even though she wasn't in a court of law, she wondered if she had committed perjury.

"Did you ever overhear him talk to a fellow member about any ISIS activities?"

"Not that I can recall," she said while she twisted a strand of her hair.

If he doesn't know by now that I'm lying, he doesn't deserve his fancy title and colored pins.

"In all of the time that you lived there, with Sargon Elbez and eight other ISIS members, you never heard them talk about takeovers, weapon purchases, or the overthrow of the Syrian government?" he asked, his voice louder than before.

Clair's stomach was in knots, and her mind ran all over the place, trying to decide what she should or should not tell him. And if he learned of her affair with Sargon, would he try to link her to ISIS?

"Once, a group there took Sargon and me. They kept us hostage for a few days. While running away from them, I was shot. Someone said it was a group called The Northern Storm."

He stared, motionless, challenging her to tell the truth. Perspiring, she took off the jacket and drank more soda.

He snapped off the recorder, tossed it on the table beside him, and glared. His tomato red face looked likely to explode.

"ISIS is a huge threat to the United States, Mrs. Stevens. Anything you tell us might help. Maybe after you've been home awhile and have had time to think, we'll talk again."

"I worked in their clinic. Hardly the hub of their operation." Her cynical voice sounded stronger than she felt.

"Do you know a man named Fakhir Kaya?" he asked.

Clair struggled to remember, but the name meant nothing to her. "No."

"A few weeks ago he became one of our informants. He told us you were at his house once while trying to get out of the country. He led us to where you were."

He helped me. After all this time, he had helped me.

"It was your husband who first learned of him, told us he thought he knew where you were."

"David? How would he know him?" she asked.

"He was in Syria, then later Turkey, looking for clues. Without him, I'm not sure we would have found you this soon."

As if in a vise, the air was squeezed from her lungs. Her eye started to twitch and the headache she already had worsened. While she was busy being unfaithful, David was here risking his life to find her.

CHAPTER 37

AT TWENTY THOUSAND FEET, CLAIR STARED OUT THE PLANE'S window, trying to calm herself. It was good to hear David's voice, but she couldn't stop thinking of Sargon's bloody death. The last two days had been a blur. First the medical exam, then the military interrogation. So many questions. He was dead. What else mattered?

The image of his shredded body flashed before her when she least expected it—in vivid color. And Ashur's wide-eyed look of surprise was something that would haunt her for a long time.

Sargon told her that things happened for a reason, that God had control of their lives. She hoped that he was with his God now, and in death, found the peace that had eluded him in life. Trying to regain her composure, Clair wiped tears from her face. She had just been rescued from a terrorist and was being returned to her husband, people would expect her to be happy.

The plane landed at Columbus International Airport amongst snow fall. When she departed the plane, the biting cold cut through her light jacket. She shielded her eyes from the bright sun and squinted as she sought out David.

But then, there he stood, good looking as always. It was all like a dream that she moved through without feeling. David rushed to her, his strong arms embraced her. While she buried her face in his neck, she felt the sob that escaped him.

How does one behave toward the person they will soon crush?

She could have stayed in his hold forever. Safe from all the questions that would surely come. But the media waited, and as much as she dreaded it, she wanted it over with.

Journalists were crammed together in a room just outside the terminal. Together with her parents and Darcy, she walked in, holding David's hand. She was immediately besieged with questions, fired all at once. One reporter from CNN spoke above the rest.

"Do you feel, now that your kidnapper is dead, that justice has been served?"

Clair scanned their faces—all looking at her and waiting for an answer.

"There is no justice. He was as much a victim as I was."

Her reply started a frenzied backlash of questions, every reporter wanting to know the meaning of her surprising comment. As they closed in on her, Clair became dizzy and lost her balance. She grabbed David's arm for support as she started to go down.

"Clair." He wrapped his arm around her waist. "You're as white as a ghost."

David passed her on to her mother and like the "knight in shining armor" he has always been, stepped up to the podium.

"My wife is happy to be back home, and I'm relieved and grateful to have her back. I want to thank the Navy SEALs for risking their lives to save her, and everyone who had a hand in getting her safely out of Syria. The doctors assure me she's fine. But understandably, she's feeling a little tired. So, if you'll excuse us, I'm taking my wife home."

They were escorted by Homeland Security officers to the parking garage. Everyone chatted at once, trying to fill her in on nine months of their lives in ten minutes' time. The original plan was to have dinner together at Clair's favorite restaurant. But since she felt ill, they agreed to make it another day.

Once in the car David held her tight, his head on her shoulder. Clair knew what she should do and say, lord knows she imagined this reunion often enough, but her body wouldn't cooperate, her mind was blank.

"At last, we're together," he said.

"They told me it was you. You were the one who helped find me."

She touched his face where a small scar, underscored his eye.

"I played a small role. Gave them the information they needed. I would have done anything to get you back."

She fought the urge to throw up, her stomach churned nonstop.

"I should have known you would do something like that."

Like a faucet turned full blast, the emotions that eluded her earlier, poured in, making her insides quake. It hurt to look at him, so admirable, brave, and faithful. Everything she wasn't.

"Can we go home now? I don't feel well."

David started the car and it wasn't long before Clair closed her eyes and slept. She dreamt of Sargon and their last night together, his last night alive. A gentle kiss on her cheek woke her, and she opened her eyes expecting to see Sargon.

"You're home," David said.

She looked around, a bit disoriented.

"What you went through, it had to have been awful. If you want to talk about it, I'm a good listener," he offered.

She couldn't begin to speak of Sargon, or even Ashur, without crumbling.

"Oh, maybe sometimes, but things weren't always bad for me," she said, trying to sound upbeat for his sake.

He wasn't convinced. "You were crying out in your sleep just now."

She laughed, quick and shrill. "I've been having some crazy dreams. Hard telling what I might say."

His dark eyes, filled with concern, probed her face. She laid her hand on his arm.

"You know you shouldn't have gone there, you could've been killed."

"Without you, I was dying a slow death anyway."

Guilt was a disease that spread like fire within her. Eating away, it affected her body, her voice, and above all, her mind.

"Can we go inside now?" she asked.

In the house, Clair meandered through, looking. Nothing much had changed. The wood floors and oak cupboards that had once meant so much to her now seemed run-of-the-mill. Like everything, it didn't seem important anymore.

"There's been an addition to our family, since you've been gone."

Coming out of the laundry room, he held a dog for her to meet.

"I found him in the bushes out back. Couldn't find his owner—believe me I tried."

The dog scampered over to Clair, sniffed her all over before sneezing.

Clair reached down and patted his head.

"He's not very attractive," she said smiling.

"Not at all, but we're friends now. I named him Buster. Is it okay if he stays?"

"Sure, I like dogs. And I'm glad you had a companion."

"Are you hungry? I'll fix you something."

"Maybe just some tea. My stomach is still upset."

She touched the copper pans that hung from the ceiling above the island. They looked brand new.

I see he didn't cook much while I was gone.

Moving on, she wandered into the formal living room. Their curio cabinet was filled with the Swarovski Crystal Paradise collection. Every figurine purchase had thrilled her. They say one's possessions tell a lot about a person. What did these say about her?

In the family room, she sat on their comfortable overstuffed sofa. Everything seemed so extravagant.

"I took tomorrow off work," David yelled from the kitchen. "I thought we could do some shopping. Maybe get you some new clothes."

He came in with the tea and turned on the television.

"You've been all over the news. People love a happy ending."

Stay tuned. This may not end so happy.

Flipping through the stations he stopped on CNN.

"Are you warm enough? I can start a fire if you're cold," he offered.

"I'm fine. Thank you."

You'll regret being so kind to me, once you know the truth.

They sat, staring at the television. It wasn't long before her story played out on the screen. First, at the hospital, holding an infant. Then still frames of the house where she was held. Next up, an interview with her parents as they waited for her plane to land.

But the storyline that grabbed the most attention was Clair's declaration that Sargon was a victim. It became the story within the story, as commentators guessed at its meaning.

The segment ended with a photo of Sargon, and appeared to have been taken several years ago. He wore his usual camouflage attire and held an AK-47 as he looked into the camera, a violent sneer on his face. Before she could stop them, tears slipped from her eyes and trickled down her cheeks.

"This is all too much for you," David said, turning off the television. He sat close, putting his arm around her, and tried to comfort her. It seemed surreal, being comforted by her husband while crying over her lover's death. It was all so wrong, and the first time that she had such a strong dislike for herself.

"If it's okay with you, I'd like to take a shower and turn in. I'm exhausted," she said.

His face held a confused and worried expression.

"Of course it's okay; do whatever you want."

She hugged him and climbed the stairs to the bathroom.

In the shower, she was relieved that at last, she could mourn Sargon's death in private. But once started, she couldn't stop the unraveling. Everything held precariously together by a thread, now gushed out, shaking her to the core.

Sobbing, she dropped to her knees as hot water carried her tears down the drain. Steam filled the room, enclosing her in a safe haven of invisibility, if only for a while.

She sat on the shower floor, the water raining down her back and thought of their day at the beach. Although she would soon pay the price for that day, she wasn't sorry that she had given Sargon such joy before his death.

Stepping out of the shower, she felt weak and unsteady. With her hand, she cleared the moisture and looked in the mirror. The scar on her forehead was a jagged, ugly line. Her narrow face, further tarnished by her puffy red eyes. As she studied her reflection she knew she should be grateful to the mirror for revealing only her appearance. She couldn't yet face the person inside.

In the bedroom, she found a pair of new silk pajamas in her drawer. While putting them on, she noticed David standing in the doorway.

"The shower felt good. I think I used all the hot water."

He walked over and wrapped his arms around her. They stood, awkward and tongue-tied.

"You get some sleep. I'll be up later," he said.

At the bedroom door he stopped, his stony expression unreadable.

"It's good to have you home, Clair. Sleep well."

Lying in bed, her eyes skirted the room. The cherry wood bed and dressers, handmade by the Amish, brought a nostalgic feel, as if it belonged to her in another life.

She felt relieved David had given her a pass for the night. Sometime soon he would want to have sex, she was, after all, his wife. But how could she pretend that things were the same when she held such a dark and shameful secret? She would soon have to tell him, and when she did, her betrayal would rip his heart out. It was only a question of when.

CHAPTER 38

THE NIGHT DIDN'T GO AS PLANNED. CLAIR WAS IN THEIR BED, but alone. She was back, but not entirely, and David could feel the pull. While she showered, he sat in the living room beneath her and listened to her cry.

What happened that she's not telling me?

David went to their room, stripped down to his boxers, then eased into bed.

By now he should be making love to her—he wanted to. Man, he wanted to. But something was terribly wrong, and he would wait. She looked so afraid, even now that she was home and safe from ISIS. Unable to sleep with these thoughts, it was early morning before he drifted off.

When he woke, the bed beside him was empty and cold as if yesterday had been a dream. Moving down the stairs he spotted a note on the kitchen table from Clair, telling him she needed something at the store.

He looked down at Buster.

"Did I not tell her we were going shopping today? What couldn't wait?"

While he drank his coffee, he watched as she parked the car in the garage and walked toward the house. She was too thin. Her sunken cheeks made her eyes stand out from the rest of her face. But more than just her looks had been altered. It was stupid of him to think she'd come home the same as she left.

When she entered the house Buster greeted her. His little tail wagged like wiper blades full speed as he jumped at her legs. She knelt and rubbed his head.

"I didn't want to wake you, so I left the note. I hope you weren't worried."

"Not at all," he lied. "After shopping, I thought we could go to that café near the park for lunch."

"I'm ready. You just need to get you out of your pajamas," she said.

David smiled. "Honey, you can get me out of these pajamas anytime."

He regretted saying it the second it was out of his mouth. Recoiling from his words, her eyes cast down and the carefree mood she was in, gone.

"I'll be ready to go in ten minutes," he said, kissing her cheek before he headed upstairs.

Take it easy. She's only been home one night.

When dressed, David walked into the kitchen, but Clair wasn't there. Nor was she in the living room. Starting toward the garage, he stopped short, floored by what he saw. Sitting on the step outside was Clair—smoking.

"What are you doing?" he asked, walking toward her.

"Smoking a cigarette."

"But you don't smoke. At least . . . you didn't."

"Well I do now. It helps me to relax," she said, as smoke floated from her nose.

They gave her cigarettes?

He couldn't help himself, he knew he should stay calm and take this in stride, but he couldn't let it go.

"It's just, with what happened to your sister—"

"Megan's cancer had nothing to do with cigarette smoke."

She looked up at him, frightened—like a child in the dark. What was she afraid of? She took one last drag from her cigarette before putting it out with her shoe.

"Ready?"

After a shaky start, their day together was good. At the mall, he enjoyed helping her pick out new clothes. They both laughed at some of his terrible choices.

By the time they entered the cafe for lunch they were relaxed and at ease. They ordered their lunch, and David held her hand across the table.

"I'm scheduled to go back to work tomorrow but if you'd like, I'll call my sub and get another day."

"Actually I think I might enjoy a day to myself, to get back into the groove of being a housewife."

He liked the sound of that. She just needed time. The waitress served their food, and they both began to eat.

"Darcy would like to come up and spend a day with you. Maybe the two of you could do a little more shopping."

David took a bite of his pasta. He watched Clair eat and noticed her fingernails. He couldn't remember a time when they weren't polished and manicured. Now they were jagged and short, the skin around them, red and raw.

"I noticed you're not wearing your wedding ring. Did you lose it?" he asked.

She looked down at her hand, where her ring used to be.

"I gave it to a girl to buy her way out. Sorry."

"There was a girl there?"

"She didn't live with us. I met her when I ran away."

David watched as she turned her head and stared off into the distance. The figure sitting across from him was merely a ghost of his wife.

"I never knew her name," she whispered, more to herself than to him.

"Don't be sorry, you did the right thing. I just wondered if it was lost or stolen."

Right now, it's in my dresser waiting for our anniversary to come out and surprise you.

"I never knew if she made it out," she murmured.

"It was a nice ring, I bet she did."

Suddenly she was back, and she smiled. "Always the optimist, aren't you?"

"I try to be. It wasn't easy while you were gone."

"I didn't think I would ever leave there."

He held her cold hands between his and warmed them.

"That had to be hell. I wished every day that I could trade places with you."

"That wouldn't have worked. Who would have traveled the world looking for clues?" She smiled, and David saw a glimpse of the person she used to be.

"Let's go home."

When they went into the house, David turned on the television. Clair smoked outside. When she came in he had an idea.

"I'd like to show you something." He took her hand and led her to the basement.

"I haven't worked on it lately, but I will soon. Maybe put a big screen TV over here and a large sofa over there." He raised his arms, drawing on air, trying to share his vision of what could be.

"I was thinking hardwood for the floor, but if you prefer carpet, I'm good with it. What do you think?"

She glanced around the room, appeared disinterested.

"Whatever you want. It all sounds good."

Dejected, David nodded his head. "Okay, well, I just wanted to ask if you had any preferences." She looked as uncomfortable as he felt. They glanced around the room, avoiding eye contact.

"I like your ideas, really. Carpet would be nice, making it cozy."

He appreciated what little enthusiasm she'd mustered, and smiled. "Yeah, carpet would be better. We could put speakers in all the corners for the TV and for music. You always liked to play your music loud."

The conversation turned to silence, heavy and dark like a hovering storm cloud.

How is this possible? I love her, and she loves me.

"Tonight would you like to pick up burgers somewhere?"

Her eyes fixed on his as if she too was pained by their small talk. By their need of it, to chase away the awkwardness that silence brought. He had a sense there would be frequent recurring forms of such awkwardness.

"Burgers would be fine."

That night after dinner he watched as she sat outside staring into the distance.

What's going on in that beautiful mind of yours?

He put on his coat and went out to join her, Buster at his heels.

"I've been thinking. Maybe it'd be best if I slept in the guest room for a while. Until you feel more comfortable and adjusted to being back home."

She reached for Buster, scratched behind his ear.

"That might be best, for a time."

"It's your call. No pressure," he assured her.

Going back in the house he picked up the essay papers that needed grading and went to work.

Later, the shower ran upstairs. One of the few things she had told him about her time spent in Azaz was that she went months between showers. Laying his head back, he stared up at the ceiling and listened to water run off her body. Something happened to her, so terrible she can't talk about it. But he saw it. No deep wound ever closed without a scar.

CHAPTER 39

IT WAS SO LIKE DAVID TO VOLUNTEER TO SLEEP IN THE GUEST bedroom. And although Clair was relieved that sex wouldn't be something she'd have to shirk, each and every night, his thoughtfulness brought more guilt. By the look on his face, it was clear he was hurt by her indifference, but how does she become the woman she used to be? After all she had seen and done, how does she become his wife again?

She crawled into bed, her body slowly sunk into the soft, coddling comfort of the Tempur-Pedic mattress. She and David had taken weeks researching mattresses before spending a small fortune on this one.

Although her body relaxed, her mind didn't, and she waited for sleep that wouldn't come. Finally, she threw off the blanket and went downstairs.

It was cold outside, so she sat at the kitchen table and smoked. Soon, the overhead light came on, and through squinted eyes, she watched David come into view.

"Everything okay?" he asked.

"Couldn't sleep."

"I'll make some hot chocolate," he said while he reached for a small copper pan.

Together they sat and waited for the milk to warm. She lit another cigarette.

"The sergeant I spoke with after the rescue had said you were shot. Will you tell me about it?" he asked.

She told him of being kidnapped and held by yet another rebel group. Of Tenderheart, and how close she had come to being rescued there. And how they ran.

"Were you shot then?" he asked.

She stared straight ahead.

"Clair?" he said gently.

Her body twitched as she regained her focus.

"I'm sorry, what?"

"I asked if that's when you were shot."

"Yes, as we ran away. The bullet grazed my head, and it bled a great deal, but head wounds always do. It wasn't serious."

"If you were the only doctor, who took care of you?"

She raised her trembling hand to her mouth and inhaled smoke. Then leaned to one side and looked around him. "It smells like milk burning."

He stood and went to the stove, prepared their drinks and brought them back to the table.

"I just can't believe how brave you're being about all this," he said.

She shrugged.

"Where were you on Thanksgiving and Christmas?" she asked.

"Thanksgiving I went to my mom's house. Your parents invited me over but . . . I just couldn't."

They sipped their cocoa.

"I slept through Christmas, in a hotel in Turkey."

"In Turkey?" she gasped. "So close."

While she lay on her cot, dreaming of him, he was nearby looking for her.

"Why did you sleep, were you ill?"

He rubbed the back of his neck as he tilted his chair on two legs. "Just stupid."

He told her how he fell for the lies of a thug. How he was beaten and left in the desert, then later saved by two very kind strangers.

"It was worth it. That's where I found Fakhir Kaya's brother, the man who led the military to you."

Shame filled her with a self-loathing so strong that she wanted to run away, far from his concern and all he did to save her. But mostly she wanted to escape herself, shed the memory of what she had done, and come back clean and whole. She didn't intend for it to happen, but once she started she couldn't stop crying.

"I'm . . . so sorry." Her breath, drawn in short, jerky gasps, shook her body with each heavy sob.

David put his arms around her, lifted her onto his lap, and caressed her back. Gentle and slow, he rocked her. It felt good to both cry and be held by him that, for the moment, she forgot her affair and wallowed in his comfort.

Soon, he buried his face in her neck, turned into her and began kissing his way toward her lips. She opened her mouth, welcoming his. His hand ran up her leg and moved beneath her robe. By the time she gathered her wits they were both breathing heavily, and David's hands were all over her.

"No," she whispered, wanting him, but at the same time, knowing this had to stop. He tugged at her robe, taking it off her shoulder.

He covered her mouth with his while his hand moved under her pajama top and headed toward her breast. She leaned back while she pushed against his chest.

"Stop." She stood and took a step back. He stared with a dazed look on his face.

"I'm sorry. I just . . . I thought you wanted this."

She continued to move backward, slowly shaking her head.

"If I let you love me, in the end, you'll hate me for it."

"Hate you! What are you talking about? I love you more than I ever have."

He got up taking hold of her arms.

"Clair, I could never hate you." His face, a combination of hurt and confusion.

She looked at him—really looked, straight to his soul, and found nothing dishonorable. He was still the boy she had fallen in love with. She was the one who had changed.

"I'm sorry."

She turned and walked up the stairs, leaving him standing with a shell-shocked look on his face. From now on, she would be strong and keep her distance. To allow him to think they could ever be the same was cruel.

The days passed. Neither mentioned that night in the kitchen. David was back at work, and she found herself in total control for the first time in almost a year. After spending so much time alone with no television or radio, Clair wondered if she suffered from culture shock. Everything now overwhelmed her.

Some days she would sit on the sofa, think about Sargon and their affair, and be surprised to see that hours had passed. She knew she should tell David what happened. But instead, she looked for any excuse not to. A part of her started to believe that maybe it was better if he never found out. And another day would pass with her secret intact.

CHAPTER 40

MAINTAINING THE HOUSEHOLD PROVED EASY FOR CLAIR AND she soon became bored. One day, needing something to distract her from her thoughts, she called and talked to her mom. It felt good to listen to her replay the mundane occurrences of everyday life. Clair couldn't get enough of it. No talk of war, or bullet wounds, death or betrayal.

When their conversation ended, still restless, Clair went for a walk. With no destination in mind, she started out toward the mall, past the closed factories that once employed hundreds. The buildings, rusted and deteriorated, now attracted vagrants and rats. People here were still angry over the closings, when their good paying jobs were moved to Mexico.

Crossing the street she continued along the river that led to an area recently developed. The red brick sidewalks, benches, and young trees, all lined its banks.

Clair sat down on a bench to catch her breath, paying the price for nine months of inactivity. Staring at the muddy water as it meandered by, she became mesmerized, and like the river, her mind drifted.

* * *

"David, are you awake?"

He didn't move. She rubbed his arm and raised her voice a notch.

"David, I need your help."

She leaned in, hoping he would sense movement, wake up, and help her. He had other ideas as he came to life, grabbed her arms, and pulled her on top of him.

Startled, she pounded on his chest.

"You faker!" she yelled.

He laughed.

"No need to beg, I'm all yours," he said, as he squeezed her tight.

"That's not what I'm looking for. I need your help finding my passport."

"You can't leave me if you don't have your passport."

"I'm having second thoughts about this. Do you think I'm doing the right thing?"

"The world needs people like you. As miserable as I'll be without you, you should go."

"Then you'll help me find my passport?" she asked.

"All right, but if I find it, you owe me." His bawdy look said it all as he rolled off the couch to help.

"I've looked everywhere, I can't imagine where it could be."

"Did you look in the desk?"

"Yes."

"Your underwear drawer?"

"Yes."

"The box on the closest floor?"

Clair perked up. That box was their catchall. She hurried toward the stairs.

"Oh no you don't." David gave chase, circled his arms around her waist, and moved her aside.

On the steps behind him she grabbed his ankles, tripped him up, and crawled over his body, both laughing as they raced upstairs. In the end, it was David who pulled the box out of the closet. With her passport in hand, he eagerly demanded his prize.

"Don't be a sore loser about this," he said.

She put her arms around his neck. Her tongue traced over his lips before slipping into his warm and willing mouth. She pressed her hips forward into his.

"Why would I?" she whispered in his ear. "I get my passport and you."

David took her hand, led her to bed, and then slowly undressed her, kissing each part of her body as he unveiled it. He took his time, made her want him more as each minute passed, until at last, his lust took over.

* * *

If David hadn't found my passport that day, my trip would have been delayed one month, and I would have been assigned elsewhere. And none of this would have happened. If I had asked a volunteer to wait on me while I consulted with Dr. Schmidt, I probably wouldn't have been taken. And if I had listened to the tingle that ran up my spine when I first turned onto that dark and empty street, I would have gone home as scheduled.

* * *

She replayed these thoughts so often, they grew dull with repetition and lost their original punch. She stood and resumed her walk. The temperature was cool but at the pace she walked, she began to work up a sweat.

At the mall, she decided to stop at a diner for a snack. While she waited for her coffee and Danish, she noticed a local newspaper, its pages sprawled on the table beside her. She picked it up and while eating she read, getting herself up to speed on the happenings here.

A new Staple's store opened up at the edge of town. The high school baseball coach expected great things this season with so many seniors on the team. Then, putting the last bite of Danish in her mouth she read the front page headline, "Local Woman Returned From Terror" and swallowed hard.

The article spoke of David and his work as a professor at Heidelberg College and how she put her own career on hold to volunteer in Syria. It went on to tell about the physical and mental abuse she suffered daily at the hands of her kidnapper.

And then, it reported that Sargon Elbez, a known terrorist who was wanted by the US Government for previous crimes, was the primary perpetrator in her kidnapping. Held by this ruthless murderer, it was unknown the extent of her suffering. The article concluded by applauding the Navy SEALs for their bravery in the rescue and the killing of such a monster. Clair tossed the paper on the table and left the shop.

The further she walked, the angrier she became. Why were journalists allowed to write such inaccurate stories? She had never said anything about being abused. And the part about Sargon being wanted for other crimes, was that false as well? Her head spun with this confusing information.

Maybe what was written about him was true at one time, but she knew him to be tender and kind, something she could never tell the press about. As she turned the corner for home, David's car came into view, parked in the drive. Nearing the house she paused as he came out the door and marched toward her.

"Where've you been? I thought something bad happened."

"Do I need your permission to go for a walk?"

"Of course not, but I called the house phone and then your cell, and when I got no answer from either..." His voice trailed off. His questioning face begged for an answer.

Instead, Clair took off on a dead sprint toward the house. David followed. She darted through the kitchen, into the bathroom, just making it before throwing up.

Holding her hair away from her face, David stayed with her until she stopped, then brought her a cold washcloth and a glass of water. When certain it was over she came out and sat down at the kitchen table.

"Okay, I panicked, but you haven't been yourself. I'll do everything I can to help you, but for a while could you text me, let me know where you are? And look at you, you're sick."

He kneeled in front of her and held her hands.

"Will you see Dr. Gregg and get to the bottom of this?" he pleaded.

Torment clouded his once bright eyes, and Clair wondered how she could be so selfish.

"I will. And I'll let you know where I'm going. Please don't worry about me, most of the time I feel good. But I'll call Dr. Gregg's office and make an appointment just to make sure."

He smiled, put his arms around her, and kissed her forehead.

"Thank you. I'm going back to work then if you're sure you're all right."

"I'm fine, but I might take a nap this afternoon. That walk wore me out."

After calling Dr. Gregg's office and getting an appointment for the following day, Clair went to David's desk and started up his computer. She Googled the name Sargon Elbez and read of his involvement with ISIS and his role as a leader. Of his participation in the bombing the American Embassy in Cairo where twelve people died. She found little else and nothing recent.

But when she searched ISIS, she watched amazed as her screen filled with articles, each reported one horrific act after another. She knew ISIS was callous and capable of kidnapping, obviously, but until now she hadn't known the severity of their cold-heartedness as they slaughtered their way through Syria and Iraq.

One gut-wrenching story almost had her back in the bathroom throwing up. On a Sunday morning, one month before Sargon's death, a Christian church in Aleppo was burnt to the ground. While churchgoers tried to escape the flames, they were gunned down as they came out, some on fire as they ran. Twenty-three people were killed, and twelve were children. The story didn't mention Sargon by name, only that ISIS claimed responsibility, but she had to wonder if he was there.

Meanwhile, I was having a love affair with him.

She remembered the time when Sargon had lost his brother, Jaul. He told her then that ISIS had taken four journalists out of their hotel rooms and taught them a lesson. At the time, he was so distraught she didn't ask him about it, but now wondered just how violent that lesson had been.

How could I not see who he was? I thought he was a man trapped, wanting out, and wanting to be, of all things, a farmer. Am I crazy or just unbelievably stupid? Or is it possible he really tried to change?

She read on. Of the stealing of school girls, sold to the highest bidder, of beheadings and mass shootings of innocent people, all dated throughout her stay there. There was so much she didn't know. Now her head was about to explode with information. She sat in a whirlwind of mixed feelings and sickening memories. And when she thought she couldn't feel any worse, she remembered telling reporters that Sargon was as much of a victim as she was.

What must people think of me?

She wanted to crawl into a hole and stay there.

In a stupor, she climbed the stairs to her room. Hoping to quiet her mind, she lay on the bed and covered herself, wanting a sleep that would allow her to forget what she had just seen.

When David came home from work she was still in bed, wide awake, her mind spinning ISIS horror stories repeatedly. He walked into the room with his brows wrinkled and a frown on his face. She was growing accustomed to that look of concern. He wore it so often. It was there because of her, and she hated the sight of it.

He sat on the side of the bed and took her hand.

"Are you sick?"

"Just tired."

"You look like you've been crying." He stood, his eyes bearing down on her.

"I'll get up and fix dinner," she said.

"You stay put and rest. I'll fix dinner." He kissed her cheek before he turned to go downstairs.

"Did you call Dr. Gregg today?" He stopped in the doorway and waited.

"I have an appointment tomorrow afternoon."

"Want me to come with you?"

Yes. But you've already done more for me than I deserve.

"I'm good."

David went downstairs, then later returned carrying ham and cheese sandwiches and iced tea. As they sat in bed together, he ate while she picked at her meal. Her mouth was too full of disgust to put food in it.

"Have you thought of going back to work at the hospital?" he asked.

"Yes, but not yet. I just don't feel ready if that's okay."

"You don't ever have to go back if you don't want to. I make enough to support us. I was just wondering if it might help you to move forward, put all this behind you."

She dropped her hands in her lap, a deep sigh bubbled from her mouth.

"David, I'm sorry I'm not the wife I once was. So much happened there . . . I want to tell you but . . ."

He put their plates on the nightstand, pulled her into his arms, and ran his hand over her hair.

"Don't worry about me. You're everything I want in a wife and more."

He continued to hold her until, thankfully, she closed her eyes and slept.

CHAPTER 41

IN THE MORNING, CLAIR FELT SO NAUSEOUS SHE COULDN'T eat. After David had left for work, she went back to bed. Her body still numb from all she learned. For five hours she lay, trying to uncover the truth of who Sargon Elbez really was.

At one o'clock, she slid her feet to the floor and got out of bed without an answer. She stood beneath the shower until the water ran cold, but couldn't be cleansed of the dreary spirit that filled her.

Being behind the wheel of a car seemed awkward. Aside from the short jaunt she took to buy cigarettes, it'd been a while. The BMW no longer gave her the same thrill it once had. Not when she considered how many people could be helped with the money it cost.

At the doctor's, she found the lone empty chair in the waiting room, and wasn't surprised when she waited forty minutes before taken to an exam room. When the doctor entered the room, he asked the usual questions and ordered some tests. She hoped this was a waste of his time. Aside from her nausea, she felt fine.

When Dr. Gregg came back in, he studied her chart as he walked, then paused before he looked up at her.

Come on, out with it.

"So what's the good news, Doctor?" she asked.

"Well, for everything you've been through, you're in fairly good health. A little underweight, but that can be easily rectified."

She knew coming here was unnecessary, but if it eased David's anxiety, it was worth it.

"After reviewing your blood work everything appears normal except for your pregnancy test. It's positive."

Clair froze.

What?

"Are . . . you're . . . telling me I'm pregnant?"

My periods have been sporadic for the last six months. Missing a couple seemed normal.

"Yes. That explains your nauseous stomach and the vomiting. Have you been more emotional than usual?"

I've been an emotional wreck for a year.

"A bit."

"Look," he said, "I'm aware of your situation. This baby is likely not your husband's. No one could blame you if you decide to abort it. I can set you up with a gynecologist who could perform the procedure, a simple one really. You would have some pain, but otherwise be up and running in no time. It's your decision."

"I'd like to go home and think about it," she mumbled.

"As you should. You have time—no need to rush this. When you've made your decision, either way, call me and we'll go from there."

Clair walked to the parking lot stunned. Her week had been full of shocking news. But being pregnant with Sargon's child bowled her over. How would she ever explain this to David?

Driving home, her mind so full it was hard to focus on the road. The easy way would be to terminate the pregnancy, but Sargon had already lost one child, how could she deliberately end the life of another? More pressing, how would David feel toward another man's child?

Busying herself with chores around the house while trying to think of a way to tell David this news, made her afternoon go fast. All too soon he walked in the door, and after greeting her with a hug asked about her doctor's visit.

"He said I'm healthy. And suggested some things I could try for the nausea."

"But otherwise you're well?" he asked.

"I need to put on some weight, but otherwise I'm healthy."

Relief flooded his face. "Maybe you're just not used to eating good food. Wait here, I have something for you."

He rushed out to his car, carried in a package, and handed it to her. She opened the lid on a box of luxury products, bath beads, lotions, soaps, and body sprays.

"You always liked this stuff. It might help you relax."

"How thoughtful of you. You're nicer to me than I deserve."

"Stop talking like that. You deserve everything I give you. Now, why don't you put these to good use while I start dinner?"

"I made lasagna," she said. "It's still baking. Give me thirty minutes?"

"Take your time."

As she soaked, she laid her hand on her belly. Not long ago she thought this impossible. Now she felt blessed and damned all at once.

She hadn't yet told David of her infidelity, how could she tell him about her pregnancy? Regardless, she couldn't go through with an abortion, there was no way. No matter what it would cost her, she would have this child.

On shaky legs, she came down the stairs and watched David as he set two plates on the table.

Please try to understand.

She took a deep breath and walked toward him.

"David there's something I need to tell you."

She sensed an impending disaster. One that once started could never be stopped. But she had no choice.

He set down the salad he'd made and waited.

"There's no easy way to tell you this so, I'll just say it. I'm pregnant." Then whispered, "I'm so sorry."

Her words should have packed a powerful punch, but he wasn't getting it. Then slowly, understanding seeped in, and she could see his anger grow until, with nostrils flared, he let it fly.

"Sorry? You have nothing to be sorry about. What you've been through is horrible, and if that bastard wasn't dead already, I'd kill him myself. It was him, wasn't it? It was Sorgon who raped you?"

Raped?

His words were filled with possibilities—game changers. They possessed a type of reality voodooism that could wipe out the past. Instead of correcting his misunderstanding, she took the easy way out and corrected his botched pronunciation.

"Sargon," she said in a whisper. "His name was Sargon."

CHAPTER 42

I CAN'T BELIEVE THIS. NO WONDER CLAIR DIDN'T WANT TO BE intimate. Who knew how many times that low-life had raped her.

He walked into the family room to get away. Inside, he seethed, and stood with both hands clenched. The hatred he felt toward a dead man was pointless, but his anger grew into rage and before he could stop himself, he swung his fist, hard into the wall.

Clair came running in.

"David, what are you doing?"

He raked his hand through his hair, every muscle in his body, stiff and tight.

"Hell would be too good for that piece of human garbage."

Clair stood staring at the fist-sized hole in the wall.

"David don't—"

"Don't what? There's nothing I can do."

She collapsed onto the sofa, dropped her head in her hands, and cried. He paced the floor in a fury. When he heard her sobs, growing louder and more anguished filled by the minute, he knew he had to get a grip. Sliding next to her, he took her hand.

"Listen, we'll get through this somehow. And if you decide to have this baby, I'll love it like my own."

Clair kept her face in her hands and remained silent. The timer on the oven chimed, their lasagna was ready to eat.

"Hey." He gently rubbed her back. "You couldn't help what happened to you. This isn't your fault."

He placed his hand beneath her chin and lifted her tear-streaked face.

"Why don't we try to forget the past, look forward to our future instead?"

Clair's eyes darted around the room before settling on him. She nodded her head in agreement.

"Yes . . . forget the past."

He took her hands, lifted her to her feet, and kissed her. And for the first time since being home, he sensed her ease and felt love in her kiss.

While Clair took their food out of the oven, David poured their drinks. Watching her cry was painful. She needed help. Who wouldn't after going through what she had? He knew there was something she wanted to say but didn't. And now, little by little he pieced together the horrible details of the nightmare she'd endured. They talked about having a family soon—hell of a way to start one.

They walked like zombies to the table and sat down to dinner. Neither ate much, who could after that conversation and soon, he gave up on it and laid his fork down.

"You've been through so much, I'm sure there are things you might be . . . uncomfortable talking to me about. I understand, but you shouldn't have to take this all on yourself."

He reached for her hand.

"I don't want to push you into anything you aren't ready for, but maybe talking to a professional would be good for you," he suggested gently.

To his surprise she agreed.

"You're right. I do need help with . . . everything."

She looked down at her food, pushed it around her plate with a fork.

"I have to call Dr. Gregg tomorrow anyway, I'll ask him to refer me to a therapist."

Relieved, he picked up the dishes and carried them to the sink. Clair followed him.

"It's about time I did more around here. I'll do the dishes," she said.

"Are you sure you feel okay? I don't mind doing them."

She insisted, so he relented, knowing the amount of work he needed to do before tomorrow. At his desk, he found it hard to concentrate. And although it was painful, he pictured his wife being forced to do things so degrading, it made him sick. Tears dropped from his face onto his papers. The more he thought, the angrier he became, and without thinking he snapped his pen in half. Ink splattered across his desk. He went to the kitchen for paper towels.

While Clair washed the dishes, he surprised her by wrapping his arms around her waist from behind.

"I promise, I'll never let anything happen to you again."

She turned into him and buried her face into his chest while he ran his hands over her back. As hard as this was to accept, at least he knew now, the truth behind her odd behavior. Together, over time, she would heal. And their marriage would be stronger than before she was taken.

CHAPTER 43

LYING IN BED, CLAIR STRUGGLED TO MAKE SENSE OF THE DAY'S events. When David had suggested a psychiatrist she almost leaped out of her seat, latching onto his idea as if it were a life preserver.

She knew she needed professional help—lying had become too easy. And seeing David so angry and upset, knowing that what caused it was a lie, was cruel. Yet she stood and watched it all unfold like an uninvolved bystander.

But what difference did it make how she hurt him? With the truth or a lie, she would hurt him just the same. And now, how could she take it all back? The hole she dug for herself deepened.

Despite the mess she made of their lives, she was having this baby. The next day she called Dr. Gregg, told him of her decision, and was given phone numbers for both an OB and a psychiatrist. Clair wasted no time and scheduled her appointments.

They had decided against telling anyone about the baby for now. It was still early in her pregnancy and the extra time allowed them to adjust to the idea of becoming parents.

That afternoon, Darcy called.

"Are you ready for a night out?" she asked.

"I guess so. When were you thinking?"

"I have a commitment this weekend, but I'm free the next. Are you?"

Free—my favorite four-letter word.

"Next weekend would be perfect."

When David came home he seemed pleased that she was having a night out with Darcy. Sitting in the living room after dinner, she noticed his blossoming mid-section as he slouched on the sofa. No longer the rock hard abs he had worked so hard to get. Her absence had changed his appearance as well as hers.

"David, while I was gone, did you ever think about what you'd do if I never returned?"

He turned the television's volume down and leaned back on the sofa.

"I didn't want to think that way but, yeah. This house seemed so empty without you, I . . . I don't know, I guess there were times I became pessimistic. It was then that I'd let myself consider it. But the next day I'd try to be more positive."

He moved closer to her and put his arm around her.

"The worst for me was not knowing. I imagined all sorts of terrible things happening to you. As it turns out, some of what I envisioned was real."

Oh David, what am I doing to you?

His words hung over her as they both turned and faced the television, neither really watching. When the program ended she kissed him goodnight and with a heavy heart, went upstairs to bed.

CHAPTER 44

CLAIR SAT, SWINGING HER CROSSED LEG WILDLY AS SHE WAITED to be called into the psychiatrist's office. How could she tell a stranger all that she'd done, without making herself look like a horrible person? She was horrible, no matter how she tried to pretty it up—what she did was wrong.

Before she felt ready, the receptionist called her name and ushered her in. The plush office, decorated with soft colors and dim lighting, an atmosphere that should invoke calm, did little to settle her. She could barely walk straight—her nerves had the best of her. She sat near the edge of her seat and fidgeted uncomfortably. When she settled, she looked at the woman sitting across from her.

Slim and athletic looking, Dr. Rita Burns had silver hair, cut short and spiked on top. But it was her beautiful face that drew your attention. Growing older hadn't diminished that, and Clair wondered what her secret was.

After introductions were made Dr. Burns wasted little time getting started.

"Dr. Gregg's office faxed me your history, so I have some idea what you've been through. Why don't you start by telling me what it was like being in Syria?"

Clair inhaled deeply, then let it out slow. How could she put into words what life there was like?

Finally she said, "It was . . . warm."

She stared down at the sage-green carpet, swallowed hard in an effort to open her clenched throat. When she raised her eyes she met the friendly gray eyes of Dr. Burns and gained strength.

"It was frightening. And painful. And lonely—God it was lonely."

Clair's eyes brimmed with tears. Dr. Burns handed her a tissue and a glass of water.

"After working at the hospital, I walked back to my hotel. A man got out of his car, chased me down, and hit me." She pulled back her hair, revealed her scar. "I was rendered unconscious and taken to Azaz, where I lived for the next nine months. The man responsible for my kidnapping, Sargon Elbez, is the father of my unborn child. We were lovers."

She swallowed hard. Admitting that she willingly became sexually involved with a terrorist was humiliating.

"I hadn't lived there long when two of the soldiers tried to rape me. I fought hard to stop them but was no match for their tenacity. Just when my strength was all but gone, Sargon came in. He kicked my assailant so hard that he broke his nose."

Dr. Burns hadn't interrupted or asked any questions; she didn't write or record her words. She listened, giving Clair her full attention.

"I'll never forget that man's face, or the pleasure he got from hurting me." She paused, sickened as she relived the horror of that day.

"Sargon saved me. If he hadn't come in when he did, both men would have raped me."

Dr. Burns leaned back in her chair and crossed her arms.

"Clair, do you really see Sargon as a hero? He was, after all, responsible for your being there."

"I wouldn't call him a hero, but after that day, I was never touched by the soldiers again. They rarely looked at me, so yes, I was grateful for what he'd done."

Dr. Burns leaned forward and put her hand on Clair's knee.

"It's not uncommon for someone who's been abducted to become infatuated with their abductor. Even to the point of idolizing them. It even has a name, Stockholm Syndrome."

Clair stared down at the tissue in her hand.

"I've read about that, but . . . I don't know, it doesn't seem to apply to me. As much as I regret it now, I was genuinely attracted to him; my feelings were real."

"Think about it. You were taken away from family and friends and forced to live under wretched conditions. You were totally dependent on one person for everything. And when that one person showed signs of kindness, well, it was easy to think more of him than he deserved."

Clair stared into space, thinking about Dr. Burns's words.

"Since I've been home, I've learned of many horrendous crimes that ISIS has committed. I knew they were known for their hateful ideology, but until recently, I never knew how horrible their actions were. I don't think I wanted to know. It was as if I viewed life peripherally, never seeing reality head on. It was easier that way. And . . . I just couldn't think anymore. Not about David, the past, or even the future."

Is it possible to send a patient straight from this chair to an asylum?

For a moment neither spoke.

"He told me that he wanted to change. That he would help me escape, he even hinted at leaving ISIS. Now, I don't know what to believe."

At the time, she was certain that he was sorry for what he'd done. Especially to her.

"Can't a person change?"

"Of course they can," Dr. Burns said, "but wanting to and actually doing it can be far apart. Sometimes people suffer so much, have lost so much that the anger they carry is hard to ostracize. And sometimes people are just plain bad. As for you not knowing if he was or wasn't remorseful, how could you? He let you know only what he wanted you to know. You had no outside information to base your opinion on."

Clair thought about Sargon having lost both his parents and then his wife and son. He had let her in on his sad past but gave little detail of his involvement with ISIS.

"I'm so confused, about what I did, my feelings for Sargon. Knowing what I know now, I can't believe I was so naive. I regret what I did to David. He doesn't deserve any of this."

Dr. Burns took Clair's hand, squeezed it. "Neither do you."

Her kind smile calmed Clair. She was good at this.

"I've done things since being home that I need to make right, but I'm not sure how."

"What in particular?" Dr. Burns asked.

Clair grimaced, and her face burned.

"Well, you know I'm pregnant with Sargon's child, and David knows as well. But when I told him, he assumed that Sargon had raped me. I let him believe that."

Clair expected shock from Dr. Burns, but she remained expressionless.

"Why do you think you did that?" she asked, without skipping a beat.

"I'm just so afraid of losing him . . ."

Clair squirmed in her seat and turned her glance to the floor. An icy rain began to fall, and the drops tapped the window like small pins. Winter's last gasp at holding on, before giving way to spring. At every end, there's a new beginning. She took another drink from her water glass.

"When I was first taken, I ached from being apart from David, no phone calls or emails. After time, I still thought of him, but it was without a future. I was afraid to dream of a life with him. I had only memories of our past. Now when I look at him, I'm ashamed that I let myself give up so easily. He didn't. He came looking for me—twice."

Dr. Burns leaned forward, her elbows on her knees.

"Don't be so hard on yourself. Your world existed inside that house, your view distorted. Forgive yourself first. Then ask David to."

She looked at her watch and walked around her desk.

"I think you've had enough for now. I want you to think about what we've covered today, but don't pressure yourself to understand everything just yet. It will take time. I am wondering something, though, do you still love your husband?"

"I do. But I'm handcuffed with guilt. I want David, but how do I make love to him after what I've done? I can't pretend everything is fine when eventually he'll know that it's not."

"You'll tell him when the time feels right. For now, accepting what you must do, is enough," Dr. Burns said. She made some notes, then escorted Clair to the receptionist to schedule her next appointment.

In the car, she thought of Dr. Burns's words. And wondered if her feelings for Sargon were some kind of misguided adoration. She was so confused her head hurt. Since the news of her pregnancy, she had quit smoking but desperately wanted a cigarette now, her fingernails were already chewed to the quick.

On her way home she drove past a beauty shop, its sign "No Appointments Necessary" caught her attention.

Why not?

She couldn't remember when she last crossed the threshold of a salon but desperately needed something done with her hair and went in.

When the stylist had finished her magic, the floor was covered with long, dark strands. Clair watched it being swept into a pile, and felt lighter and somehow, cleaner. She looked in the mirror and slowly raised her hand to her hair, touching its ends. The short cut made her face look full and healthy. And the layers gave her hair bounce. She couldn't help smiling as she drove home, catching a glimpse of herself in the rearview mirror.

She parked the car, entered through the back door, and was greeted by a familiar smell. Pizza. Until then, she hadn't realized how hungry she was.

David came down the stairs, fresh from his shower. He stopped short when he saw her. Hair that just this morning had hung the length of her back was now cut short and tucked behind her ears.

"I love it. You look great," he said.

"You really like it? It's a big change."

"Sometimes change is good, better than before."

Their eyes met, and in that moment, she was consumed by profound and eager hopefulness. Together, they would make this work.

"Did the therapy help?" he asked.

"Are you wondering if I'm fixed yet?"

"No, I . . ."

She touched his arm and smiled. "It's a start. I like Dr. Burns and will see her again Friday," she said, tucking stray hairs behind her ear.

David looked relieved.

"Your courage amazes me. It's what will get us through this." He kissed her forehead then embraced her. She laid her head on his shoulder, basking in his love.

"Hungry?" he asked.

"I'm starved. I saw the pizza and almost started without you." They both sat at the table and filled their plates.

"Remember how much pizza we ate in college?" she asked.

"Yeah. Remember when I entered that pizza eating contest? I was nauseous for days. And all for a T-shirt that advertised the place."

They both snickered at the memory, and for the second time today, Clair felt weight being lifted from her. She had much to think about, but not tonight. Tonight she would enjoy the good food and the even better company.

CHAPTER 45

Clair spent the next day sifting through her conversation with Dr. Burns. David might understand her depraved behavior if she explained it to him the way Dr. Burns had. Maybe their marriage was strong enough to withstand this. She felt her resolve strengthen, and when the time was right, she would unload her guilt and tell him everything.

In the meantime, she would try to be his wife again. She drove to the grocery store, getting what she needed to make a meal he would enjoy. With her mood buoyed, she dove into her meal preparation with gusto, and before she knew it, David pulled into the drive.

He walked into the rich, buttery smell of chicken roasting that filled the air. And when he saw her up to her elbows in flour, rolling pin in hand, he looked both happy and surprised.

"Whatever you're cooking smells delicious."

"It's time I fixed us a decent meal, apple pie included." His smile warmed her heart as he closed the gap between them. She shut her eyes and tilted her head in anticipation of his kiss. Instead, he ran his finger through the flour and smeared it on her nose.

"And here I was, prepared to give you a kiss that'd make your toes curl." She shrugged her shoulders, turned to walk away.

"Oh no you don't." He pulled her close. His mouth was warm and she could taste the sweet residue of the soda he'd been drinking. Suddenly, he turned it up a notch, pulled her tight against him, and kissed her with such passion, it took her breath away.

When their lips parted, Clair's head was spinning. She wouldn't be able to put him off much longer, it had to be obvious that she wanted him.

"I better fix dinner while I'm still able."

With a devilish grin, David turned to go upstairs, whistling as he climbed the steps. Clair watched him go. She loved him. No matter what she thought or felt while gone, she has always loved him.

At dinner, while chewing on a bite of chicken, she mulled over the idea of blurting the truth out now.

"I think with Dr. Burns's help, I'll come to understand what I felt . . . and what I did."

He didn't take the bait, squeezed her hand, and kept eating.

"I don't think I'll ever be the woman you married. I've changed, for better or worse."

"Give yourself time. You've only had one session."

"Aside from what I experienced, I can't forget the suffering of those poor people. I'm not sure exactly what I can do, but I want to do something more for them."

He stopped eating and looked at her.

"That's admirable Clair, but you've already done more than most. I hope you aren't thinking of going back."

His hand lay on the table, purple and swollen from his fight with the wall.

"No, at least not anytime soon. But if there's something I can do, to bring awareness to people here who possess influence and money, I'd like to do that."

"Right now I think you should focus on yourself for a change. Then focus on me."

They both laughed. And in that moment, she knew that miraculously a part of who she was before still lived. She reached across the table and took his hand, kissing the bruise.

Later that evening, Clair joined David in the living room. He held her hand as they watched TV.

"The Buckeyes are playing," he said, taking a bite of beef jerky.

"Okay."

"Well, we always eat beef jerky when the Buckeyes play, you know that."

"Ugh. I don't think so."

"All right, but if they lose, it's on you."

She huffed, rolled off the couch, and walked into the kitchen. When she came back she had a stick of jerky in her hand.

"That's my girl," David said with a smile.

She laughed, and he put his arm around her as they watched the game. It felt so much like life before Syria when everything was perfect that Clair believed somehow everything would turn out fine.

For the remainder of the night, she embraced the warm glow of love she was feeling.

Tomorrow. I'll tell him the truth tomorrow.

CHAPTER 46

THE NEXT WEEK FLEW BY. CLAIR HAD HER APPOINTMENT WITH the obstetrician whom Dr. Gregg had recommended and liked him immediately. She also had another appointment with Dr. Burns and with her help, she felt less anxious, more certain of what she wanted. By the time the weekend arrived, Clair felt more like herself.

On Saturday, David woke early and was preparing his famous blueberry pancakes when Clair came down the stairs.

"I think you're trying to fatten me up," she said.

"Guilty. I just hope I don't gain weight along with you. You may have noticed I put on a few pounds while you were gone."

A lot happened while she was gone. But as sad as their lives had been, Clair needed to shake off thoughts of the past. Darcy would be arriving later, and she had much to do to make both the house and herself, presentable.

"Do you know where you two are going?" David asked.

"I don't, but you know Darcy, she has everything planned, including where we're stopping for dessert on the way home," she said.

"You look happy."

"I feel happy, thanks to you."

It was true, he filled her with joy.

"Are you going to tell her about the baby?"

"I might. I guess it depends if the opportunity arises. But she's always been able to make me talk. As teenagers, I could keep secret my latest crush for weeks until Darcy got me alone."

They laughed, knowing what a talker Darcy was.

"You're beautiful, you know."

Her heart skipped a beat before finding its rhythm. She stepped forward, into his arms and rested her head on his chest.

"I better let you get ready. Darcy will be here soon."

Clair smiled up at him, gave him a quick peck, but then David pulled her close and deepened their kiss. When they parted she shook her head at him.

"Shoo," she said, patting his behind, "before you make me late."

"Yeah. I'm always doing that," David said sarcastically.

Clair was notoriously late. It happened so often she made a joke of it by blaming David. Brightened by the light conversation, Clair felt better than she had in a long time. When Darcy got there, she was still upstairs putting on the finishing touches. When ready, she started for the stairs, but stopped short when she heard Darcy talking to her husband.

"How are things going?"

Hidden at the top of the stairs, she listened.

"Better. It was rough at first like we didn't know each other."

"Do you think it's possible she's been brainwashed? I mean that comment she made about her kidnapper being a victim. Where did that come from?"

David sighed. "I don't know. I know she has a lot she's dealing with now."

"Like what?" Darcy asked.

Clair bounced down the stairs smiling.

"Sorry to keep you waiting. Ready to go?"

Their evening started well. She couldn't remember when she had laughed so much as they rehashed old times. After dinner, they went for a drink in a bar downtown.

When they entered, right away Clair felt old. The place was filled with college students. Most squeezed themselves onto the dance floor while the music blared.

As they walked to a table, her shoes stuck to the floor with each step. It reminded her of the grubby linoleum in the Azaz house.

"Would you rather go somewhere else? Maybe a place where we can hear our own thoughts?" she asked Darcy.

"Why? This place is great. You wanted to party."

When in Rome . . .

Clair smiled and ordered a glass of wine.

David was concerned about her drinking alcohol while pregnant, but she assured him a glass or two of wine would not hurt the baby. It was sweet of him to care so much. When their drinks came, Clair wanted to tell Darcy about her pregnancy.

"I have something to tell you," she began. "I'm going to have a baby."

"You mean someday?" Darcy asked.

"I'm pregnant now. Just ten weeks. David is the only one who knows. And now you."

"Ten weeks? Clair, my God, were you raped?" She took Clair's hands in hers, her eyes tearful as she waited for an answer.

Instead of keeping with the lie she had David believing, Clair for once told the truth.

"No."

Silence ensued. Clair watched Darcy's face as understanding registered.

"I had an affair with Sargon Elbaz. I know it's hard to believe but . . . it happened." Clair's face burned with the shame she felt. Saying it out loud it sounded cheap and dirty.

"You fell in love with your kidnapper?" Darcy asked. Her eyes brimmed with disapproval.

"It wasn't love. At the time, I thought it could be. It's hard to put into words, but he was nice to me, made it a habit to come to my room and talk. With no one else, I looked forward to those visits."

Clair took a sip of her wine, hoping she made clear how this could happen to anyone.

"Whether or not it was love, I wanted him. I can't say I was forced or tricked into it. I'm working with a psychiatrist now to figure it out."

"Does David know about this?" Darcy asked.

"No. I mean, he knows that the baby is Sargon's but he assumed I was raped. I guess it was just easier to let him think that," Clair said.

"Oh Clair, what are you going to do?"

"I don't know. David's been so good about everything. He told me he'd be the best dad possible, and I believe he will. But if he finds out that the sex was consensual, well . . . it won't be good."

"You have to tell him. He deserves to know," Darcy said, a look of disgust on her face.

"I know, and I plan on telling him. I just haven't found the right time."

"Poor David," Darcy said.

Poor David? I thought we were friends.

The waitress stopped at their table, and Darcy ordered another round.

"I know David deserves better, it's just that things have been tense between us since I came back, and it's just starting to get better. I guess I'm afraid he might leave me."

"If you don't tell him now, you never will. Your whole marriage will be a lie," Darcy snapped.

Clair took another sip of wine.

"David and I have gotten close while you were gone, and I'm not sure I can keep this from him," Darcy said, matter-of-factly.

Clair couldn't believe what she was hearing, and wondered just how close they had become. The last thing she had any right to be was jealous, but right now she was consumed with it.

"I'll tell him the truth," she said, louder than intended. "But I need time to find the right words."

The second glass of wine started to affect her. She had last drank alcohol the night before she left for Syria. A romantic evening with David.

"Darcy, I figured you of all people would support me. I guess I'm not the only one who's changed."

"I can't support you. What you did to David was wrong. I was here with him. I know how much he suffered. And you, over there . . . having an affair. It's just not right." She slapped her hand on the table.

"You make it sound as if I was on spring break. For crying out loud—I suffered too."

Clair noticed the couple at the table beside them eavesdropping and lowered her voice.

"I'm not trying to make you understand. Your mind is already made up about me. All I can do is ask that you give me a couple of days to find the right words. I will tell him."

They both decided to call it a night and left for home, the promising night of fun was dampened by their argument.

Once inside the house, Clair was relieved to see that David had gone to bed. Darcy tossed her a trite "sleep well" then hurried up the stairs. Clair pulled a chair away from the table and sat, desperately wanting a cigarette.

Trying to find a good way to tell David the truth was not going to be easy but she had no choice, Darcy made that clear. She should have told him the day she came home.

Someone was descending the stairs. Expecting Darcy, coming back to apologize, she was surprised to see David, wearing sweat pants and bare chested.

"Not ready for bed yet?" he asked as he entered the room.

"I'm still a little wound up."

"You're home kind of early. Hope you had a good time," he said.

"We did. It's just . . . nothing's like it was before."

David took her hand, helped her up, and then rested his hands on her shoulders.

"You can't help being a little different. Who wouldn't be—going through what you did? But you're still the woman I love, despite any differences. I love you, Clair, and there's nothing you can do to change that."

Wanna bet?

He lifted her chin and kissed her, deep and hard. All her anxiety melted away like snow thaw on a warm day. No more worries about the past or what she should do in the future. She wanted him and was tired of fighting it.

Her palms skimmed over his shoulders, on their way to his chest. Hard, and fresh out of bed warm, she pressed her hands flat against him.

As he gazed down on her, his hand moved under her blouse, his fingers traced the lace that trimmed her bra. With his thumb, he rubbed her breast through the silky material. She inhaled sharply and closed her eyes, free of all restraint.

"I love you, David."

He slid his powerful hands over her bottom and scooped her up. Her legs wrapped tight around his hips while their kiss went on forever. With one swipe of his arm, he cleared the table before laying her down on it, then kissed her with such longing she could taste the raw need in him. As he yanked at her blouse the material give way in his rush to remove it. She tugged at his shoulders, urging him closer. And when at last, their clothes lay scattered across the floor, they rode the waves of pleasure that for so long had been denied them. It was a feeling of being taken to ecstasy on a new level. She had never felt so loved.

CHAPTER 47

IT HAD BEEN AWHILE SINCE DAVID FELT THIS HAPPY. WITH HIS beautiful wife in bed with him at last, things were now as they used to be. He listened to her shallow breathing and was comforted knowing she lay just a few inches away. It wasn't long before he too closed his eyes and slept.

The next morning, he woke before Clair, and quietly crept out of their room. At the back door, Darcy stood, putting on her shoes.

"Leaving so early?" he asked.

"Hope I didn't wake you. I've got some work I should take care of before Monday. I wanted to get a jump on the traffic."

"Can I fix you breakfast, a cup of coffee?" he asked, then moved to block her view of Clair's bra on the kitchen table.

"No thanks. Tell Clair goodbye for me."

David watched as Darcy got into her car and drove away, puzzled by her unexpected departure. He shrugged and hurried back up the stairs, in hopes of picking up where they left off last night.

* * *

She was awakened by a soft kiss and opened her eyes. David lay on his side next to her. His hand braced his head, and his smile touched his deep, dark eyes.

"Sleep well?" he asked.

She stretched then ran her hand down his arm before resting it on his hip.

"I had a weird dream."

"Oh? I hope nothing bad."

"I dreamt we made wild love, on of all places, the kitchen table."

He flashed a big smile.

"That is crazy. Were you happy . . . in your dream?"

"Umm, completely."

She remembered Darcy and started to get up, but David pulled her back.

"We have company. Don't start what you can't finish," she said.

"That didn't stop you last night."

She laughed and swatted his arm.

"I still can't believe we did that."

"Well, today you don't have to worry. Darcy left early," he said.

"In that case . . ."

She placed her hand behind his neck and pulled him toward her mouth. A rush of heat flooded her body as his hand swept past her stomach. Unlike the night before, they took their time, melting their bodies together into one.

It was after ten when they emerged from their room, famished. Clair pulled bacon and eggs from the refrigerator.

"Our lovemaking, it's the one thing that hasn't changed. We're still perfect together," she said.

David took the bowl of eggs from her hands and set it on the counter.

"It was worth the wait."

She moved into his arms.

"I didn't want this until you were ready. When I saw how much you were hurting, I knew it would take time. Now, I can't get enough of you."

He held her while she stared over his shoulder.

Please don't ever stop wanting me.

They took their breakfast back to their bed along with the Sunday paper. It had become a ritual for them to spend Sunday mornings being lazy together. It was noon when they emerged, ready to work.

David tore up the floor in the basement and installed a wet bar while she worked on turning one of the spare bedrooms into a nursery. They both were so happy that Clair started to believe David could forgive her lies.

Monday came all too soon. Before he left for work, David kissed her goodbye.

"Eight hours is too long," he said.

"I'll be here waiting."

Another kiss.

"I can't leave you."

"Then don't."

He glanced at the clock on the wall, kissed her again.

"Promise you'll be here when I come home?"

"Promise."

He walked backward out the door, his eyes locked in on her. Her palm pressed flat against the glass as she watched him go.

After she had watched him drive away, she readied herself for her eleven o'clock appointment. This time, instead of feeling apprehensive, she couldn't wait to talk to Dr. Burns, hoping she would again ease her guilt.

While driving, the nausea that started after breakfast worsened. She eventually had to pull off the road and throw up. When the retching finally stopped, she sat up and scavenged through her purse for tissues. The bitter taste in her mouth had her digging further for gum. She settled instead, for a wrapper-less mint, and after picking off the fuzz, popped it in her mouth.

She was late getting there, and the receptionist called her in right away. Her body fell into the comfortable chair, and in a huff, she released the air from her lungs. Her shoulders lowered as she began to relax.

"Did you have a good weekend?" Dr. Burns asked.

"I slept with David," Clair blurted out.

Dr. Burns smiled. "Well, he is your husband."

"Then why do I feel so sleazy? I should have told him the truth first, and then, if he still wanted me, we could go from there."

The hope that she had was starting to dissipate, and in its place, apprehension.

"I keep messing this up."

Dr. Burns sat, with her finger tapping her lips. "Yes, you do need to tell him, but I think you're forgetting one very important point. You are the victim here. You didn't ask to be taken from your husband, and you lived under extreme duress for nine months. Under those conditions, you made some mistakes. Tell him, and then the two of you, working together, can try to mend the damage caused by this tragedy."

Maybe I'm not such a terrible person.

"Clair, can you see yourself having an affair with someone now?"

"Never. I love my husband."

"Then stop blaming yourself and move forward. Whether it be with David or without him you are going to have a child who will need you."

Her words jolted Clair like a slap to her face.

My child needs me.

"I guess I should start thinking of more than just myself and David. I'll tell him of my affair soon, and ask his forgiveness. It sounds easy saying it to you."

"Regardless of the outcome, you'll feel better having it over with. I can prescribe some medication for anxiety if you'd like. One that is safe to take while pregnant," Dr. Burns offered.

"Thank you, no. I need to learn to deal with life sooner or later."

They talked at length about what she had done, and her feelings for both men. All too soon her time was up.

As she walked toward her car, her step had a little more bounce to it, her head held a little higher. She would face her fears and tell David the truth, soon.

CHAPTER 48

ON THURSDAY, DAVID DROVE TOWARD HOME AFTER WORK, eager to see Clair. It seemed unbelievable but soon he'd be a father. Downtown, he stopped at one of the shops Clair frequented, and found a wooden cradle, perfect for the baby's first few months.

Happy about his purchase and excited to show it to Clair, he hurried home. He could hear her upstairs in the bedroom, so he quickly set it up in the nursery. When she stepped into the hall he pulled her into his arms. "I've got a surprise for you."

"Last weekend wasn't jaw-dropping enough?" she joked.

Taking her hand, he led her to the nursery.

"What do you think?" he asked, pointing to the cradle.

That I'm married to the sweetest man in the world.

"It's perfect. Thank you."

She leaned into him and with his arm around her, they stood admiring the cradle.

"I'll be happy either way, but if it's a boy, I'd like to teach him the things my dad taught me. Not just sports, but how to treat women, how to be a man. My dad was the best."

She smiled and nodded. Then reached her hand to his soft dark curls. In college, he wore his hair long and she used to love to run her fingers through it. She told him she could never marry someone who had such gorgeous hair, and it wasn't right to be jealous of your spouse.

"I think I'll go for a run before dinner. Want to come?" he asked.

"No, you go ahead. I'm a little tired." *And I need to plan what to say to you. Tonight's the night.*

Later, they sat together in bed reading. Clair took a deep breath, prepared herself for the worst, and began.

"David, we need to talk."

He set his book down and waited for her to speak.

"I've not been honest since I've been home," she swallowed hard, "you need to know the truth."

Her eyes jumped from the book he'd been reading to the wall behind him, to her hands—anywhere but his eyes.

"Sargon didn't rape me."

Clair straightened the blanket and with her head down, she glanced at his face. His expression slowly shifted from bewilderment to comprehension.

"Please understand, he was all that I had there. I was in another world, and I believed I'd never see you again."

She rubbed her temple where a headache mounted an attack. He sat like a statue, stiff and unmoving.

"I was so lonely, and eventually we became friends. I didn't plan for it to happen, but near the end of my stay there . . . I had an affair with Sargon."

Finally, she spoke the whole truth—naked, cold, and as fatal as a soldier's knife. When she laid her hand on his, he jerked it away. Then stood, his red face disfigured, and a vein engorged in his forehead.

"You're telling me that you wanted him?" His look was one of contempt. "The man was a murderer. He kidnapped you . . . and you couldn't stop yourself from having sex with him?"

His voice rose, high and loud. "Forget that you were married. How could you stoop so low? He was a terrorist, for Christ sake!"

He paced the length of the bedroom, rubbing the back of his neck.

"If you weren't pregnant, would I have ever learned the truth?" His cold, dark eyes pierced her heart. If not for her pregnancy, would she have told him? She would like to think yes, but wasn't sure.

"David, as awful as it sounds, I needed him. But in therapy, I'm learning that maybe it was just some sort of worship I felt because he was nice to me. I . . . I don't think I'm explaining it quite right, but maybe you can come to my next appointment and talk to Dr. Burns. She says I have—had—Stockholm Syndrome."

"He was nice to you, are you kidding me? He robbed you of nine months of your life."

In all the times she imagined this conversation, she never saw the look of total disgust like she saw in him now.

"Haven't I gone through enough torment? And all the while I was here, not knowing if you were dead or alive, you were screwing your kidnapper."

David threw his head back. His laugh, ugly and raw, sounded nothing like him.

"What a fool I've been," he spat. "I understand you feeling lonely, I felt that too. But when I had the chance to be with someone else, I chose not to."

Desperate to stop this free fall she tried again to make him understand.

"I love you. I have always loved you. I made a huge mistake, and I'm sorry."

He leaned against the wall and stared down at the floor.

"You're right when you say you aren't the woman you used to be. I don't even know you."

He slammed the bedroom door as he walked out and moved back into the guest room.

CHAPTER 49

CLAIR GLANCED AT THE CLOCK ON THE NIGHTSTAND. EIGHT thirty. David would be at work by now. She hadn't slept much with so much to think about. Mostly, of what she could say that would undo the damage.

Things couldn't have gone worse, she should have explained it better. But no matter how she said it, the facts remained the same. She had been unfaithful to her husband, and then lied to him about how her child was conceived.

In the past, when her life was in crisis, she would turn to Darcy for advice and support, but not this time. Their friendship had changed. Clair suspected it was Darcy whom David referred to as his "chance to be with someone else."

She needed to talk to him and try to mend this mess. David was a forgiving person, maybe, in time he would come to see why she did what she did. Then they could put this behind them.

She ran her hand across her flat stomach.

Soon my baby will grow here. My baby.

It still surprised her when she put those two words together. She would never know for sure if Sargon would have left ISIS had he lived. But she did know that his child would know love and peace, and have every opportunity to be different.

David just needed time. Maybe a couple of days without her would help him sort through his feelings and, if unable to forgive her right away, at least understand how she could do such a thing.

Clair crawled out of bed, went down to the kitchen, and picked up her phone. The sound of her mother's warm hello eased her tension.

"How would you feel about having company for a couple of days?"

"Wonderful. Will David come too?"

"David has work to do, it will just be me."

"Is everything all right?" her mother asked.

"Yeah, I'm fine. I'll pack a few things and be on my way."

She threw some clothes in a bag, then taking a piece of paper from his desk, she wrote David a short note telling him where she would be and when she'd be home. She prayed that the days apart would give him the time he needed to understand her. If not, she would throw herself at his feet and beg for his mercy, anything to make him forgive her. She had lived almost a year without him, and it nearly made her mad. Giving up was not an option.

CHAPTER 50

David stood in the kitchen, Clair's note in hand. In no mood to talk, he was glad she had taken off. He crumbled the note in a ball and tossed it in the trash, got a beer out of the refrigerator, and dropped himself on the couch.

Sure, he still loved her, but the truth of her deception had knocked the life out of him. Was it even possible to make things right?

That night, he lay in bed thinking of Clair—her lies and her betrayal. And then he would remember how good it felt to have her in his arms, and he'd long to have everything the way it used to be. They were so good together, how could she do this to them?

On Saturday, he rented a truck and loaded it with the basement flooring he had ripped out last weekend. When finished, he took a sledgehammer and tore down a wall, each swing of the hammer powered by anger and hate. He welcomed the physical pain to his arms and back, hoping it would somehow overcome the greater pain of Clair's deceit. But he didn't stop there. He had more to give, and went to work destroying the new bar he had just installed, pounding over and over until it was nothing but a pile of kindling. When the dust settled he dropped to the floor, exhausted and covered with sweat and dirt, just as distraught and unsettled as before he started.

On Sunday, he lay on the sofa, rehashing everything that had happened over the past months, trying to make sense of it all. And clinging to one thought above the rest: *she's made such a fool of me.*

Before ready to face her, he watched as she parked her car in the garage and walked toward the house. She set down her bag as she stepped in.

"Hi. I'm glad you're home. We need to talk."

He leaned against the counter, his arms crossed along with his ankles.

"Oh, now you want to talk. Well I don't."

He pulled a leash out of a drawer and snapped it on Buster, walked around her and out the door.

Does she expect me to forget this? Go on as if everything were the same?

After miles of walking, with nowhere to go, David went home. Besides, he didn't think Buster could take much more of it. When he entered the house, he heard the shower running upstairs and took the opportunity to get clothes from his closet for work the next day.

On his way to the guest room, Clair stepped out of the bathroom in front of him. Their bodies collided, and he almost knocked her off her feet. Wearing nothing but a towel, it was impossible to touch anything but bare skin as he stopped her from falling.

"I didn't know you were home," she said, steadying herself.

"I just got in."

As he made his way to his room, she shouted out to him. "David, please, let's sit down and talk about this." Her voice quivered as she pleaded with him.

With his hand on the door knob, he looked back at her. The night of her confession, the night that he'll forever remember as the end, he had felt something inside him shift and break loose. Life no longer made sense—if he couldn't trust her, then who could he trust?

She stood in the hall, a tight grip on her towel, and a hopeful look on her face.

"I have nothing to say."

He entered his room, leaned against the closed door, and felt his stomach fill with acid. The scent of her soap lingered on his hands. Fresh from her shower her skin was damp and warm.

We had it all, why would you do this?

All week, they moved around each other like strangers. Worse than strangers, there were no polite quips or easy smiles. By the time the weekend rolled around, David's nerves were frazzled raw. The tension was so thick that Clair dropped and shattered dinnerware—twice.

He wasn't holding up much better. Hurrying to get out of the house before she came downstairs, he dropped a full gallon of milk on the floor, spilling most of it. Something had to give.

He needed out. He couldn't think straight living here, and couldn't remember the last night he slept more than a few hours. After work on Friday, he entered the kitchen where she stood at the sink, and told Clair of his decision.

"I can't live like this any longer," he said, as he leaned against the counter.

She spun to look at him. She moved slowly toward the chair facing him and hesitantly sat down. A spark ignited in her tired eyes.

"I can't either. Listen, I know this is hard, and you have much to forgive, but I promise you won't regret it. I'll do everything I can to make this up to you." She looked at him with a face full of optimism.

"What? Clair, I meant I can't take living here anymore. I'm moving out."

Her agonized exhalation tugged at his heart.

"Please stay." Her soft voice trembled.

Oh God, don't beg.

Unable to look at her, he stood facing the stairs. "I . . . can't." Every cell in his body wanted to turn back and promise her everything would be all right. But he didn't believe it. Not now. He hurried up the stairs, away from her. Away from the pain of being near her, knowing that life would never be the same.

The next morning, he met with a realtor who handled rentals near campus. With the way college students moved in and out of apartments, it wasn't hard to land one. When he came back home, Clair was gone.

Walking through the house he collected his things, put them in a suitcase, and the next morning while Clair still slept, David took Buster and moved out. It didn't take long to move his few things into the small apartment. When finished, he sat looking at his pathetic new home. The used furniture with its torn upholstery and the warned carpet, stained from careless teenagers, all made a good analogy of his life.

"Well boy, it isn't much, but it's ours now. Like it or not."

Sitting on the sofa, he stared at his hands and wondered what she was doing now. He hadn't eaten today and should make a move to get some groceries. Instead, he threw his legs on the couch, lay down, and stared at the stains on the ceiling.

This will definitely take some getting used to.

On Monday, he found it difficult to keep his focus while teaching, but somehow got through the morning. During lunch, he noticed several missed calls from Clair. He turned off his cell and forced his attention on his next class and the homework assignment he hadn't yet reviewed. At some point, they would have to speak, he just couldn't yet.

After his last class, he went to his office. But after staring at the same papers, with little accomplished, he succumbed to his abstraction, packed his briefcase, and turned off the light.

While he locked the office door, his phone rang.

"Hi. How are things?" Darcy asked.

"Everything's great."

"You don't sound convincing," she said.

"Cut the crap, Darcy. You know, don't you?" he asked.

"Why are you upset with me? I haven't done anything but support you."

David didn't want to hurt her feelings, but he wasn't sure who he could trust. "What all did Clair tell you?"

She sighed loudly. "I know that Sargon didn't rape her."

"I bet you got all the juicy details."

"When she first told me about it, I begged her to tell you. And this is the thanks I get."

She's right. This wasn't her fault. "It's been a rough couple of days. I moved out yesterday."

"Moved out? Oh David, that's terrible. But I can't say that I blame you. I still can't believe what she did. Is there anything I can do?"

"No. It's just hard. All this time, I thought she was sad because of the horrible things that were done to her. Instead, she likely mourned her lover's death. How does someone get over that?" His voice cracked as he fought his emotions.

"I have to tell you," she said, "Clair has changed. She isn't the same sweet person she was before she went away."

David's stomach clenched tight. No matter what Clair had done, he still couldn't listen to someone else bashing her.

"I've got a lot of work in front of me. Can I call you later?"

"Sure. Call me anytime," she said.

He hung up the phone, discouraged. Darcy was supposed to be Clair's best friend—were all women traitors? He should call his dad, he would have good advice. But they hadn't talked in over a year, it would be awkward. No, he would have to get through this on his own. His world had turned upside down, and there was nothing anyone could do to change it.

CHAPTER 51

COCOONED IN DARKNESS, CLAIR SAT ON THE SOFA, NUMB, completely absorbed in a stream of thoughts and reminiscences. All it took to unleash her grief was to find his dirty sock, left under the bed, or a sports magazine on the end-table. Reminders of what she had—of what she destroyed.

While staying with her parents, Clair had put together a strong case for herself, practicing every word she would say. But the opportunity to plead it never came.

How do you talk to someone who refuses to listen?

She left voice messages, text, and emails and checked her phone obsessively for replies that never came. If they couldn't work this out, life would again become unbearable. No longer was she the confident woman she once was. Nor was she the person who lived in captivity, frightened and clinging to the one man who had said he cared. Maybe, who she was lay somewhere between, but without David her identity was unclear.

There was so much to regret, but she now wondered if she had it to do over, could she have done things differently. Maybe not, but she could have been honest about it and told David the truth from the start.

She slept on the sofa these days. Their bed held too many memories. When she wasn't thinking about all she had lost, she lay down and dreamt of it. And when she felt she could no longer stay in an empty house all day, she decided to go to work.

It felt strange at first working at Mercy Hospital and having at her disposal all that modern technology had to offer. But she adjusted fast and smiled, thinking of what she'd worked with before.

One evening while in the bath, David phoned her.

"I've been thinking about things," he said.

She sat, straight and still.

"I've been thinking too."

She thought he would say, *I love you. We can get through this, our marriage is worth fighting for.*

"We'll need to put the house on the market. After you have the baby of course."

"Oh. Of course." She dropped the towel she held.

"I'll contact a realtor soon, he'll need to look at it."

"You're not wasting any time. How can you be so sure about this? For God's sake, give us time to work this out."

Water dripped from the faucet in large drops splattering noisily into her bath, one after the other. The sound was like her blood as it dripped off of her scalp onto the concrete. Would her past ever stop haunting her?

"Look, I just wanted to give you a heads up," he finally said.

"Considerate of you," she snapped, before ending the call. She had planned that when they talked next, she would beg him to forgive her. But his words hurt.

How can he talk so matter-of-factly about our marriage ending? And why sell the house so soon? He's not even giving us a chance.

With a burst of energy she hadn't felt in months, she decided to clean. Starting upstairs she stripped the beds and threw the sheets in the wash. She dusted and vacuumed and scrubbed. When she finished upstairs, she carried her supplies to the first floor and tore into it.

It was close to midnight when she put the last of the food back into the sparkling refrigerator. Exhausted, she sat at the table and admired her work. Order was a security she had created for herself. But on this night, it failed her. She laid her head on the table and wept.

* * *

The next day, she decided to face the inevitable and called her parents. It was difficult for them to understand the reasons behind her separation, even after Clair painfully told them her embarrassing story. Taking her side, they thought David was being unreasonable. The news that they would soon become grandparents should have been a joyous event, but even that fell flat.

The weekends were the worst. Loneliness consumed her, as she counted the minutes until it was over. On Saturday morning, she sat in the kitchen drinking tea when the doorbell chimed, interrupting her thoughts and cutting through the silence that filled the room. Lieutenant Colonel Gerald Wolfe stood on her threshold, just as starched and shiny as before.

"Lieutenant Wolfe, this is a surprise."

He smiled brightly.

"Forgive me for coming unannounced. I had business in the area and thought I'd tie up some loose ends."

His cheerful demeanor didn't fool her.

"You had business in this small town?"

"Cleveland. May I come in?"

The last thing she felt like doing was to talk to this busybody.

She took a step back, allowing him to walk around her into the house.

"I have an appointment soon. I hope this will be quick."

He pulled a chair from the table and made himself at home. She reluctantly sat across from him.

"Mrs. Stevens, the last we talked, you were having difficulty remembering. I thought maybe being back home may have helped you."

"I told you everything already. If that's why you came, you've wasted your time," she said.

"I talked with Mrs. Elbez, shortly after you were rescued. She told me Sargon had plans to move his family to Iraq."

What?

"Mrs. Elbez is . . . his mother?"

"His wife."

Dear God.

"Are you sure, because I overheard Ashur tell someone his wife was dead."

"Nope. His wife of ten years, along with his six kids, live in Tartus."

"Six children?"

That explains his many trips there.

"He had seven. One died in an explosion in Damascus. Anyway, I thought we could try this again."

How could he? The lies . . . and me, falling for it all.

Lieutenant Wolfe sat his ominous recorder on the table.

"In the nine months that you were with Sargon Elbez, did he ever talk to you about ISIS?"

Did he ever really care for me?

"Dr. Stevens?"

She slowly turned her face and met his eyes. She despised this man, coming here, making her feel worse when she didn't think that was possible.

"He told me they were getting out of Azaz to focus on Iraq. They took control of the airbase and oil fields there. And they've stolen hundreds of American weapons that were given to the Iraqi military. They have connections with people in the US. I don't have names but I overheard talk of informants here."

He didn't move as if afraid he'd break the spell and she'd quit talking.

"Have you ever been to a member's home?"

"Yes. In Efrin. Yusuf Tlas. I don't know his position with ISIS, but he's high up."

"Did Sargon have anything to do with the murder of the four French reporters in Aleppo?"

They killed them? She was comforting him for the loss of his brother after they had killed innocent men.

"Not directly, but he may have ordered it."

"Is there anything else you think I should know?"

His small, beady eyes along with his by-the-book attitude, repulsed her.

She looked out the bay window, past the back yard into the distance.

"Unless they have use for you, they never keep prisoners alive."

He turned off his recorder and stood.

"Thank you."

"I'll see you out."

He stopped at the door and gave her a sympathetic smile.

"Don't be too hard on yourself. You're not the first person to be fooled by the likes of him."

"Goodbye, Lieutenant."

She knew he meant well, but she had enough.

Once he stepped out, she swung the door shut, leaned her back against it, and closed her eyes.

Sargon has a wife? And kids?

This news shouldn't hurt her, but it did. His lies ripped her to pieces with their sharp humiliation and cutting disrespect. But more, they made her feel small.

As the weekend dragged on, Clair felt her insecurities rise. There was something about being alone that had always made her feel unwanted. Her melancholy carried her up to the nursery, the one room that had no past, it offered possibilities. Determined not to know the sex of her child, the decor was neutral. She sat in the oversized rocker, centered between a six-foot giraffe and a white wicker changing table, and imagined her life with a baby.

She looked forward to bringing her child home, this home. She realized then that she didn't want to go along with David's plan to sell. Now that she worked, she could afford to stay here. That is if he would agree to sell her his half.

She started to envision raising a child here, as she had when they first bought the house. And although she held out hope David would be a part of it, she would live her dream, with or without him.

CHAPTER 52

ANOTHER WEEKEND ALONE. THINGS WEREN'T MUCH DIFFERENT for David now than when Clair was missing. Except that he lived in this tiny apartment instead of his nice home. Who said life was fair?

He sat alone with his headache, his retribution for over-drinking the night before. The seltzer tablets he dropped in a glass of water, sprayed his face as he watched it dissolve.

With nothing to do, and feeling claustrophobic, David leashed Buster and went for a walk. He didn't have a destination in mind when he left but as if drawn by some unknown force he found himself in front of his house. A car he didn't recognize, sat in the drive.

Pretty early to have company.

Jealousy ran rampant through his mind. He spun around and walked back to his apartment, feeling worse than when he left.

Trying to forget what he just saw, he reviewed his lesson plans for the upcoming week. In the kitchen, he grabbed a soda and stood at the window, looking down from his third story view. It was busy outside, students always had someplace to go.

He started to turn away when movement from inside the building next door, caught his eye. They were one floor down, the top pane of the window was curtainless, allowing him to stand and watch as the young couple kissed. It wasn't long before the boy pulled off her shirt.

She stood before him as he dropped to his knees and unfastened her pants, pulling them off, one leg at a time. Her beautiful body mesmerized David, holding his gaze as he watched her lover kiss his way up her body. Seized with pleasure, the girl tilted her head back, her eyes closed.

David leaned forward, watching, until her eyes flew open and met his.

He flung himself back, tripped, and landed flat on his back. *Please don't let her recognize me.*

His heart rate rocketed. On weak knees he crawled away from the window, then stood, yanked the window shade down before he dropped on the sofa.

With his face in his hands and Buster beside him, he sat burning inside.

"I've got to get a life."

* * *

On Monday he was extremely busy, always the case at the start of a semester. The beautiful day was in contrast to his mood. Walking past the house had been a bad move on his part and now he couldn't get Clair off of his mind.

He needed distraction from his misery, so on Wednesday, when Darcy called, he was happy to hear from her.

"Hey, Darcy."

"How are things with you and Clair?" she asked.

"We haven't talked in weeks, and that was business. But I've been thinking. Maybe I acted too fast."

"What do you mean?" Darcy asked.

"I wonder if I should call her and make sure she's okay," he answered.

"I've talked to Clair, I don't think she's ready to patch things up, if that's what you're thinking."

"I thought . . . she acted like she wanted me back the last time we talked."

"Maybe. But that wasn't the impression I got from her."

"It's just as well I guess. But . . . I do miss her."

"I'll do anything I can to help you," Darcy said.

"Are you doing anything this weekend?"

"Not much. What do you have in mind?" Her high pitched voice revealed her excitement.

"I don't know, maybe meet for dinner, somewhere in Columbus. I could use a night out."

"Alexander's at seven?" she suggested.

"Sounds great. See you then."

Darcy had probably just saved him from more humiliation. It was a crazy idea anyway. He would always have trust issues. How could they resume their marriage without trust?

The rest of the week flew by, and when Saturday night came, David was a little tense; he arrived at the restaurant early. It was crowded, but he found a stool at the bar and had a drink while he waited. This suddenly didn't seem like such great idea.

When Darcy walked in, heads turned as she sauntered by on her way toward David. He had always thought she was cute but never looked at her the way other men were doing now. Her short dress and high-heeled shoes showed off her sexy body.

"Sorry I'm late," she said, kissing his cheek.

"I'm early. Can I order you a drink?"

They sat at the bar and waited for a table.

Their conversation was light and, for the most part, funny. She had a great sense of humor and in no time, David was relaxed and having fun.

After dinner they had another drink. He was very aware of her hand on his leg as they huddled close together and talked. When finished, David paid the waitress and walked Darcy to her car.

"I had a great time."

"Who says it has to end?" she asked.

David laughed. "If I have another drink I won't be able to drive."

With the smile still on his face, Darcy leaned in and kissed him. Her body pressed firm against his. If she wanted his attention, she got it.

"Don't go home to an empty apartment tonight."

He felt himself weaken. After his weird behavior watching his neighbor's private encounter, maybe a night of fun sex was what he needed.

"Hey, we both need someone tonight, why not each other?"

Why not? I'm separated from my wife. And she didn't waste any time finding someone new.

But the truth was, he still loved her. Sleeping with her friend was not something he could do—to Clair or to Darcy.

"Let's not rush this. I had a great time, but I should probably go home now."

Darcy never gave up on anything without a fight. She linked her hands behind his neck, her bottom lip puckered in a mocked pout.

"Don't you find me attractive?"

"I do, along with every other man in the restaurant. Hell, I even saw some women drooling when you walked by."

Her head fell back, and she laughed, a deep, sexy sound that hit him below the belt. This wasn't easy. He took hold of her arms and stepped away from her embrace.

"Look, I thought I was ready for this, but I guess I'm not."

He covered his face with his hands and tilted his head back, released a loud sigh before dropping his hands to his side.

"And if Clair found out, it would kill her."

"After what she's done to you, why do you still care?" she asked, annoyed.

"Why don't *you*? I'm sorry, but you grew up with Clair, you were practically sisters."

She crossed her arms, the night air was cool, and in the slinky dress she wore she looked cold. He took off his jacket and put it around her.

"I shouldn't have come here tonight; it was selfish of me. I was lonely, and I needed someone . . ."

He leaned against her car, put his hands in his pockets, and lowered his head.

"My feelings are pretty muddled right now, I can't explain them. You're a beautiful woman, Darcy, and the right man is waiting for you, but it probably isn't me."

Without looking at him or saying a word, she tossed his coat at him and got into her car. He stood in the parking lot and watched her drive away.

David found the nearest McDonald's and ordered a large black coffee for the ride home. He agreed with Darcy, what Clair had done to him was horrible, but he didn't have it in him to get even. Now, he just wanted it to be over with and move on. Soon the closing on the house would be completed, then their divorce. After that he would try to put all of this behind him.

Walking past their house was a stupid move. In the future, he would avoid that part of town all together. Maybe he should think about getting another job, move elsewhere. There were plenty of colleges that needed professors, and with nothing holding him here, he would consider all his options.

CHAPTER 53

CLAIR RAN HER HAND DOWN HER YOUNG PATIENT'S NECK, feeling his glands and lymph nodes. The boy, a good-looking fourteen-year-old, was hospitalized with mononucleosis but was rapidly recovering.

"I'm having the IV removed today."

He gave her a hopeful look.

"When can I get back to soccer practice?"

"That may be awhile."

He raised his arms and dropped them, released an exaggerated moan.

"Hey Doc, you're pretty good looking, got a younger sister?" His said playfully.

"That does it. I'm discharging you tomorrow. Every medical journal specifically states that when teenage boys start thinking of girls, they're well enough to go home."

"Yes!"

At the nurse's station she charted his discharge orders, then walked to the elevator. In an hour, she would see patients in the clinic and wanted to go to her office to finish some paperwork.

While she waited, a man came up beside her just as its doors opened. They stepped inside together and when she turned to give this stranger a polite smile, she found herself looking into very familiar eyes. David looked as surprised as she was.

Her heart took off on a sprint.

Why does he have to look so good?

David spoke first: "How've you been?"

"Okay."

Her mind raced to come up with something brilliant to say, but the elevator came to a stop too soon. As he stepped out he turned to her.

"I hope everything goes well. With the baby I mean."

She looked down at her growing stomach and rubbed her hand over it. Their eyes met before the doors closed between them and she moved upward. When she reached her floor, she punched the button to go back down, where David got off. If ever she needed courage, it was now.

On the second floor, a man in a bathrobe walked by her, pushing his IV pole ahead of him. An elderly woman inched her way forward in a wheelchair, her eyes roamed the room in quick, twitching movements. A few nurses stood at their station, talking. But David was not among them.

Leaning in close, Clair spoke to the woman in the wheelchair.

"Can I help you?"

She glanced up and smiled.

"I'm lost. My room has to be here somewhere, but they all look alike."

Clair pushed her over to the nurses. When they finished their gossip, they glanced up and got busy in a hurry.

"Dr. Stevens, I'm sorry I didn't see you. Can I help you?" one nurse asked.

"You obviously didn't see this patient either. She's lost. Which room is hers?"

A bright red covered their faces as they shuffled through papers, looking for the room number.

"Mrs. Garber is in room 316. I'll take her." The nurse said with a sheepish smile.

"I've got this." Moving around them Clair wheeled the woman toward 316, and glanced in each room for David as she passed.

Once she had Mrs. Garber where she belonged, she continued her hunt, looking and listening for signs of him. Just when she thought she'd been mistaken, and David had gotten off on a different floor, she heard his voice and gravitated toward it.

He was in a patient's room, visiting. Clair hoped it would be a quick one, her break was almost over, and she had a busy afternoon ahead of her. With her eyes fixed on the room's entrance, she almost toppled a medication cart as she backed away, and decided it would be safer to sit near the elevator and wait. Ten minutes later David walked toward her.

"David, can we talk?"

His head jerked in her direction, surprised.

"All right, but I don't have long."

She stood, at a loss for the right words. The atmosphere here was all wrong for what she really wanted to say.

"I've been thinking. Now that I'm back to work and can afford it, I'd like to buy the house."

"You want to buy our house? Isn't it a little big for you?" he asked.

"We bought the house because it was a perfect place to raise children. Now that I'm going to have one, I want him or her to grow up there. Listen, just think about it and have it appraised. I'm not asking for any favors and will pay market price."

And I love you and want you to move back in with me.

"I'll look into it. Is there anything else?"

Indifference sprung from him like a fountain.

"No . . . I guess not."

For a minute they stood, awkward and silent.

"I'll call you when I have the numbers."

She nodded before he walked away. Leaving her with a sour taste in her mouth.

He acts as if he couldn't care less about me. Is that how he really feels?

She took a deep breath, headed toward the elevator and back to work.

When her day was over, she couldn't wait to go home, get a bite to eat, and go to bed. But once there, her mind settled on her conversation with David.

He seemed so eager to get away from her. But he'd have to call soon with a price on the house. Then she'd get another chance to explain what happened in Syria and perhaps, make him understand and forgive her.

A week passed, David had arranged for the appraisal and she looked forward to his call. On Wednesday, her day was a busy one. A car carrying three children, all under the age of six, crashed into the back of a pickup. The mother had been drinking and would face charges, but all would live. Children's Services was called in, and soon foster homes would be arranged for the three of them. Clair hoped they could stay together. As sad as it was, at least these children would have a home and food. She had met so many while in Syria that had neither.

Her lack of sleep the night before, coupled with her crazy day had her drained. She picked up some fast food for dinner and sat in front of the television, eating. When she headed to the kitchen to unload the dishwasher, she noticed the flashing red light on her answering machine and listened as a very stoic David relayed the price of the house. She almost cried as yet another opportunity to explain herself was lost.

CHAPTER 54

DAVID STUFFED HIS HANDS IN HIS COAT POCKETS AND KEPT moving, killing time before going back to his cramped apartment. He had begun walking as a way to shed a few pounds. The weight he had gained while Clair was gone slowly melted away, he walked now to clear his head.

Seeing her at the hospital last week had conjured up feelings he couldn't shake. Standing in the elevator, so close to her, he felt the stir in his groin and couldn't flee fast enough. Now, he slowed his pace as he neared her house—so much for his vow to stay away.

Why did she need such a big house for just the two of them?

Standing across the street, cloaked in darkness, he hoped to catch a glimpse of her. From there, he watched her, talking on the phone as she walked, her face flooded with a beautiful smile. She took something from the refrigerator and left the room, turning the light off on her way out.

He'd seen enough and walked back to his apartment. Sitting on the sofa, he pulled out his phone and dialed the familiar number, knowing she was home.

"Hi. Did you get my message?"

"Yes. The price sounds fair. What's next?"

Her voice, even when aloof, had a kind undertone.

"I have the paperwork in order. Should I drop them off at your lawyers?" he asked.

"I'll look at them myself. Would you mind dropping them off here?"

David hesitated, not wanting to risk being alone with her. The possibility of his body betraying him like it did in the elevator was a strong one.

"Please. It's important to me," she pleaded.

"Will tomorrow night work?"

"Tomorrow night would be perfect. Thanks."

David sat, long after hanging up, thinking about her. Going into the house where he no longer lived would be strange. He rose, returned to the work that lay spread out on the kitchen table, Buster hot on his heels. He patted the dog's head, glad that he had him.

"You'll always be loyal, won't ya?"

The next evening, he put on a heavy coat and walked the two miles to the house. All the while, thinking of her and what he would say. Briefcase in hand, he fidgeted with the keys in his pocket and waited for her to answer.

"Hi. Thanks for coming." She invited him in and led the way into the living room. They both sat down.

"Can I get you something to drink?" she asked.

"No thanks."

Opening his briefcase, he pulled out the papers and pretended to study them, not really seeing any of it.

"Here's the documents. My lawyer marked where you'll need to sign. That's just the beginning. We'll still have more to sign at closing," he said all business like, as he handed her the massive stack.

"Thanks. I'll go over them later."

"I guess if I have to sell the place, it's better you buy it than have strangers living here. Are you sure you can keep up with a house this size?"

"There'll be plenty of work but what I can't do, I'll hire out."

"You probably won't be alone for long," he said. His chipper voice letting her know it was fine with him.

She shot him a dirty look.

"Why would you think that?"

"I happened to go by one Sunday morning, saw a car parked in the drive. It's none of my business what you do. I just thought if you had a man around it would be easier for you."

Her frown deepened as she glared at him.

"That car belongs to my mother. It's new. I'm not dating, and I'm certainly not sleeping with anyone."

"Like I said, it's none of my business." He smiled, knowing he was being an ass but couldn't stop himself.

Blinking back the tears, Clair took a deep breath.

"I said on the phone that I wanted to talk to you about something, other than the sale of the house. And as hard as it is for both of us, I think this needs saying. I want you to try to understand what happened to me while in Syria." She wiped the tear that spilled from her eye, cleared her throat, and continued.

"When I was first taken I had hopes of freedom. When months passed and I still lived there, I began to believe I would never leave. Did I tell you most of my time was spent in darkness?"

"No."

"There's so much I left unsaid, which I now regret." She paused, tried to put together the right words. "Darkness was my punishment for trying to escape."

"And yet, you still slept with the man," he said bitterly.

She paused, her lips pressed firmly together. David felt sorry for her but she caused this and he didn't mind pointing out the bad choices she had made. It was her fault they weren't together. And why was it important to her that he understand if she didn't want him back?

Clair stood and walked to the kitchen, plucked a tissue from its box and blew her nose. She returned to the living room, just as her phone started to ring.

"I'm expecting a call from the hospital. I'll be just a minute," she said.

"I should be going." He stood, closed his briefcase.

"David, please, this won't take long."

The ringing stopped.

"Some other time, I have plans."

He turned to leave, and then stopped, ran his fingers through his hair as he looked back at her.

"While you were gone, I imagined you being beaten, raped, and even murdered. Then you came home and I let myself believe that maybe your suffering had been psychological, less physical."

He closed his eyes and took a deep breath.

"When I learned you'd been raped, I thought the worst. Torture on a daily basis—it consumed me. I blamed myself for letting you go, for not getting you out sooner. And then, you tell me it wasn't rape after all. Why Clair? Why would you let me believe that?"

For a split second, their eyes met. Then, he turned and walked away. A sob escaped her lips, but he continued moving away from the sight of her. But the distance did nothing to erase her from his mind.

* * *

As David sat in his apartment, thinking of her, his heart ached. Not just for him, but for the both of them. And all that was lost.

CHAPTER 55

AT THREE O'CLOCK A SHARP PAIN IN CLAIR'S ABDOMEN WOKE her with a jolt. The bed was wet—her water broke. She sat up but the pain was so severe it took some time before she could stand.

She staggered toward the bathroom, stopped to knock on the door to the spare bedroom. When her OB told her four days ago that they would have to do a C-section, her mother packed a bag and came right away. The doctor told Clair she had a condition called placenta previa and a vaginal delivery would be dangerous. The C-section was scheduled two days from now. This wasn't good.

"Mom, wake up. I'm in labor."

In the bathroom, Clair was shocked to see her pajamas covered with blood. The sticky red liquid ran down her legs and puddled between her toes. These pains weren't labor.

"Mom," she yelled in a panic.

Her mother rushed in, dressing herself as she walked.

She stopped at the rooms' entrance and stared at the bloody footprints smeared across the white floor tiles. She quickly took charge and threw some towels on the floor.

"Lay down, dear. I'll call an ambulance."

"I'm scared," Clair cried, "I can't lose my baby."

She did as she was told and lay dizzy and shaking inside. *I can't lose my baby, it's all I have left.*

* * *

After she had made the call, Barb sat on the floor beside Clair and cradled her head on her lap until help came. She was losing so much blood. She rubbed her hand over Clair's forehead, tried to remain calm and reassured Clair that everything would be all right. Inside, she was terrified that this would end badly.

What's taking so long for them to get here?

When the ambulance finally got there, Clair was barely conscious.

By the time Barb got to the hospital, Clair was already being examined by an obstetrician. She paced the floor frantically. And when a nurse came out to talk to her, Barb grabbed her by the arm.

"Please, tell the doctor, if he can only save one of them, let it be Clair."

"They're doing everything they can to save both and are preparing her for surgery. Will you sign the consent?"

Barb quickly scribbled her name and watched the nurse rush back to the operating room. There was nothing she could do now but wait. She dropped herself on a plastic chair and prayed that her daughter would live.

Maybe David should be told about this, after all, they were still married. If he would come here, it might give Clair more reason to fight, more reason to live. Especially if her baby doesn't make it. She took out her phone and called his cell. After several rings with no answer, she was forced to leave a voice mail.

Hours later, Clair's doctor came in the waiting room.

Barb stood, shaking inside.

"Is she all right?"

"We think she'll be fine. And you have a beautiful grandson." She cried with relief.

"Thank you so much, I thought the worst."

"Well, we did have to do a hysterectomy. I'm afraid she won't have another child. You look tired, why not go home and rest. She'll be under the anesthesia for several hours. I'll wait until you're back before I tell her."

Barb thanked him again and went back to the house to rest, grateful that this daughter would live.

* * *

Dressed and ready for work, David poured himself a cup of coffee before he left the apartment. He unplugged his cell from the charger and was about to put it in his pocket when he noticed he had a message—from Barb.

"David, Clair's at the hospital, in surgery now. She's lost so much blood . . . I . . . I'm not sure the outcome. I just wanted you to know."

Lost so much blood? She must be having her baby.

David flew down the steps to his car and sped to the hospital. When he finally found her room, he stopped in the doorway and took in the pitiful sight of her. Lying in bed, her face as white as the bed sheet, IVs in both arms, and one pumped blood into her. He slowly walked toward her.

Oh, Clair. You've been through so much.

He took her hand, as cold and clammy as death, and held it. What he felt now was akin to the night he got the call, telling him she was missing.

You made it through Syria, please, don't give up now.

A nurse came in the room and checked on the IVs.

"Is she going to be all right?"

"Are you a relative?" she asked.

"I'm her husband."

"Oh." She looked at him suspiciously. "I didn't know . . . I mean, yes. She gave us a scare, but she should be fine."

David sighed with relief. *Thank God.*

"How about the baby?"

"The baby is beautiful. Would you like to see him?"

David looked down at Clair, smoothed her hair away from her face. He shook his head.

"No. No thanks."

He walked out of the room, past the bewildered nurse, and on to work.

CHAPTER 56

CLAIR LOVED HIM FROM THE MOMENT SHE HELD HIM. WHEN she looked at him, she saw Sargon, the splash of Asian descent obvious. Her mother was so proud. She pointed him out to complete strangers from behind the glass of the nursery, embarrassingly boastful of her first grandchild.

While Clair nursed him, his little fingers wrapped around one of hers, and she thought of all she had lost from her affair with Sargon. Now, she held in her arms her tremendous gain.

The doctor had been in earlier, explained the surgery and told her there would be no more children. As much as it grieved her, she was grateful that her son was alive. Knowing that he would be her only one made him all the more precious.

She wanted to give him both an American and Syrian name, and Carter Hakeem Stevens seemed to fit him fine. On his birth certificate, Sargon Elbez was listed as his father. It was hard to fathom, but maybe someday David would come back and Carter would have a man to look up to. But for now it would be the two of them, and she would work twice as hard to make sure her poor past decisions wouldn't hurt him.

A week after she had brought Carter home, she sat at the table with her mother, eating breakfast.

"I think it's time I go home," her mother said. "You're going to be fine."

"I hope so. This job is much too important to screw up."

Her mother gave her a hug and with a wide grin on her face said, "Honey, there isn't a mother alive that hasn't thought at some point they should have done things differently. We do the best we can and hope it's good enough."

"Wow, that takes some pressure off," Clair said laughing. "But seriously, I look at him and already I'm afraid something bad could happen. I almost panic thinking about it. How did you make it through losing Megan?"

It was a while before her mother answered. With a faraway stare, she gathered old memories.

"I hope you never have to go through that. As a parent, you take for granted that your child will outlive you. When that doesn't happen, it's devastating. But you go on, one day at a time. After a while, it gets better. And of course I had you, which helped. I'm just so thankful I didn't lose another. You had me pretty scared."

They embraced. Sharing the bond of motherhood connected them in a way they hadn't known before.

"One of my biggest regrets was that I was so occupied with Megan, I didn't spend time with you. And I wasn't much of a mother after she passed either."

Clair looked at her mom and noticed she had aged. She had been through so much. She didn't need to carry any guilt because of her.

"You were a good parent. Like you said, you did the best you could. I'll always remember a wonderful childhood, and I want you to remember it that way too."

In the driveway, Clair waved goodbye. As much help as her mother had been, she looked forward to having her son all to herself.

Looking at his round little face, she tried to imagine him as a boy. Despite the fact that he was conceived under dire circumstances, she would do everything to shape his character into a kind and thoughtful man—like David.

When old enough, she would tell him about his father, maybe in a way that would shield him from hearing the worst. It would be difficult for him, to accept that his father was a terrorist, but she wouldn't lie. If she had learned anything from all this, it was that lying made matters worse.

The house no longer felt big and empty. A family lived here now and would for a long time to come. She wondered if somehow David knew she had given birth . . . if he had kept track of the months that passed since she had come home.

Off work for two months, she would devote that time to her son, willing him to feel her love as she had with Hakeem. She especially liked the night, when he would wake up and need her. And couldn't get enough of his soft coo while he nursed. She wouldn't trade these moments for anything.

When the time to go back to work neared, she became anxious, not wanting to separate from him. But she couldn't stop the inevitable and made plans for Carter's care. A coworker had recommended a woman who provided child care in her home, and after meeting with her, Clair knew she would take great care of her son.

While ironing, Clair looked down at him, sitting in his carrier. His chubby cheeks and bright eyes made him irresistible, and it would be hard not to spoil him.

She had been through so much over the past year and a half, but right now, she considered herself the luckiest woman in the world.

CHAPTER 57

DESPITE THE JOY CARTER BROUGHT TO HER LIFE, CLAIR STILL felt the void left from David's absence. She had tried to talk to him, but he didn't want to hear her excuses. She climbed the stairs and eased a sleeping Carter into his crib.

"I guess it will be just you and me buddy," she whispered.

Why did she think it could be any different? She had done the unthinkable to a man who deserved much better. While she sat alone, she thought of one last ditch attempt to keep them together. If she couldn't say what needed to be said face-to-face, she would write it. And after reading her letter, if he still couldn't forgive her, she would wave a white flag with no more resistance.

It was midnight before she finished putting into words, all she was feeling. Time would tell if it would make any difference. She walked outside to her mailbox, set her letter inside, and felt relief that it was done.

The next day, not wanting to be alone, Clair took Carter to her parents' house for the weekend. They were exceptional grandparents, and it filled her with joy to witness the love they felt for him.

On Saturday they insisted on taking her on a shopping spree, to get a few necessities. When finished, they came home with a stroller, a high chair, and enough clothes to last until his first birthday.

That night her mother asked about David.

"Have you talked to David lately?"

"No. Not since he came over with the contract on the house. But I sent him a letter explaining what I did and why. We'll see if it does any good."

"I bet it will, once he hears your side of it."

Clair shrugged. "I don't know. He was devastated, as a child, when his mother had her affair."

"Well you aren't going to give up are you?"

Clair sighed. "If he doesn't respond to the letter, for my sake and Carter's, I need to."

On Sunday evening, she was back home and unpacking her car when she noticed a large package on the front porch. After changing Carter's diaper, she laid him on a blanket spread on the living room carpet and brought the package inside.

It held a baby's bathtub, filled with every bath accessory imaginable. At the bottom of the box, a card from Darcy.

Her way of apology. I knew she would eventually.

When she settled Carter in for the night, Clair took her phone to the sofa and called Darcy.

"Thanks for the gift. He doesn't have a tub, and all that went with it. Who knew a baby needed so much?"

"I'm glad you like it. Sorry I haven't been up to see him. I bet he's cute," Darcy said.

"I may be prejudiced, but yes, he's very handsome."

They both laughed. It felt like old times.

"Remember when we swore we'd never have babies if it meant getting married to some gross boy," Darcy said, then laughed again.

"I remember. But right now I would take David back in a heartbeat if he ever forgives me."

"Yeah, I don't know. He's pretty hurt."

"Would you help me?" Clair asked." Maybe talk to him, convince him that I'm sorry. That I love him and want him back."

Clair waited for an answer.

"Darcy? Did you hear me?" she asked.

"I don't think I'm the right person for the job," Darcy said.

"Why not? You know us better than anyone. I think David would listen to you. He certainly hasn't listened to me."

Darcy sighed heavily.

"I'm sorry to be the one to tell you this, but David just wants it to be over," she finally said.

"Oh."

"He can't get over what you did. He was worried sick while you were gone. We spoke often, and I helped him get through the tough days. Once, he was so upset that I came up for the weekend, and we went to Cleveland to the wineries—"

"Sounds like he was really distraught," Clair blurted.

"Oh Clair, I'm sorry, really I am. But I think it would be best if you forgot him," Darcy said.

Clair loved David. And probably always would. But how could she make him love her in return?

"Thanks, Darcy, for telling me this. It's killing me now, but I needed to know how he feels."

After they said their goodbyes Clair turned off her phone and lay on the sofa waiting for tears that never came. Instead, the reality of living her life without David brought a sudden and powerful panic. How could she live without him? Could she really raise her son, alone? This was all wrong. And although she appreciated Darcy telling her the truth, she felt that something had happened between the two of them while she was gone and wasn't sure she could trust her anymore.

On Monday, Clair was back to work, and their lives fell into a routine that brought the stability they both needed. Now that she had a stroller, she took Carter for long walks in the evenings. He seemed to enjoy the ride, and she was glad for the exercise.

As days turned into weeks, and still no response to her letter from David, the sinking feeling of hopelessness took over. That is, until the day of the house closing. She rose early, showered, and styled her hair the way David liked it, parted on the side and tucked behind her ears. When she finished applying her makeup she looked in the mirror, then added a touch of gloss to her lips. Satisfied, she put on the new blouse she bought.

Her sitter didn't work on Saturdays, so she packed Carter up and started out. While she drove, she thought of David and the heart-racing, heartbreaking feeling that came with seeing him. As long as she still loved him, he would always provoke a mixed bag of emotions in her. Would she ever not love him?

When she entered his lawyer's office, she was greeted by the receptionist.

"I'm Clair Stevens. I have an appointment with Mr. Williams this morning."

"Good morning. If you'll follow me, Mr. Williams is ready for you."

Clair purposely walked slow and steady, her head held high. Despite her dry mouth, she put on her best smile as she entered the room. At the end of a long table sat David's lawyer. The eight other chairs were empty.

"I must be early. Would you prefer I wait in your reception area until David gets here?"

Mr. Williams stood, pulled a chair out for her.

"No, you're right on time. Mr. Stevens came earlier. He had another appointment this morning."

Clair felt herself shrink.

"Not to worry," Mr. Williams assured her, "he has signed the necessary papers. All we need now, to make it official, is your signature. And a check of course."

When all was reviewed, signed, and notarized, Clair felt joy now that she owned the house, but also felt dejected. Did David really have an appointment, or was it more that he couldn't stand the sight of her?

A few days later, Clair received an envelope with Mr. William's return address on it. She assumed it was a copy of the deed, but instead she held their divorce papers. Clair knew this day would come. But still, it hurt to see their names, typed neatly on page one, as the couple who had failed.

She pulled open a desk drawer, threw the papers in, and slammed it shut. It could wait. She was in no hurry to be free of him. This would be her last defying moment. One that could only last so long. In time, she would surrender and make final the divorce she adamantly rejected.

CHAPTER 58

DAVID'S DAY WAS BAD FROM THE START. DURING THE NIGHT, the electricity in his building went off, yet again. Just long enough to throw his alarm into a different time zone. Lucky for him, the students who lived in the apartment above, woke early. Their music, played at a deafening pitch, jolted him awake with just enough time to dress and hustle off to work.

Around ten o'clock, he got a call from a university in Oregon, where he recently applied. They were looking for someone with more experience and wouldn't even grant him an interview.

Right before lunch, his lawyer sent him a text. He needed David's signature on a few more papers by four o'clock when the courts closed. Soon his marriage would be just a memory.

At noon, he rushed to his car and drove to the office of Williams, Williams, and Stein for probably the last time, leaving him twenty short minutes before his next class. The receptionist greeted him as he walked in.

"Professor Stevens, hello. Is Mr. Williams expecting you?"

"Yes, he has some papers for me to sign. I'm on my lunch break and wanted to stop in quick and take care of it," he said, trying to hurry things along.

"He's on the phone right now but if you'll have a seat, I'll tell him you're here."

David thanked her, then paced the waiting area, twirling his keys. There was no chance of him getting lunch now. When at last Mr. Williams came out with the papers, David hastily looked them over before adding his signature.

As he left, he wanted to feel the relief that should come from knowing the end was in sight. But instead he felt sick. His head pounded, and he felt nauseous—to the point he wondered if he indeed was coming down with something.

He looked at the clock on his dashboard. He'd have to move fast. While he sped off, he thought of Clair. She should have told him the truth the day she came home. Or at least soon after. It still would have hurt, but in time, he could have accepted it. Without giving him a chance, they would never know if they could have worked this out.

David slammed the brakes and stopped his car just before he ran a red light.

"Damn it."

He glanced at the clock again, dropped his hand on the armrest.

"Come on."

A sign posted "No Right On Red" but when he saw that it was clear, David punched the gas and turned onto Hedges Street. In his peripheral, a blur of pink and white moved toward him from the right of the road.

It happened so fast, a flash of bicycle and little girl in front of his car in an instant. He stomped the breaks, tires screeched, and the sickening thud of his front bumper making contact jarred his insides. David's face slammed hard against the

Returned Broken

steering wheel. When he looked up, she lay spread eagle in the street.

Throwing the car into park, he got out. Before long a whirl of commotion surrounded him, as the mother cried and people gathered. Police and ambulance sirens blared, and the small body of a little girl lay lifeless on the blacktop—because of him.

Numb, he stood totally inept, watching as they loaded her onto a stretcher and into the ambulance. On shaky legs, he walked over to the paramedic.

"Is she alive?"

"Yeah. Your nose is bleeding, you all right?" he said, as he handed David some gauze.

"Do you think she's going to be okay?"

"Don't know yet. You're gonna have to get out of the way."

He jumped into the ambulance as its sirens screamed. David stepped aside. When he walked back to his car, a policeman stood waiting.

"This your car?"

"Yes."

"I need to see your license and registration."

David got into his glove box and gave the officer what he asked for.

He sat in his car while the police ran his background report. When he handed back his license the cop looked at David's shirt.

"Where'd the blood come from?"

"My face hit the steering wheel when I braked," David said.

"Was your seat belt on?"

David lowered his head and shook it. The cop made note of it.

"I've talked to two witnesses who said you were speeding. One said he saw you run the red light. How fast were you going?"

David shrugged his shoulders.

"I don't know, not too fast. I stopped at the light, before turning."

"Didn't read the sign, huh?"

The officer scribbled more.

"I'm going to ask you to park your car, come with me to the station."

David went from nauseous to a dizzying sickness.

He parked in a lot across the street, turned off his car, and laid his head back. He knew it was his urgency to sign the divorce papers that caused this.

A tap on his window pulled him back into the here and now. He stepped out of his car and was escorted to the backseat of a cruiser while people stood watching.

The police station was loud and chaotic. He was lead through a maze of office cubicles before being seated in a chair and introduced to Sergeant Faulkner.

"Mr. Stevens, is it?"

David nodded.

"I'll need you to fill out this form. At the bottom, in your own words write what happened."

"Am I being charged?"

"As of right now, just the seat belt violation and running a red light. But if the child dies, you could be charged with involuntary manslaughter. That carries a sentence of ten to sixteen months in prison. Minimum."

Prison. Jesus, my life's such a mess.

"There's also a chance the child's parents could file a civil suit to cover medical expenses and such."

Filling out the form was tough. With questions like, "Were you speeding?" and "Did you drive through a red light?" to answer, he felt like he signed his own death sentence when he answered yes to both.

When he had all the information he needed, Sergeant Faulkner stood.

"Don't go out of town without checking with us first. I'd get a lawyer if I were you."

I just came from one.

"I'll have someone drive you back to your vehicle."

Once in his car, David called Dean White and told him what had happened, minus the possibility of prison time, and that he needed a few days off work. Then drove straight to the hospital.

Walking through the emergency entrance, he glanced around at the disorder. It was crowded. People sat waiting, sharing their ailments with one another. There was no sign of the girl's family.

Across from the waiting area, four sets of curtains hung. Hidden behind them, the seriously sick and injured. Those that qualified as emergencies—the girl.

He moved at a snail's pace, outside of the curtains, eavesdropping until he found the room he was most interested in.

The phrase "please don't die" played over in his head as he listened. From the hodgepodge of words, those that made it through the curtain, he learned the child was still alive. Her name was Julie, her mother repeated it between sobs. And then, a voice, as familiar to him as his own. Clair.

If anyone could make that child better, he'd put his money on her. Pacing the floor, he hung on to every positive word that filtered out to him. Suddenly the curtain flew open, and a team of nurses rolled a gurney out, taking the girl to the elevator while her mother clung to the bed rail, her short legs had her running to keep up.

As the room emptied, David scanned each face looking for Clair. The last to come out, she held a laptop, making notes as she walked and didn't notice him until he spoke. "Can I talk to you?"

She stopped and looked up from the laptop with beautiful eyes.

"David, what are you doing here? There's blood on your shirt. Are you—"

"The girl. Will she be all right?" he asked.

"I've ordered tests. Until I get the results, I'm not sure. Do you know her?"

"Not really," he said, raking his fingers through his hair. "I was driving the car that hit her."

"Oh no," she murmured. "How did it happen?"

"I was in a meeting, running late and driving back to campus and I . . . I didn't see her." He sighed, stuffed his hands in his pockets.

She looked at him through narrow eyes.

"Let's go where we can talk."

She led him to a room at the end of the hall and closed the door, poured him a cup of coffee.

"Where did this happen?"

"I was driving down Sycamore Street, and had just turned onto Hedges toward campus. Like I said, I was late, and my mind was on something else and . . . I couldn't stop in time." His voice choked. He swallowed some coffee.

"That girl could die because of me. And if she lives, will she be the same?" He buried his face in his hands, his elbows on the table.

"The police have witnesses who say I ran a red light and was speeding. If she dies, I could go to prison."

Clair gasped.

"The poor kid, if she dies I deserve prison."

"Were you speeding?"

"I don't know. I was in a hurry."

She sat beside him.

"Let me tell you what we're doing for her. Right now she's having a CT scan. Because she's still unconscious we're looking to see if there's any damage to her brain. Once we have those results we can decide if surgery is needed and proceed from there. She has some cuts, some bruises, but the head injury is our main concern. Why don't you go home and I'll call you with any news?"

He shook his head. "I'm staying. And if I get a chance, I'd like to tell her mother how sorry I am."

"That's not a good idea. Promise me you won't talk to her mother today. You're both upset. If you start telling her you're sorry, you were late and distracted, on top of the possibility you were going too fast, this will not end well for you. I understand how you must feel, but you can't talk to anyone. Agreed?"

He dropped his shoulders and nodded.

"If you insist on staying, you can wait in my office. It's on the third floor. I'll call up and have someone let you in. When

I see the results of the CT, and after we put our plans in motion, I'll come up and we'll talk."

With her hand on the doorknob, she paused. "Sycamore, isn't that the street your lawyer's office is on?"

He didn't say what she already knew. Their eyes met, locked in a telling gape, before she turned and left the room.

CHAPTER 59

WHILE IN CLAIR'S OFFICE, WITH NOTHING TO DO BUT WAIT, David pondered the disaster that was his life. His failed marriage, his ambivalent career, and now this. He thought of Clair, in the arms of another man. Jealousy still grabbed him by the throat when he traveled that path. Why did she do it? Why did anyone?

He spun in her chair and faced the window. Looking out, he stared into the distance, and thought back, years ago.

* * *

He was twelve, and had just eaten lunch in the school cafeteria. While going back to his classroom, his stomach lurched and emptied itself all over the hall floor. A quick-thinking woman, who earlier had thrown beets on his plate, now threw powder over his vomit. At least once a month a kid would throw up and the stuff they put on it smelled worse than the vomit. The kids called it puke powder. They sent him home.

As he entered the house, music played. Lou Rawls' smooth deep voice singing "Lady Love" made him cringe when he heard it. He followed it to his parents' room. The muffled sound of his mother's voice escaped through the closed door. He assumed she was on the phone. His dad, a long distance trucker, was on the road.

What he wouldn't give if he could forget what he saw next. There, in his parents' bed, his mother with a strange man, their clothes sprawled across the floor. His mom screamed at him to get out. The man struggled to cover himself while he met David's stare. Unable to look away, and with his mother still yelling, he threw up on the carpet before running to his room and locking himself in. His world had just been rocked.

A week later his dad moved out. David visited him every other weekend. Over time, their strong bond weakened, his visits grew further apart, and nothing was ever the same. Eventually, his mom married Jerry, who never got over the awkwardness of what David saw that day. He couldn't remember the last time he spoke to his dad.

* * *

The door opened, he spun the chair around as Clair entered the room.

"How is she?" he asked.

"The CT shows swelling in her brain. She'll need surgery to release the pressure and remove any fluid. We're waiting for the surgeon to arrive from out of town. And then, we wait and see how she responds."

David went weak. Brain surgery. What would that do to her? He knew from the years with Clair that it would be risky.

"She's lucky on one count. She has you for a doctor. I'd like to stay until it's over if that's all right."

Under the fluorescent light, Clair looked tired. Dark circles had formed under her eyes, lines that weren't there a year ago, sprung from their corners.

"You can use my office. I'll stay until the surgeon comes, brief him on what's transpired to this point. Then I need to pick up Carter from the sitter's."

Ashamed he had never before asked her son's name, he tried to make up for it.

"I like the name. It sounds strong."

"His full name is Carter Hakeem Stevens. I hope you don't mind us keeping your name."

"It's your name too," he said.

They both stood silent until Clair started for the door.

"Clair, wait," he said stopping her. "Thanks for your help. You've been great."

She looked at him through questioning eyes, her lips closed tight. Whatever she was thinking, she kept to herself.

"Let's hope we have good news tonight," she finally said before she walked out.

"I'll see you tomorrow then," he spit out hurriedly before the door closed.

He felt the chill she left in the room. What did he expect? Until today, he hadn't shown much interest in her life. But he thought of her—he always thought of her.

Hungry and bored, he started out to find the cafeteria. On the first floor, he continued down halls and past waiting areas like a mouse in a maze he followed sign after sign pointing the way to food.

Just before reaching the cafeteria, he passed by the hospital chapel and glanced in. Julie's mother stood talking to a priest. Recognition lit up in her puffy eyes as they met his. Her face drooped as if a strong gravitational force pulled at her flesh, and she held the priest's hand like a lifeline to God. Breaking the connection, he moved on, hoping to avoid any confrontation.

At the cafeteria, he stood in line looking down at the food, wondering how long it had sat under the warming lights. He hadn't eaten all day so, as unappetizing as it looked, he put food on his plate.

Carrying his tray to a nearby table he sat down and bit into a rubbery hot dog. His empty stomach gurgled—it knew better. Things got worse when, within minutes of sitting, Julie's mother appeared. Her long black hair, pulled back in a rubber band, was frizzy and windblown. She wore gray sweat pants and a T-shirt, the image of a ballerina along with the name of a dance studio, on its front. She stood wringing her hands, and a weak smile draped across her face.

"Do you mind if I sit down?" she asked.

He stood and pulled a chair out for her.

"Mr. Stevens, right?"

Afraid to admit to anything, David gave her a nod.

"I've been wanting to talk to you. Julie has just learned to ride a bike, and I walked beside her until she started to pedal faster. In a few seconds she was out in front and I was running to keep up. I warned her to stop but . . ." She opened her purse and dug, found the tissue she was looked for, and dabbed her eyes.

"What I'm trying to say, Mr. Stevens, is that this is not your fault. She was in the street before you could stop."

David was touched by this woman's sincerity. After all she was going through right now, she took the time to comfort *him*.

"I know your daughter's name is Julie, but I didn't get her last name."

"Hernandez. Julie Hernandez."

"Mrs. Hernandez, it's good of you to take time away from your family to console me. If I had your courage, I'd be in that waiting room comforting *you*. I'm so sorry for what happened today. If there's anything I can do, please tell me."

"You can pray for her."

"I will." And then added, "My wife is her doctor here."

Surprised, she gave him a big smile. "I didn't know. She is so good with Julie—all of us. Please, come back to the chapel with me. I would like my family to meet you."

On the way, David wondered if he could stoop much lower. Not only had he led her to believe he was happily married to Clair, but allowed her to treat him like some sort of celebrity because of it.

He sat with Julie's family while they waited for news of the surgery. A religious bunch, he would often see one of them praying with rosary beads in hand. An hour after he joined them, the surgeon entered the room.

"Mr. and Mrs. Hernandez?" He said, skirting the room for the parents he had not yet met. They got up and approached him.

"How is our daughter?" Mr. Hernandez asked.

"Surgery went well. We drilled a small hole in her skull, behind her ear. Then inserted what's called a VP shunt to remove the fluid and release the pressure. The swelling should go down. The next twenty-four hours will tell us more."

Good news. But he had made it clear, she wasn't out of the woods yet. Before he left, David gave Mrs. Hernandez his card with his address and phone number. "Please, call anytime if I can help."

After saying his goodbyes, he went straight to Clair's office, locked the door, and went back to his apartment. Tomorrow he would be at the hospital early, check in with the Hernandez family and talk to his soon-to-be ex-wife.

CHAPTER 60

C**LAIR EXAMINED** J**ULIE AND, FOR THE FIRST TIME SINCE THE** girl came in, felt hopeful. The surgery went well and Julie's eyes darted behind closed lids, a good indication the brain was busy working. All they needed now was for her to wake up and talk to them.

She left Julie and went to the waiting room where her family sat huddled together. After giving them the promising report, Julie's mother took Clair's hands in hers.

"We owe you a great deal for taking such good care of our daughter. Thank you."

"Most of the credit should go to Dr. Hill, the surgeon. But from here on, I'll be the one monitoring her progress. Any questions or concerns should be directed to me."

She received more gratitude from them and a big hug from Mrs. Hernandez. "I feel so bad for your husband; he is such a nice man. Carrying around so much guilt is not good for him."

Clair stood, arrow-straight, a forced smile on her face.

Why were they talking to David and how do they know that, technically, he's still my husband?

"He was wonderful last night, waiting for the surgeon with us, praying."

David praying?

"I haven't yet talked to David, but I will."

Believe me, I will.

She promised to meet with them later, and then walked away, wondering at all she had missed last night. She didn't have to wait long to find out, David paced the floor outside her office.

"Have you seen Julie yet?" he greeted her.

She unlocked the door and motioned for him to come.

"I did. She's doing well, but we won't know anything for sure until she's conscious."

"I plan on hanging around today, maybe see her awake," he said.

"It appears you made quite an impression on the Hernandez family," Clair said. "What were you thinking? From what I gather, they aren't blaming you. But if they change their minds, which given time to think, and if Julie doesn't respond well to the surgery they might, they could use anything you said last night to hang you."

"I tried to avoid them, but Mrs. Hernandez saw me walk by the chapel and followed me. She told me it wasn't my fault and asked me to go back to the chapel with her."

"Keep in mind," she cautioned, "we don't know how this will end for Julie. If you must talk to them, guard your words."

"I will. Thanks."

"I have patients to see. You can stay here, just lock up when you leave."

"What time do you break for lunch?"

"Around one."

"Will you meet me back here then?" he asked.

David looked a mess. His nose was swollen and bruised. He looked as if he hadn't slept and he needed a shave. Against her better judgment she agreed.

"If I have news on Julie, I'll tell you then."

As she walked away she couldn't help feeling sorry for him. She sensed his neediness, but how much of herself should she give him? Right now he was vulnerable, but once on firmer ground emotionally—what then?

She had many patients to see and the morning passed quickly. She saved Julie for last in hopes that, given the extra time, she would find her awake.

Flowers and balloons filled the window ledge and stuffed animals sat on the nightstand, waiting for her to wake and enjoy them. Unfortunately, she remained unconscious. Clair examined her again, encouraged to see her limbs thrashing about. It wouldn't be long. Mrs. Hernandez sat beside Julie, holding her hand.

"Mrs. Hernandez, there's something I'd like you to do."

"Please, call me Gloria." She appeared eager to do anything Clair asked of her.

"Could you get some books, maybe Julie has a favorite story, and read to her. Sometimes when a comatose patient hears something familiar it causes them to think and to regain consciousness sooner."

"Oh yes. I'll have my husband get some books from home. She loves to be read to."

Giving a family member something to do was important. Instead of sitting there helpless, they felt a part of the healing process. Gloria needed that.

When Clair got off the elevator on the third floor, she smelled food. Not just the usual hospital food, but an aroma that shouted delicious. And the closer she got to her office the stronger the smell. When she entered, she couldn't believe her eyes.

The white table cloth and Italian food were a familiar scene. And for a moment, Clair was elsewhere. On a roof, overlooking a river, drinking champagne. David had just proposed.

"What's all this?" she asked.

"I want you to have a decent meal, my way of saying thanks."

All right, so he appreciates my help, nothing more. This probably isn't the time nor place but could he at least acknowledge my letter.

"So much food and so little time. I better get started."

"How's Julie doing?"

"She isn't awake yet, but there are more positive signs it will happen soon. She's moving her limbs and that's encouraging."

"That is good news. I need to get back to work tomorrow. But I'll come when I can."

She nodded, then dove into the scrumptious food. Things got quiet in a hurry. It was one thing to have a conversation about Julie while standing, ready to take off when finished. But here, sitting down to lunch together had them both tongue-tied.

"Thank you for this, it's the best lunch I've eaten here." She stood.

"I've had the food here; that's not such a compliment," he laughed. "Clair, you've been great—"

A shrill beep came from her pocket, she pulled out her pager and glanced at it.

"I've got to go."

He stood, his eyes met hers before she rushed off to the ER. It was good that they could be cordial now, but she couldn't allow herself to hope for more. Yesterday, she signed the divorce papers and mailed them. After hearing David had been at his lawyers, why prolong the inevitable. He could have his divorce.

CHAPTER 61

THREE DAYS PASSED WITH JULIE STILL IN A COMA. DAVID SAT in her room and listened to her mother read *The Cat in the Hat* when she opened her eyes. The first word out of her mouth, "Mama." Clair had been paged and came immediately, ran Julie through a series of tests, and with everyone holding their breath she looked to Mrs. Hernandez.

"Everything appears to be good. I want her to stay here for a couple more days, make sure she doesn't have any complications. I'll remove the shunt tomorrow and I'm optimistic she'll be fine."

You could almost feel the air go out of the room, their sigh of relief so great. As they gathered around Julie, David sidled next to Clair.

"I liked seeing you at work. You're a wonderful doctor."

"It doesn't always work out this well, but thank you. How are you doing?"

"Well I drive a lot slower now. I don't think I'll ever get the image out of my head, though."

"In time, you'll think of it less often. And if that doesn't happen, I know a good psychiatrist if you need one." Her beautiful smile reached her eyes.

"Sounds like the charges will be dropped. Just a fine for not wearing my seat belt, turning right on red when it was posted not to. The police thought it unlikely I got over twenty-five miles per hour in such a short distance. That and Gloria's account of what happened saved me. And of course, Julie survived this—thanks to you."

"You give me too much credit, but I'm glad for you," she said.

"I'm glad we're friends, Clair."

They stood as if they were the only two in the room, gazing at each other. Breaking the spell, Julie called out to Clair, who moved quickly to her bedside. "What is it, Julie?"

"Will you sleep with me tonight?" Julie asked.

The room erupted with laughter. Clair sat on the bed and took Julie's hand.

"I'd love to, but I have a baby who needs me. But I promise that first thing tomorrow I'll come here to see you."

Julie crinkled her brows and crossed her arms.

"I don't like babies."

Again more laughter. Clair told Mrs. Hernandez's that she would see Julie in the morning, and told them all goodnight. She gave David a quick smile and left the hospital.

Rain pounded the concrete as Clair walked toward the parking lot. She picked up her pace and ran, pulling the hood of her coat up over her head, she splashed through puddles on her way to her car. This time she didn't mind the privileged benefit of front row parking.

Before Syria, she took pride in being a doctor, the respect given her from strangers, once they found out she was "Doctor

Stevens" and not just Clair. Now, she just wanted to be like everyone else. After seeing how devoted and selfless the Syrian doctors were, she felt embarrassed by the status being a doctor brought her here.

She eased her car onto the highway, trying to see through the downpour. Her mind drifted back to Julie's room, where David said he was glad they were friends. Friends? Really?

After all they'd been through, she could never be just friends. She loved him too much. Besides, she still hurt. She had poured her heart out in that letter, begging him to understand and forgive her, but it meant nothing to him.

Baffled by his behavior today, she decided to put thoughts of David aside as she turned into the lane that led to her son.

CHAPTER 62

BACK IN HIS APARTMENT, DAVID SCANNED THE CLUTTER THAT was his home. His running shoe, torn to shreds and scattered across the floor, was proof of how unhappy the dog was with his absence, and added to the dismal decor. He couldn't wait to move out of this dump.

On Friday, his lawyer called, telling him that he received the signed divorce papers from Clair, in two weeks it would all be over. And on Monday he got news that all but ended any chance encounters with her. A college in Sacramento offered him a job too good to turn down.

The days passed, turning into weeks. His divorce became final and his plans to move west were set in motion. But before he moved, he would need to pick up his suits that were still at the house.

He dialed Clair's number.

"Are you busy?"

"David?"

"Yeah. Would you mind if I came over and picked up the rest of my clothes?"

"Tonight?" she asked.

"If it's okay, I'd like to come now."

Her baby cooed in the background.

"Yeah, I guess," she said.

This would probably be the last time he'd see her. The finality of it hit him hard. Even after the divorce was final, he somehow felt comforted that she lived just a couple of miles away.

When he arrived, she opened the door before he rang the bell.

"Come in," she said.

"Sorry for popping in like this but I need my suits."

She nodded and stood quietly, looking at him.

"Still upstairs?" he asked, as he pointed upward.

"Oh, yes. Go on up."

On the way to the closet, David walked past Carter sleeping in the cradle he had purchased. Not so long ago, he had big dreams of being a dad. Their bedroom hadn't changed much. Except their honeymoon photo no longer stood on the nightstand—probably tossed in the trash.

He threw his clothes in a large garbage bag, started for the stairs, and then stopped. He couldn't resist. Standing over the cradle he looked down at her son. He reached out and touched his soft arm.

"Take care of your mother for me."

He swallowed hard past the lump in his throat.

"You and I would've gotten along just fine."

Asleep, Carter hummed with each exhale. His mouth found his fist and he sucked on it.

On heavy legs, David trudged down the steps.

"I think this is all of it."

She leaned against the counter with her arms crossed.

"I got a new job. A small college in Sacramento."

Her hands dropped to her sides as she stood, straight and stiff.

"Sacramento?"

"Yeah, well, new beginning, I guess."

Their eyes met and held. Clothes tossed in the dryer. The clang of zippers and buttons as they hit the metal drum of the dryer filled the thick silence that had taken over. Neither knew how to say goodbye.

"Good luck, David. I hope you'll be happy there."

It was hard to breathe as he nodded goodbye, walked out of his home, and away from the life that had meant so much to him. It shouldn't end this way, but it was too late to take back all they had said and done. He kept walking.

A few days later, he sat on the sofa going through his mail. Most of it bills and a letter—from Clair? Scribbled on the back, a note.

Found this in the box beside yours. The kid had moved out and I hadn't checked it until now. Hope it wasn't important. Bob.

His landlord. Flipping the envelope over, he looked at the date. Almost three months ago. His heart stopped as he sat, holding the envelope, staring at the familiar writing.

Slowly, he opened it and pulled out the note.

Dear David,

I wanted so badly to explain to you, make you understand how I could still love you and at the same time do what

I did. I've made a mess of things and I can't tell you enough how sorry I am. But hear me out, read this note, and then, if you still want your divorce I'll accept my punishment. But if you find it in your heart to forgive me, please pack your bags and come home. I'll be waiting with open arms.

David read the letter in shock. *All this time she's thought I had read this.*

While with ISIS for nine months, I had two people to talk to. Ashur and Sargon. Everyone else hated me. There, an American woman is the lowest of species. I was so lonely I ached for any conversation I could get. Over time, Sargon would come to my room and we talked. I needed that.

I would have been raped twice had he not stopped it. And I was grateful. The two of us were captured by an opposing rebel group. You know that is when a bullet grazed my head. But what you don't know is that as I lay on the hard concrete bleeding, I embraced death. I couldn't take anymore and waited for them to come and finish me off. Instead, Sargon came back for me, picked me up, and carried me as he ran. For that, I will forever be grateful. In a place where I had no companion and no love, when he offered both, I took it. I knew it was wrong, but I couldn't stop myself.

I have no good reason for letting you believe I was raped, except for the fear of losing you. Being without you for over a year, I couldn't risk destroying what we had finally started to recapture. Clearly I was wrong in doing so.

I never stopped loving you David, but I did give up believing that I would ever see you again — my biggest regret.
Please try to understand. I'll be waiting.
Love, Clair

He dropped back against the sofa, stared up at the ceiling. He viewed the whole matter through a prism of new understanding, and wondered what, if anything, he should do about it.

CHAPTER 63

For two days, David mulled over Clair's letter but was still unsure what to do. When he was at the house, she didn't seem too friendly, maybe things should be left as they were.

That evening, just as he sat down to dinner, his phone rang.

"Mr. Stevens?"

"Yes."

"This is Gloria Hernandez, Julie's mother."

"Oh, Mrs. Hernandez, how are you?"

"Wonderful, now that Julie is doing so well. Her birthday is on Sunday and we are having a party for her. We would like very much if you and your wife could join us."

David couldn't come up with a quick excuse.

"Can I talk to my wife and get back to you?"

My ex-wife, who lives across town.

"Sure. No need to call me, just come if you can. It starts at two o'clock."

After telling her they would try to make it, David sat, thinking this might not be a bad thing. He threw on his jacket and headed out the door. The closer he got, the more doubt cluttered his mind. What if she didn't want to talk to him, or worse, what if she had company?

All too soon he stood on the sidewalk in front of Clair's house. His feet, like lead, kept him at a standstill.

I've accused you of taking the easy way out, but you've been the brave one. I stand here afraid you'll reject me, but you're raising a child alone. And the courage it took for you to write that letter . . . you're amazing.

He took a deep breath and with his head down, marched forward ready to face what would be. But as he neared the door, Clair started out, walking backward as she eased a stroller down the steps.

He moved in quick. "Can I help you with that?"

Startled, she turned. "David, what are you doing here?"

"Coming to see you." Kneeling, he removed the blanket from the baby's face.

You're a lucky guy to have such a wonderful mom.

"He has your nose."

She tucked the blanket back around Carter and stood to start their walk.

"Do you mind if I walk with you?"

"I guess not."

They walked in silence for several minutes before Clair said, "If you're here for your tools, they're in a box in the garage."

"That's not why I came. I received a call from Julie's mother today."

"Is Julie all right?"

"She's fine, just another year older. In fact, she's so good that her mother's throwing her a party on Sunday, and she's invited us both to come."

Clair continued to walk, her focus on the sidewalk in front of them.

"David, why did you allow the Hernandez family to believe we were still together?"

He took a deep breath, let it out in a huff.

"I don't know. At the time, I felt so guilty, she started gushing about how wonderful you are, and I guess I wanted to be a part of you. To hold on to your coattails, and in some sick way feel good about myself."

Neither of them spoke as they walked toward downtown. She stopped in front of the Java Cafe and turned to David. "When Carter and I walk on cold days, we stop in here to warm up. If you want, you can join us."

He held the door as she pushed the stroller inside the warm coffeehouse. Once seated she removed his blanket and a sleeping Carter stirred, stretched and opened his mouth in a big yawn. They both laughed at the comical expression only a baby could pull off.

After the waitress had taken their order, David began his plea. "Come to the party with me Clair, it will be fun. Julie would love to see you and meet Carter. We don't have to stay long, but I think we should go."

She looked at him as if he'd grown horns.

"I have plans Sunday. Please give Mrs. Hernandez my regrets."

David sighed, then waited until the waitress served their drinks.

"Are your plans so important that they can't be changed? It would mean so much to them to have you there."

Clair tapped her fingers on the table.

"All right. We'll go. But if they ask any questions about where we live or anything about us as a couple, I'm telling them the truth."

"Fair enough. I'll pick you up at two o'clock then."

"And I can't stay long."

"You have a date or something?"

"It's really none of your business, but on Monday I'm speaking in front of a congressional hearing to drum up support for the US involvement in Syria. I want to practice my presentation."

He sat, wide-eyed and speechless.

"Wow, that's great. Tell me more about it."

"I'm not the only one, but I want to share my experience with them, let them know what I saw firsthand, how truly horrible life is there. We want them to approve arming the democratic opposition in Syria. And do something for the persecuted religious minorities, stranded in Iraq."

He looked at her so long she blushed.

"You're unbelievable."

"Hold your applause until I actually get something accomplished."

The waitress brought their cinnamon rolls and they began to eat.

"Have you talked to Darcy lately?" Clair asked.

David washed down his mouthful with coffee, unsure of what Darcy might have told Clair.

"No. Not since we had dinner, weeks ago."

She was probably still mad at him.

"David, she told me the two of you spent the weekend together while I was gone, and now you've had dinner together. Are you dating?"

"She spent the weekend, but we didn't sleep together. I hope she didn't imply that." His voice shot out in a high pitch.

"Not in so many words, but it made me wonder."

"She spent the weekend in the guest room. I was starved for company—"

"Oh I totally get that," she said.

Their eyes met. Her words jolted him like a splash of cold water. Here he had family and friends. A job. And still he was so lonely. In Syria, she had none of that. No one.

I've been such a hypocrite, feeling so superior while appalled at what she'd done.

"It doesn't matter anymore. Nothing's like it used to be."

He wanted to scream, "We could be!" But that would be a lie. For whatever they did, together or apart, they were not the same two people. Like a rock in the river, shaped by the current that washed over it, life had changed them.

They stood. She bundled up Carter, and they walked back to her house in silence.

He helped lift the stroller up the steps and into the house, said goodbye and walked back to his apartment. He could no longer deny it, he wanted her back. But time had given her independence and she embraced it—no, she thrived on it. She had taken a horrible experience and used it to make things better. And what he had once seen as crippling, he now saw as a change in her for the good.

I thought she had the most to lose from this divorce, but it's me—by a mile.

On Sunday, he would say to her what he should have said sooner, pride be damned, and pray it wasn't too late.

CHAPTER 64

WHILE SHE ATE DINNER, CLAIR FRETTED OVER THE UPCOMING party. She knew that while at the hospital, David had needed her, but he doesn't now. That was made clear by his plans to move west. Showing up today insisting she go to Julie's party, confused her.

What does he want from me?

She looked at Carter, laying in his carrier on the table. "That man is hard to figure out. Maybe he's worried if he goes alone, he'd have to tell the truth for once."

On Sunday, Clair put Carter down for his nap earlier than usual. She wanted him well rested with a good disposition for his first party.

While he slept, she wrapped Julie's present. Her anxiety grew as she imagined being alone in the car with David. Like the elevator, there was no escape if things got uncomfortable.

Carter's cries ended thoughts of David, and she hurried upstairs to get him. Holding him, she cuddled her face next to his, his little finger squeezed her cheeks, tickling her face. She laid him on the floor and dressed him in a brown corduroy jumper with a monkey on the front.

"I'm going to love showing you off."

It had been awhile since she'd been to a party, and once she convinced herself that David's intentions were harmless, she became excited about going.

"Now," she said, "we'll try to make Mommy look good."

Carrying Carter to her room, she quickly put on her new designer jeans and blouse, bought for this occasion. Standing in front of the mirror, she noticed her hair had grown thick again. The weight she had gained filled her out in the right places. All in all, she didn't think she looked half bad.

True to his word, David rang her bell at one fifty-five. Unlike her, he was always prompt.

"Come in," she said, as she opened the door. "I just have to pack a few things for Carter. Do you mind watching him for a minute while I run upstairs?"

"I think we can get along," he said. His gorgeous eyes, deep and dark, pulled her in and held her. It was one long and embarrassing moment before she looked away.

Gone a short time, she spotted them as she descended the stairs. David held Carter close to his face, talking softly as he walked around the room. Tears pricked her eyes as she watched the two of them together. It wasn't fair that Carter would miss out on a great dad because of her. She swallowed hard and continued down the steps.

"Did he cry?" she asked.

"Not at all. He's just too irresistible to leave be. You must be very proud."

"I am. You know, when I first found out I was pregnant, Dr. Gregg suggested an abortion. I admit that for a minute I thought about it. But I knew I couldn't live with myself if I did. Now, I look at him, and it scares me how much I love him."

For some reason, she wanted him to know that although she had many regrets, having Carter would never be one of them.

They took Clair's car since it had Carter's car seat. She also wanted the added distraction of driving, hoping it would alleviate the awkwardness of being so close to David.

"You look beautiful." he said.

Awkward!

"Thanks."

"I'm glad you agreed to this. Julie will be happy to see you."

"I'll see her at her appointment next week, but the party should be fun."

They drove the next few miles in silence. She chewed on her bottom lip, and he tapped his fingers on the armrest. When they turned into the Hernandezes' driveway, Julie came running out to greet them. She took Clair by the hand and led her into the house, leaving David to carry Carter. She looked so remarkably well Clair almost forgot how close she came to being severely disabled or, worse, dead.

At first, Julie seemed a bit jealous of Carter, but once Clair allowed her to sit on the sofa and hold him, she warmed up to him. Mrs. Hernandez took pictures of the two of them, and seeing them together, saddened Clair, knowing that Carter would never have a sibling. He would never know the bond that she and Megan had shared.

David struck up a conversation with Julie's uncle, a history buff, and spent much of the party dissecting and debating the fallout from the Civil War. The poor man. David had written his dissertation on the Civil War. There wasn't much he didn't know.

After they had eaten cake and ice cream, Julie wanted to show everyone her skills on the new bicycle David had given her, so they all bundled up and went outside.

"Nice of you to get her a bike," Clair said.

"It was the least I could do since I totaled the bike she had. Things could have turned out so much worse when I think about it." He shook his head.

"Try not to dwell on what could have been."

Her words, a double edge sword, made them both uncomfortable and quiet.

Near the end of the party, Gloria sat down with David and Clair to chat. Their family was large, and being a good hostess she wanted to make them feel included.

"Clair, was Carter a newborn when you adopted him?" she innocently asked.

Speechless, Clair wondered if this was another misconception David had led Gloria to believe. But when she looked at him, he appeared just as dumbstruck.

Of course people would think he was adopted, with his dark skin.
Clair took a deep breath. "He isn't—"

"The adoption papers haven't been signed just yet, but I hope to see my lawyer soon, speed things up," David interjected.

Poor Gloria looked bewildered. "He is a beautiful baby and is fortunate to have you both as parents."

What is going on here? What adoption papers?

If looks could kill, David would be dying a slow and painful death.

After they had said their goodbyes and strapped Carter in his seat, she wasted no time before lashing out at him.

"Would you stop with the lies? It's one thing for you to allow them to believe we're still together, but what you said in there is a flat-out lie, and I won't be a part of it. Especially when it's about my son."

"Then make it the truth," he said calmly.

It was all she could do to keep her attention on the road, so at her first chance, she pulled into a parking lot and turned off the engine.

"What are you talking about?"

He took her hand and held it. "I love you, and I want us to be a family."

"I don't believe it," she said, pulling her hand away from him. "After all this time, why now?"

"I want you back."

"What? So soon after the divorce you had to have. And what about Sacramento?"

"To hell with Sacramento. I want us all together and will do whatever it takes to win you back."

She fell back against her seat and turned away from him, looked out her window at the cars moving past.

"How do I know you really love me? Tomorrow you may change your mind," she said, her voice cracking.

He dropped his head back and rubbed his forehead.

"I've lost you—twice. It took a while for me to realize it, but I need you, Clair."

Taking off his seat belt, he turned toward her, his hand firmly on her shoulder.

"I never said I stopped loving you. I couldn't deal with what you did. I was hurt and . . . I don't know, afraid. Part of me felt like I did years ago when my mom cheated on dad."

He took his hand off her shoulder and looked down at his feet.

"We both have said and done things we wish we hadn't, but if you give me a chance, I'll show you every day how much I love you."

He looked sincere, but how could she be sure.

"But Darcy said you didn't want to reconcile."

"What? She told me you didn't want to," he said.

They sat there, surprised at how Darcy had betrayed the both of them.

"Is Darcy in love with you?"

"I don't know. Maybe. That doesn't excuse what she's done here."

No wonder she couldn't help me. But she didn't have to lie.

"It was when I read your letter that I realized how unfair I've been to you," he said. "I cared more of my suffering than yours. I've been a jerk."

Her eyes narrowed as she studied his face.

"When you read my letter? You couldn't even acknowledge that letter, why bring it up now?"

"Because I just read it a few days ago."

She sat, unmoving. All this time she had imagined him reading it, waiting for a call that never came, and feeling hurt and rejected.

"But I mailed it months ago."

"It landed in the box beside mine by mistake. My landlord just found it."

He took her hand, rubbed his thumb across it.

"Can you forgive me for being so stubborn?"

Forgive him?

Crying, it took a moment before she could speak.

"Before you say another word, you should know . . . there were complications when I gave birth to Carter. I can't have any more children."

His eyes opened wide then softened, filled with sympathy.

"I'm sorry. That had to be tough to hear. But you know, there are lots of kids who need a good home, parents who would love them. We could adopt."

She knew that Syria was full of such kids.

"Are you sure about this?" she asked.

"I've never been more certain of anything."

Reaching his arm around her shoulders he pulled her close and kissed her, long and slow. When their kiss ended, he took his shirt sleeve and wiped her tears.

"I love you, Clair. I wish I could have accepted things sooner."

Just then, Carter let out a loud burp, causing them both to laugh.

"Things will be different," he said.

Then he took her hands in his.

"Will you give me another chance?"

She had just gotten her life in order and didn't want it disrupted. But in her lap, he laid a life-changing offer, the chance at a do-over, a mulligan. They wouldn't be sitting here divorced if her past decisions had been different. She looked into those deep brown eyes of his and knew what she had to do. She felt strength in his hands, strength that passed on to her.

"Do you really want to adopt Carter?"

"As soon as possible."

"I love you so much," she said.

Their eyes locked, and a tightness crept into her throat as tears welled in her eyes.

He pulled a small box from his coat pocket and lifted the lid. Inside was a diamond ring, surrounded by sapphires. Her ring.

"Where did you get this?"

"I bought it from a man in the streets of Mardin. I asked him where he got it but couldn't get a straight answer. But I had to have your ring back."

My ring. If it made it to Turkey, chances are, the girl did as well.

"When you asked me about it, you knew."

"I knew you no longer had it, I didn't know how it got away from you. I planned to surprise you with it on our anniversary but . . . we were apart at the time."

He shrugged.

"So, will you marry me?"

She smiled and cried at once.

"Yes. A thousand times yes."

About the Author

JUDITH KELLER WAS BORN AND RAISED IN RURAL OHIO, where she still resides with her husband, Dean. From an early age, she has had a strong love of literature and wrote her first short story at age ten. She wrote sporadically as an adult until, as a loving grandmother of five, the many opportunities for storytelling prompted her to pick up her pencil (computer) and write again. Today, she continues to share her love of writing by serving as a member of her library's foundation board and literary club, and also by being a part of Romance Writers of America, an association dedicated to helping writers build careers in the romance genre.